This book is dedicated to my biggest fan and supporter.
I love you, Mom.

- 1 -

The forest was a blur on both sides of Harvey Chase as he dodged and weaved around trees. His legs pumped at an unprecedented level, adrenaline pushing him faster. Had anyone ever been this close to success?

He and his men had started to run when they heard the trap snap shut and saw a blur heading away. Whatever the thing was, it frustrated Chase and his hired team for nearly a week. Chase even began to question the hunt completely.

He had spared no expense in hiring the men that claimed to be the foremost experts in their field. They certainly charged enough. Their trap, which required constant adjustments, seemed unable to fool their prey. The beast was agile enough to steal the bait without springing the trap when the trigger would allow, and intelligent enough to throw a rock and set off the trap when the trigger was made sensitive. The majority of the attempts were made when Chase and his men had drifted off to sleep, which meant it was watching them.

Chase skidded to a halt and examined the foliage to his right. He thought he saw the blur of a figure beside him, keeping pace with him, maybe even moving faster than him. He stopped a moment, eyes searching, ears piqued high enough to hear a mosquito's wings, but there was no sign of anything.

He burst back into a sprint, intent on catching his men ahead of him.

Aside from the hired experts, Chase had brought a team of his own personal security. Nothing too involved. Three men, all people he had worked with in the past and, more importantly, guys that he trusted. They had dropped from the lower branches in the trees when the trap sprung. Chase had been higher up and took an extra moment to climb down.

Chase's earpiece crackled for an instant before he heard the voices of his men up ahead.

"Anyone got a visual?"

"Had one. I'm on its tail. Bugger's massive!"

His men wouldn't lose the beast, Chase willed. They weren't half the disappointment the supposed experts turned out to be. Chase had shown some impatience during one of the trap resets. The lead expert, Ted Wilson, turned to him with his fists planted on his hips and a revolver, which looked extremely out of place, hanging off his belt. It was that same revolver that had been fired randomly into the trees when the expert got spooked one night.

"We're trying to catch something that's never been caught before," Ted said. "There's going to be some trial and error before we catch him."

Chase shook his head. "Not *him*. *It*. It's not a person. It's a bloody Sasquatch."

For months, Chase had spent every day sorting through

sightings of the Sasquatch, Bigfoot, Yeti, Abominable Snowman and all other similar creatures. Decades of reports revealed one thing. The sightings came in clusters from a particular area, and then they would drop off in a day or two. Eventually, the sightings would start again in the same area, but not for months, sometimes years.

Phone calls, letters, and even rumor patterns showed consistent activity in a wooded area in Pennsylvania. He queried the locals about men of experience with the fabled creature. The majority of those who were willing to talk on the subject mentioned Ted's name.

It was getting harder for Chase to push himself. His body was trying to refuse the demands that sent pain into his legs and ribs, but he refused to stop. There was some light ahead of him, where the forest thinned into a clearing.

He staggered into the clearing and placed his hands on his knees, breathing hard. The clearing led to foothills which flowed into one of Pennsylvania's mountain ranges. The foothills had several well-beaten paths among the plateaus. Rocks, dirt, and thirsty vegetation were in every direction. Thin clouds of dust led up one of the paths, and Chase forced himself to follow them before they disappeared.

After a moment or two of climbing, Chase spotted one of his men coming toward him.

"What happened?" Chase called between his panting.

"We think we've got him pinned down, sir."

"It," Chase said, and motioned for his man to lead on.

The man led Chase farther up the mountain to a small plateau where the other men stood with their guns trained on the side of the mountain.

"He's in there, sir," one of the men said.

"It. Where?" Chase asked.

The man nodded toward the side of the mountain. Chase stared but only saw dirt and rock.

The man awkwardly bent down to pick up a rock, making sure to keep his gun trained, and threw it at the side of the mountain. Just when Chase expected the rock to bounce off, it continued forward, ruining a perfect optical illusion that hid a small opening. His eyes went wide. If he had stared for a week he wouldn't have found that opening.

"You're sure it's in there?" Chase asked.

"We watched him . . . uh, it . . . go in there."

"Okay," Chase said with a big smile. "Shall we go in then?"

All three of the men remained silent. Their eyes bounced from Chase to the cave opening and then to each other, never staying in one place for longer than a second.

He approached the man closest to the cave opening, and met his eyes. After a moment, the man broke eye contact and looked to the ground. Chase was disappointed. These were some of his best men.

Chase pulled the man's handgun from its holster and flipped on the gun's mounted flashlight. The gun felt strange in his hand. The unexpected weight caused him to hold it awkwardly. It didn't matter. He only needed it for the attached light. His men stared at him in disbelief as he approached the cave.

"Sir?" one of the men said in monosyllabic protest.

Chase smirked and stepped into the cave. The opening was just large enough for Chase to step through, though he had to duck down. By the third step, darkness swallowed him. He kept the flashlight moving, mainly on the ground, to keep from breaking an ankle on a stray rock or sudden dip in the cave floor. It wasn't what he had been expecting. It was immaculate.

If Chase had walked into a bear's cave, he would have found several signs on its inhabitants. Food remnants, droppings, claw marks and maybe even the bear itself. In this cave, he found nothing.

Less than nothing. It seemed that someone had taken the time to break off stalagmites and stalactites. There weren't any stray rocks either. Was it his imagination or was the cave nearly free of dirt and dust?

Shuffling echoed from behind him. His men had finally found their testicles. Either that or their shame had driven them into the cave.

He continued forward, expecting to see a sign of life, but each step just brought more of the bare cave. *There must be another way out*, Chase thought. Just as he was considering turning around, a crude orange light flickered from deeper in the cave. As he got closer, he saw that the light was coming from around a corner. *This isn't the beast's living room, just its foyer*, Chase mused with a smirk. The orange flickering glow was paired with a sporadic crackling sound. Chase's smile grew. He never considered the beast would be capable of making a fire, but the unmistakable smell confirmed it was a campfire.

Cautious, yet confident, Chase rounded the corner at the end of the cave and took in the scene still with a smile on his face. Moments passed and everything he had seen in the past week began to make sense, questions being answered by the evidence in front of him.

"I've got to be honest. This isn't quite what I was expecting."

– 2 –

Mythical Tours' mid-afternoon excursion glided across Loch Ness's surface with the gentle chug of its engine. Paul Allen, captain of the boat and one of the owners, was always thankful when the tour went unmolested. It usually remained that way when he kept the boat away from the south end of the loch.

The tourists seated on the boat pulled their coats tighter around their shoulders against a gust of wind cooled by the surface of the loch.

Wendy, one of Paul's guides, stood from her seat and turned to face the passengers with a microphone in her hand and a smile on her face.

"Welcome, everyone, to the Loch Ness sight-seeing tour. My name is Wendy, and I'll be telling you a bit about one of the most famous bodies of water in the entire world."

The tourists gave a kind, yet unenthusiastic round of applause.

"Scotland has many lochs. The Loch Ness is second biggest in surface area and the largest in volume. In fact, the Loch Ness holds more water than all the lakes in Great Britain combined. Its great depth is a big contributor to the water temperature as well. It averages 5 degrees Celsius, the same as most refrigerators, even during the hottest weather. It's not just resistant to heat. Loch Ness has also never frozen, even in the coldest of winters. Warmer water cycles from the deepest part of the loch, constantly replacing the colder water near the surface."

Wendy paused for a few moments while the group gazed around at the water. A few of them leaned over to a friend to clear up a misunderstanding caused by either someone not knowing Celsius temperatures or a difficulty understanding Wendy's accent.

"I don't imagine many of you took this tour to hear about the water in the loch as much as the thing that swims in it."

The people erupted in a round of laughter.

"Nessie!" Wendy said enthusiastically.

The word was met with more applause.

"Loch Ness is home to one of the most famous and fabled creatures in the world, the Loch Ness Monster, affectionately named Nessie by the good folks of Scotland. The first sighting was believed to have been made by an Irish monk, Saint Columba, back in the 6th century. The monk claimed a water beast attacked a man in front of his very eyes. When the monster went after a second man, Saint Columba made the sign of the cross and demanded the beast to go back where it came from. The beast went under the water as if pulled down by ropes.

"Since then, there have been hundreds of sightings. Numerous specialists, scientists, and other curious parties have come to the loch in efforts to find the monster or, at the very least, some evidence of its existence. Some believe Nessie is a surviving descendant of the dinosaur known as the plesiosaur. Others believe that it is simply a creature that can not, and will not, ever be explained."

"That's a load of shit, it is," a man's voice called out. The voice was gruff with a thick Scottish accent.

Wendy, along with all the tourists, looked around to find the man to whom the voice belonged.

Wendy put on her best polite smile. "Please, sir, try not to interrupt the tour. Thank you. One of the most famous images of Nessie was taken in 1934. It's commonly known as the Surgeon's Photograph."

"I said it's all a load of shit," came the voice a second time.

Again, everyone looked around for the source of the criticism. Wendy determinedly carried on. "Yes, the photograph was proved a hoax, but please, sir, don't disrupt the tour. I won't ask you again."

"Or what?" the man said.

No one had noticed the smaller vessel that had pulled up beside the boat, but floating in the water a few feet away from Wendy and the tourists was an elderly man in his personal motor boat.

Captain Allen spotted him and put a hand over his eyes. Wendy smiled and walked to the side of the boat.

"These people paid for this tour, so if you don't mind, you're ruining the experience for everyone." Wendy smiled even larger. "Thanks for your co-operation."

Before turning back to the tourists, Wendy quietly approached the captain.

"He's back," she whispered.

"I noticed," the captain replied. "Keep going. Try to distract the lot of them. If I have to give refunds on another tour because of that old git . . ."

"Call the police, why don't you?"

"You know he'll be long gone by the time they get here."

"Fine. Keep us moving and see if you can stay away from him."

Wendy turned back to the tourists with the biggest smile she could summon.

"Apologies, folks. Let's continue. Some of the most conclusive evidence collected so far came from sonar experiments. One study returned an echo so powerful it would have taken a twenty-foot whale to reproduce a sound of the same intensity."

"Everyone knows the Loch Ness Monster doesn't exist!" The old man kept pace with the boat, making every directional change the captain made. His smaller boat was quick enough to stay with them no matter where they went. Their only hope was the old man losing interest and going home.

Again Wendy asked the man to stop, far less politely, and again the old man followed the boat and criticized her commentary.

The tourists joined in as well, throwing comments back at the man and even throwing things at him. Laughing, he scooped their garbage out of the water with a fishing net.

"You lot are throwing all this trash into the loch and you're yelling at me?" he said with a grin.

"I'm very sorry, folks. We're going to head back now and I'll be more than happy to give you each a free Nessie doll for the inconvenience."

The old man watched the retreating tour boat. His crooked grin turned into a crooked smile as the noise of the boat's engine faded away.

His name was Rory Stewart.

Rory baited the hook of his old fishing pole and cast his line out into the water. He set the rod down in his boat, taking extra care to make sure it wouldn't be pulled into the water if a fish tried to swim away with his hook.

He glanced over his shoulder at the boat, which was getting smaller by the moment. That particular boat was from a business five miles up the loch. There were three of them, constantly sending their boats around the loch.

"Idiots," he spat. "Morons. Travelling all that way to look at some black water as if a dragon was going to swim up from the bottom to say hello. Idiots." Rory continued to mumble on, his words becoming completely unintelligible even to his own ears.

He knew a lot of the tourists would complain enough to get a full refund, which the businesses hated. One of the business owners had even tracked Rory down once and demanded he stop causing trouble.

"Tourism has become a major part of Inverness-shire," the man had whined at Rory. "You keep this up and people are going to lose jobs."

"I only disturb others when I've been disturbed," Rory had replied without paying the man much attention. "Your boats are loud. They scare the fish away."

"It's a big loch," the man had said, placing his hands on his hips attempting to make himself an authority. "Go fish somewhere else."

"If it's such a big loch," Rory said, placing his hands on his own hips in mock, "send your tours somewhere else."

That didn't stop the old man from seeking the tour boats out and chasing them off once in a while.

He was still grumbling when his fishing rod began to dance on the steel bottom of his boat. With a single motion, he snatched up the rod and began reeling in the line with an experienced hand.

Rory pulled a salmon out of the dark water and set it down on the bottom of the boat. He looked at the fish critically as it jumped and slapped around.

"A bit small," Rory admitted to himself. "But you'll do."

Ten years ago he wouldn't have hesitated to throw the fish back and wait for something bigger. A decade later, he grew tired early in the day. If he stayed out fishing for too long, he wouldn't have the energy to finish the rest of his chores before the day's end.

The boat's engine coughed to life at the pull of its cord, and Rory steered the boat toward the small house that he called home on the southwestern shore of the loch. Some people would call his house a shack or maybe even a hut. Those were the same people that would pay good money to get on a boat and stare at black water.

Rory deftly guided his motorboat to a stop beside the small dock that he had built. A German shepherd sat on the end of the dock and greeted Rory with a single bark.

"Did you miss me then, boy?" Rory asked, laughing as he secured the boat. He held up the fish for the dog to see. "I've caught us a world-class dinner, I have." The dog barked once more, wagging his tail.

Modest was a kind word to describe Rory's house, but it was more than enough room for a man and his dog. He had a large kitchen/living room, a small bedroom, and an extra room he used for storage. The walls in his house were bare. He had little desire for decorations and even then he couldn't convince himself to spend money on something that was only for looking at.

His furniture was just as plain as his house. Functional.

Connected to his property was a fenced-in field where he raised a small flock of sheep. Rory was a man of little need, but the wool and meat from the sheep combined with the meager salary he got for keeping grounds at the Fort Augustus golf course allowed him to buy the few supplies he needed.

Behind the house, Rory had built a shed. It was almost the same size as his house. Half of the shed was used for working with his sheep, though it also housed a lot of storage. The other half he had converted into a greenhouse where he kept a vegetable garden.

Rory cleaned his catch and put the filets in some salted water before setting about his evening chores. He fed the sheep, and gave each one a check for signs of disease. After a quick tending of his garden, he pulled a few carrots and potatoes to have with his fish.

Rory took the vegetables and fish and made a simple stew, which he and the dog ate with some bread.

After tidying up the kitchen, Rory sat out by the shore in an old lawn chair and looked out over the water, as he did most nights.

The loch was always so alive. When the wind brushed across the surface of the water it created ripples which would make the moonlight dance. On the nights when the wind was still, the loch became a perfect mirror of the night sky. Looking at the loch was just as good as looking up at the stars. The occasional fish would leap from the water and make a splash, momentarily marring the surface, but the mark quickly healed.

Each night the loch would put on a display for Rory, never the same but always familiar.

It wasn't uncommon for Rory to sit outside long enough to fall asleep in his lawn chair. Those nights he'd wake up while it was still dark with a sore back and a stiff neck and stumble to his bed.

This night he didn't fall asleep. He just watched and waited.

– 3 –

The near-permanent state of the *UK Observer*'s office was a mixture of noise and motion. Reporters were either on the phone taking an interview or checking facts, while others were clacking away at their typewriters. Still others were walking prints to a co-worker's desk for a critique and a discussion or rushing to get to the scene of their next story.

The newspaper employed roughly twelve reporters, though a few were freelancers. They all shared a common work space littered with mismatched desks. None of them considered asking for an office since a good reporter shouldn't be at the office long enough to need one.

One of the few personal offices on their floor belonged to Martin Edwards, the Editor-in-Chief.

Edwards was mostly viewed as a lazy man. He kept his office door closed most of the time in an attempt to appear busy. Those who entered his office without being asked were met with a look that asked, *why are you bothering me?*

Sitting in his office, with the door closed, he looked across his desk at one of his longest-employed reporters. This was a reporter that everyone, employees and readers, seemed to love. No one ever had a complaint about him and he always finished his assignments on time with consistent quality. Edwards hated him.

"Alex Stafford," Edwards said, reading a letter he held in his hands, "seems to have a wit and a unique voice that is truly rare among publications in England. I enjoy his articles so much that I always read them first, no matter which page they appear. As fact, if I find myself short on time on any day, they are the only parts I read. Without exaggeration, Alex is the reason I keep renewing my subscription to the *UK Observer*. Many thanks, Susan Anderson."

Edwards dropped the letter onto his desk as if the page was covered in filth. He looked up at Alex in a very similar way. Alex gave Edwards his full attention and even wore a satisfied smile as he did it.

He knew his boss didn't like him. It wasn't something that the editor-in-chief hid from anyone. Edwards had certain political views. Strong views. Alex rarely shared those views. Whenever Edwards asked him to spin one of his stories or columns to prevent from embarrassing a politician, Alex would refuse. If Edwards took it upon himself to make changes to one of Alex's pieces, Alex would change it back before it went to print. It wasn't difficult to be the last one with access when Edwards went home at four o'clock every day. Also the fellows down in pre-print liked Alex a lot more than Edwards.

Alex had no doubt that Edwards would love to fire him, but there was nothing the editor-in-chief could do. The readers loved him, and the advertisers knew that the readers loved him, which meant the advertisers loved him too. Since the advertisers loved him, the paper's owner loved him.

"Another great letter of praise," Edwards said, putting on a fake smile.

"Agreed," Alex said.

"And that's how I know I can confidently give you a rather challenging assignment."

"Challenging?"

"Yes," Edwards said, hiding a yawn behind an overweight fist. "There's a story I keep hearing about over and over again, but every retelling is varied from the last. I need someone to look into it and get the facts straight."

Alex shifted in his seat. He was intrigued, but cautious knowing how little faith Edwards had in him. "All right. What's the story?"

"I knew I could count on you. By all accounts, there are mysterious forces at work in Scotland. These forces are scaring all the tourists away. One report said it was ghosts of the highlands. Another said the loch has a mind of its own. One person even said old Nessie herself is parading around disguised as an old man." Edwards laughed until he snorted. "I need you to find out the real story."

Alex stared at the man, waiting for him to stop laughing. "Is this a joke?"

"Not at all."

"You want me to go to Loch Ness?"

"Yes," Edwards replied, chins jiggling as he nodded.

"In Scotland."

"There's only one Loch Ness."

"To find out what's scaring tourists?"

"Now you've got it. You don't find it intriguing?"

"It sounds like a load of bunk. Honestly, Martin, this is the kind of story the rags would make up. It'd be right on the front page beside the double-headed alien baby. It's rubbish."

Edwards leaned forward with a smile that was genuine, but the man's eyes spoke only of malice.

"Not if it's true."

*   *   *

"The man's an absolute loon," Alex said later that night as he was packing his suitcase. "He's completely lost it."

Loren sat on the bed and watched him pace about the room packing the occasional item while ranting about the intelligence of his boss, which was quite low if Alex's comments were an indication.

"You know why he wants me to go, don't you? It's Scotland. People love reading my articles when they're about something interesting. If he gets me to start writing about Scotland no one around here is going to give a piss about anything I write. Not to mention ghosts and other shite he was trying to sell me on. This is just another attempt to find a way to fire me."

"Maybe you just shouldn't go," Loren suggested.

"I have to go, Loren. If I refuse to do my job, I'd be handing him the perfect excuse to fire me."

Loren searched her mind for the words she wanted to say, but they weren't there. At least not the right words. Maybe they were the right words, but she couldn't seem to put them in the right order. Maybe the right words didn't exist.

She had moved in with Alex a few months before. With their work schedules, they didn't spend much time together. Most days it seemed Alex only did two things. He worked and he slept.

Loren couldn't blame him. Alex loved his job. She wished

she loved her job in a similar way. To her, her job was just that. Alex lived his job like a lifestyle, which meant Loren being left out more often.

"With your reputation, your level of talent, maybe you could get a job with a different paper. One that respects you more and doesn't send you all over the place," she suggested.

"You're probably right, but it's really only the one guy who doesn't respect me. It would be tough to walk away from the *Observer* now. I feel like I really helped build it up to what it is, you know?"

"Maybe you could help build up another paper. Or how about working on that book of yours?"

"I can't. I know you probably don't understand, but I just can't."

She had heard the story many times. Alex hadn't been with the *UK Observer* from the beginning, but for the past ten years his articles had helped elevate the paper's sales. With better sales came better advertisers. With better advertisers came more money. In his time there, the office had moved twice, both times to expand into a larger and more prestigious location.

Loren stood on her knees and pulled him over to the bed, wrapping her arms around his neck.

"What would you say if I wanted you to stay with me?" she asked.

"Sweetheart, I know you want me to stay. I want to stay, but I can't."

"What if I said I didn't want you to go tonight or ever again? What if I asked you to always be here with me?"

"What? Like here in the bedroom? That doesn't sound too bad."

Loren laughed and gave a small shake of her head. "I mean

like in the same city. Never farther. No more airplanes. No more hotels."

Alex pulled away from her and continued packing his suitcase.

"That's not fair," he said, anger rising in his voice. "I would never ask you to leave your job. I'm supposed to leave mine because I have to travel once in a while?"

"Once in a while? Alex, you're gone all the—"

"It's my job."

"Do you just love your job or do you love being away from me, too?"

He finished packing his suitcase in silence. Every move he made, every item he placed in the bag, every step he made around the room seemed as though it was amplified through a speaker, echoing in her ears.

"Do you have to leave tonight?" Loren asked quietly. A tear rolled down her cheek. She quickly rubbed it away with the heel of her palm, hoping Alex hadn't seen it. The way she suddenly found his arms around her made her think he had.

Keeping one arm wrapped around her, he grabbed the phone from the nightstand and dialled.

"Hello. I have a flight to Glasgow tonight. Is there anything leaving in the morning?" There was a pause as he waited for a response. Loren gave his hand a gentle squeeze. "I see. Anything in the afternoon? Even later tonight would help." A shorter pause and Alex's voice dropped a little. "Thanks anyway."

He hung up the phone and wrapped his other arm around her, kissing her on the cheek.

"I'll call you as soon as I get there, okay?"

She forced a smile and nodded, hoping that the brave face she put on would be convincing enough for him.

He grabbed his suitcase and hugged her before leaving the apartment.

Loren stretched out on the bed and placed her hands on her stomach. She looked down her body and wondered when she would start to show.

- 4 -

Out of all the holes in the Fort Augustus Golf Club, the seventh was Rory's favorite to maintain. Partly because it was on the rear edge of the course and the only people who were normally close by were golfers playing a hole. Most of the holes ran parallel to the others, which meant being surrounded at times by three sets of golfers. Worst of all, the links closest to the clubhouse were usually watched by a gallery of players who had finished their round and were content to sit on the club's bar patio calling out remarks and greetings to fellow players.

The other reason was because the seventh required the most skill and care to tend well. The slopes caused him to constantly adjust the deck on his riding mower, and the foliage at the edge of the course was thickest, demanding ever-vigilant attention.

Rory parked the lawnmower in the small shack on the edge

of the course where he kept all his maintenance equipment, and checked his supply of seed, fertilizer, and herbicides.

As was his custom on the days he worked, he ate his lunch as he walked back up to the clubhouse, saving the crust of his sandwich for the fish between holes one and two. He admired his work as he went. Though he couldn't be credited with creating the rises and dips, or the small bodies of water, a well-tended golf course took something functional and made it beautiful.

Granted, the beauty was harder to see when a perfect shot plummeted into a bunker of sand, or when a putt ran too fast across a shorn green, but it was still there.

Fort Augustus was a small club, just like the town it shared a name with. In the average year, the club had less than 100 members. Sitting behind the pro shop counter was one of Rory's co-workers, Claire, the course's pro shop attendant, general manager, and club pro. The latter position didn't usually go over well with new male members, but Claire could improve almost anyone's game with a few pointers. Those too stubborn to take her advice soon found themselves humiliated after being outshot by a woman in her sixties.

"Afternoon, Rory," she said with a smile.

Rory sheepishly tipped his hat. "Afternoon."

"All done for today, then?"

"Aye," he replied. "For a few days, most likely."

Rory had been doing the job long enough that he made his own schedule. He knew when the grass would need to be cut before it started growing.

"Who's going to be here to keep me company?"

As much as he liked the upkeep on hole seven, talking with Claire was always the best part of his day. Claire and Rory were close in age. Ten years at most. His old-fashioned side never allowed him to ask.

"I'm sure you'll have no shortage of people to talk to, Claire. You never do."

"Oh, sure, but none of them hold a candle to you, love."

He often wondered if her flirting meant any authentic interest in him. In her position, she flirted with dozens of men in a day, but they all saw it as her doing her job and being friendly. Why would Rory look at it any other way?

"I'll see you, then," he said with a smile and a wave. "I could use a few more bags of fertilizer, I could. When you make your next order."

"Anything for you, Rory," she called after him.

*   *   *

The brakes on Rory's old pick-up truck squealed as he came to a stop outside of Morton's, a general store in Fort Augustus. There were a few other stores in town, but the owner of Morton's, Rob Morton, had become a friend of Rory's, and Rory preferred dealing with friends over businessmen.

The bell rang overhead as Rory pushed the door open. Rob quickly appeared from the back of the store.

"Uh, oh," Rob said with a smile. "If it isn't my cheapest customer."

"You're lucky I don't take my business somewhere else where they know how to treat a fellow."

Rory first met Rob when his car had broken down a mile from Rory's house. Rob had walked to find a phone to call a tow truck. When he knocked on Rory's door, the old man told him he didn't have a phone and didn't need one. Despite his brash demeanor, Rory drove the pair of them back to Rob's car and had begun tinkering under the hood. Within ten minutes the car was running again.

Living out on his own, Rory had become pretty proficient in fixing his own truck. Rob told Rory to come by his shop if he ever needed anything. Rory had been going to Rob for all his supplies ever since.

"How's the family then?" Rory asked.

"Fine, fine. Son's still got no job. Just sits around the house all day."

"Kids!"

"Will you be needing anything from the back storage today?" Rob asked.

Rory shook his head and entered the aisles, checking off items in his head as he took them.

"I've got some mail for you. I'll get it."

Rory came to such an abrupt halt that he nearly fell forward from the change in momentum. "Really?" he said only loud enough for himself to hear.

With some effort, he turned his attention back to the store shelves. Unable to focus on the things in front of him, Rory shuffled up to the front and laid his items on the counter.

Rob handed Rory the mail, and put his groceries into a paper bag.

The first envelope produced an automated letter from a bank telling him all the reasons why he should open a checking account with them. He crumpled the letter and envelope into a ball and pitched it into the trash bin behind the counter.

"How do these people even know to send me mail here?" he mumbled.

"Those people will send mail to anyone, anywhere. I got one a month ago addressed to me dog."

The second letter was from a distant cousin who had moved to England when Rory was still a boy. She was writing to let him know an uncle of Rory's died. An uncle he had never even met.

"No more mail for me, Robby?" Rory asked.

Rob shook his head.

"You sure? No other letters?"

Rob released a big sigh and looked Rory in the eye.

"Don't do that to yourself, Rory. You know there isn't a letter. There won't ever be one. Not unless you send one, and maybe not even then."

Rory looked down at the floor, searching for something that wasn't there.

"I suppose," he said. "How much do I owe you?"

"Eleven pounds." Rob pushed the bag of groceries across the counter.

"Eleven pounds?" Rory did his best to sound offended. "For some bread and milk?"

"I haven't changed my prices in two years, you cheap old bastard. You know that."

"It's a wonder I even have eleven pounds left after dealing with you for so long."

Rory took the bag of groceries and winked at Rob before heading for the door.

"Take care of yourself, old man."

The bell rang again as the shop door closed behind him. The bell announced the door reopening a second later when Rob called out to Rory.

"Rory! I almost forgot," Rob said, jogging the short distance between them.

"What's that?"

"A guy came through the area earlier asking about tourists being scared away from the loch. Started talking about ghosts and monsters. Thought he was crazy, I did. But then he came back a bit later and started asking about an old man hassling people by the loch. You don't suppose he'd be talking about you, do you?" Rob grinned.

"Who me?" Rory gave his best impression of innocence. It was a little over the top. "I'm just a harmless old man."

Rory walked away with a slight bounce in his step. Rob watched him go, knowing that the old man was anything but harmless.

*   *   *

On the drive home, Rory wondered why a man would be asking about him. At first, he was concerned that it might have been a policeman, but he dismissed the thought. A policeman wouldn't ask around town. He'd just drive down to the loch and slap a pair of handcuffs on Rory. And if Rob had thought it had anything to do with the law, he would have mentioned it.

He thought about the tour boat he had pestered a few days earlier, but most of those people knew exactly where to find him, not that they bothered anymore.

A man was standing on Rory's porch, knocking on the door, as Rory brought his truck to a stop in the lane way. Rory was about to find out who was looking for him and why, whether he wanted to or not.

Climbing out of his truck, Rory tried his best to ignore the man standing in front of his house. The man was younger, though most men were younger than Rory. He was well dressed, which meant he lived in a bigger city where fine clothes meant something. He watched Rory, but waited to be addressed. He'd be waiting some time.

Rory headed for the back of his house, walking fast, with his head down.

"Excuse me?" the man called.

The man's accent was British. Straight from London, Rory guessed. Instead of stopping to answer the man, Rory walked even faster. In situations like these, he could always claim to be hard of hearing or sight, if the need arose.

"Excuse me?" the man persisted and walked after Rory. "Sir!"

Rory stopped and turned so abruptly the younger man almost ran into him.

"Aye, what is it?" Rory demanded.

Taken aback from such a direct approach, the younger man blinked a few times before he was able to find his words again.

"Do you live here?" The younger man motioned toward Rory's shack.

Rory looked around his property as if he were seeing it for the first time.

"Maybe."

"Well, either you do or you don't."

"I suppose I do. Who are you?"

"Oh, I'm sorry," the man said with a nervous laugh. He jammed a hand into his coat pocket and produced a business card, which he thrust into Rory's hand. "My name's Alex Stafford. I'm a reporter for the *UK Observer*."

Rory took the card, holding it on the edges, unsure if he was handling it properly. It seemed such a foreign thing for a man to carry. He had rarely seen a use for pieces of paper so small.

"A reporter, huh? I suppose you've come looking for the monster."

"Of a sort," Alex admitted. "Have you heard of a man, who lives near the loch, scaring off tourists?"

Rory studied the younger man as he weighed possible replies.

"Aye, I've heard of him," he admitted. "Comes out of nowhere, that one. They say he's dangerous. Strong as an ox and smart as a fox. At least that's what the people around here say. He doesn't just scare off tourists though. Hunters, scientists, reporters even," Rory said, giving a cryptic look to the younger man. "I've never seen him myself."

"I've been talking to people all around Inverness-shire. They all say that you are that man."

"Me? Ridiculous. I'm just an old man. I'm not capable of such things."

"That's not what people have been saying," Alex said with a smirk. The son of a bitch was actually enjoying bothering an old man.

"Now you listen here," Rory looked down at the business card still in hand, "Stafford. I don't have to stand here and listen to your accusations. Some of us do real work for a living. I'm busy and I have things to do."

Rory spun around and continued toward the back of the house. He rolled his eyes when he heard the reporter's footsteps following him.

Rory's dog, who had been chasing the sheep, noticed the arrival of his master and came running over. After a quick sniff of his owner, the dog wandered over to Alex with his tail wagging.

"Don't be so friendly to that one, Graham. He'll accuse you of driving a car or some nonsense."

"The dog's name is Graham?" Alex asked.

"It's what I called him, isn't it? Something wrong with the name?" Rory didn't have to try to sound angry.

"Nothing. Nothing at all. I guess I'm just used to dogs being called Spot and Rover."

Rory went into his greenhouse and checked the moisture of his soil and the progress of his vegetables. He picked a section of squash that was ready and made a mental note to replant the section after a few days.

He was only a little surprised to see Alex standing just inside the greenhouse looking around.

"I can tell you're from the big city. Everyone there has completely forgotten their manners," he spat.

Taking the point, Alex stepped out of the green house, but stood just outside the door. Rory felt like smiling at the look of shame on the reporter's face.

"The people around here said your name is Rory?"

"That is my name," he admitted.

"Well, Rory, I've got several eye-witnesses that say you pester people in this area until they've no choice but to leave. Can't you just tell me a little bit about that?"

"Liars. All of them."

Alex continued on as though Rory hadn't said a word in reply. "I talked with some people who claimed to know of you. Some said you'd gone a little crazy a few decades ago. Others said you were just bored and looking for a way to entertain yourself. A few even said you were looking for a way to protect ol' Nessie."

"There ain't no such thing as a Loch Ness monster," Rory stated.

There was a moment of silence between the two men before Rory turned and stalked off toward his herd of sheep. Alex followed a few seconds later, once he had regained his composure.

"Those damn tourists come here and they make all kinds of noise. They walk around the whole area like they own the damn place, especially the American ones. A few years back, a man walked into my house! He said he thought my house was a damned souvenir shop. So, aye, maybe I hassle the occasional trespasser. It's nothing they don't deserve."

"So now you're admitting it?"

Rory gave Alex a look that said he shouldn't bother asking such a stupid question. The reporter began scribbling on a notepad. Rory shook his head and began inspecting his sheep, one at a time. He selected one and patted it gently on the back. Bending down, he grabbed the sheep's four legs in his two hands and hoisted it up onto his shoulders. The sheep bleated in surprise and then was quiet again.

"Look, I'm not trying to cause trouble for you," Alex said, noticing Rory was trying to walk away again. "I'm just asking a few questions."

Rory, with his new shadow, walked to the shed where he set the sheep down on the floor. He grabbed a shearer from a nearby shelf and started separating the sheep from its wool.

"Maybe I find questions to be troublesome," Rory said with a growl.

"Have you ever thought about asking the tour companies in the area to keep away from your part of the loch?" Alex asked, raising his voice over the sound of the electric shearer.

"None of that loch is mine. It's everyone's. And no one's. But that doesn't mean people can come here and do whatever they want," Rory called back. "Doesn't really matter, anyway. If it's not them it's the brain-dead fools that come thinking they're going to hunt down the monster."

"I thought you didn't believe in the Loch Ness Monster."

"I don't. But they do."

Rory placed the shearer back on the shelf, gathered up all the wool from the floor and put it in a sack. Then he grabbed a large hunting knife. Forcing the sheep to lie down on its side, he quickly dragged the knife across its throat. Blood poured out of the wound as the sheep thrashed around.

"Oh, God!" Alex blurted out, turning away from the massacre. "I wish you had said you were going to do that."

Rory chuckled. "City boys." He hung the sheep up over a bucket and left the shed. Alex quickly followed, glancing back over his shoulder at the dead sheep, its blood still dripping into the bucket below.

"Do you, um, get many," Alex sputtered, flustered by the butchering, "hunters?"

"More than you might think," Rory said. "Some call themselves scientists, or researchers. In the end, they're all after the same thing, and what they want doesn't even exist."

Alex continued to follow Rory as he threw a plastic tarp into the bed of his pick-up truck. Rory went back into the shed. Alex waited a few feet away, keeping his eyes on the grass. The old man carried the sheep carcass over to his truck and dropped it onto the tarp.

"So you really don't believe? You don't even think it's possible?"

Rory got into the truck and leaned out of the open window. "Stafford, I've been out here for over thirty years. If there was something in that water, I think I would have seen it by now."

Alex didn't seem to be completely convinced. He nodded and looked around as though the answer he was looking for would suddenly appear. "What's with the sheep, anyway?" He motioned toward the bed of the truck with his head.

"Disease," Rory spat. "Can't risk it spreading to the rest of the herd. No one will buy a diseased sheep. Got to get rid of it."

Alex stared at Rory for some time. The old man got the impression that he was waiting for some kind of confession.

"If you wouldn't mind, I have just a few more questions. It won't take long."

Rory grinned at the reporter and stomped on the gas pedal.

The old truck's tires spun, kicking up dirt and a few stones. The old man laughed at the city boy in the rear-view mirror who stood wiping at the fresh dirt on his clothes. Rory whistled a tune and drove along the shore of the loch. It would be dark soon and he had a delivery to make.

– 5 –

By the time Alex returned to his hotel room he was convinced it was time to go back to London. During his career, he had been given few assignments where there simply wasn't a story.

A few years earlier, Alex had been sent to talk to a man who was protesting outside of the royal palace. The man was all alone and wearing a sandwich board that read, *Only I have the antidote.*

Alex expected the man to be in handcuffs by the time he arrived in front of the palace. Instead, there were three policemen huddled in a circle a distance off trying to decide what their next move would be.

Alex walked past the policemen and approached the man wearing the sign.

"Good morning," Alex said with a smile.

"Hello," the man said, staring up at the sky with a smile.

"That's an interesting sign you've got there."

"Aw, thanks. Anything that might help my cause, right?"

"What cause would that be?" Alex asked.

"Are you serious?"

"I don't know what antidote you have, what disease it cures, and how that's related to any cause."

The man slowly looked down at the sign he wore and began cursing.

"Bloody kids!"

The man with the sign was nothing more than a homeless man. His original sign had said, *The one homeless guy who doesn't like booze or drugs.* According to the homeless man, some kids must have come by and painted over his sign while he slept. When the police had questioned why he was marching in front of the palace, he said he just liked the view.

In Scotland, Alex was facing another situation where there was nothing to write about.

No one in England, or even Scotland for that matter, wanted to read about a cranky old man who got on people's nerves over noise complaints. Even though Alex got the impression that the old man wasn't telling him everything, to make a story out of it would be like writing fiction. Even if the old man started telling it all, there just wasn't a point to writing a story about it.

Alex picked up the hotel room's telephone and dialled his boss's home. Normally he would have waited until the morning to call, but Alex wanted to get on a plane tonight.

"Who's this?" Edwards said, sounding miserable.

"Hey, Martin. It's Alex."

"What is it?"

"I just wanted to give you the heads up. I should be back in the office tomorrow afternoon."

"You've got the story?" He sounded surprised, borderline shocked.

"There's no story here. There are no forces at work here. It's just some cranky old man badgering people. There's just no body to this. It's a footnote, at best."

There was a long silence on the other end of the phone.

"The *UK Observer*," Edwards began, pronouncing the name as though it were royalty, "does not make a habit of employing reporters that can't get the stories we want. You say there's no story, I say you're not looking hard enough. Humor me, please. Give it one more day. If you still believe there's no story, fine. Give me a call and we'll get you on a plane back home."

It was Alex's turn to be silent. The Edwards Alex knew had left the conversation and a more reasonable Edwards had taken his place. Alex had known Edwards to be overbearing, lazy, manipulative, and a dozen other negative things, but never reasonable.

"Perhaps I could have another look," Alex forced himself to say.

"I thought you might reconsider."

Without another word, there was a click in Alex's ear.

- 6 -

Thirty years earlier, a forty-one-year-old Rory stood on the shore of Loch Ness staring out where the water, dark as the night sky, and the horizon disappeared together beyond his sight. Despite having lived in Scotland his entire life, he had never once come to see the famous loch.

Even on that night he hadn't intended to take a sight-seeing trip. He had left his home unable to face her any longer, unable to face the things that he had done, the person he had become.

The drive from Perth had been long enough that he felt almost sober. His last drink, one of too many, had been consumed in his living room. Unfortunately, he hadn't been sober enough to keep his car from slipping off the road and scraping against a guardrail. The sound of metal on metal caused him to panic and jerk the steering wheel away from the noise and sparks only to smash directly into the guardrail on the other side of the road. Only this time, the rail brought the car to a halt. His doors had been crushed inward forcing him to exit out of the broken driver-side window. When he stood up and brushed the broken glass off of his clothes, he noticed Loch Ness in the distance.

Rory stepped over the guardrail and headed straight for the black water as though it were calling to him. When he reached the shoreline, he walked the perimeter, never taking his eyes off the water.

It was beautiful. The atmosphere of the loch sank in, erasing all the commotion in his mind. He thought about his life. He wondered how far a man could fall before he hit the bottom. Was there even a bottom? If Rory wasn't already at the bottom of his, he didn't think he could handle sinking any lower. He'd sooner sink to the bottom of the loch in front of him.

Some people were low for their entire lives. That would have actually been easier to handle. Rory once had everything a man could want and, slowly, it was all taken away from him.

If he was honest with himself, not all of it was taken. Though some was unjustly taken away, the rest he had pushed away all on his own.

While he walked, and contemplated both past and future, he heard something rise above the surface of the water. He immediately thought it had been a fish jumping out of the water, but the sound had been too subtle, quieter than a whisper, and there was no corresponding splash of the fish re-entering the loch. He squinted into the darkness and searched the surface of the inky water.

The moon was out, but it wasn't bright enough to give Rory a clear look. All he could see was a black shape gliding along the water. Whatever it was, it was moving at the same speed as Rory.

A fish wouldn't stay above water for so long, and the shape appeared to be too large for any kind of bird. He started to wonder if it was a sea otter, or maybe even a seal. He had heard stories of odd sea life making it into the loch from its inflows. Of course, there were other stories, much harder to believe, that he had heard as well.

He wondered if it was just some old wood that had been submerged until that moment. On the surface, it would continue to float along with the loch's currents.

As he finished that thought, the black shape stopped and changed direction. After gliding across the water for another few seconds, the shape got a little bigger, more of its mass being revealed, and then disappeared under the surface.

Rory stood on that spot for hours. Every problem he had been dwelling on was pushed out of his mind. There wasn't a concern that troubled him any longer. He was still standing in that spot when the sun rose.

He found a nearby fisherman who gave him a ride into the nearest town, Fort Augustus. The local mechanic got his car running again, though the body was still badly damaged. It had been time for a new one anyway. When he got back home, he would sell it to a scrap yard and get something else.

As he drove away from the loch, he felt a sense of loss. The grief he had been feeling over the state of his life had been waiting for him on the road and once again he struggled to find hope, and this time he was sober.

Rory turned around and went back to Fort Augustus. He sold his car for parts and scrap back to the mechanic who had just finished fixing it. The man must have thought Rory had lost his mind. He wasn't completely wrong.

A sense of excitement and invigoration filled him and made it difficult to breathe. He was leaving everything behind. A part of him knew he should have felt ashamed, but feeling good was so overwhelming, especially after feeling low for so long.

After some searching, he found a modest little house near the shore of the loch. It appeared that no one had lived in it for quite some time. Rory moved in immediately.

With the money he got from selling his car, he bought a few sheep to tend. A few months later, he had an arrangement with the owners of the Fort Augustus Golf Club. His new life was filling out. Everything seemed easier, and he was surrounded by the most beautiful place he had ever experienced.

He tried not to think of his old life. He was always met with guilt and shame when he did.

Every once in a while, Rory would return to the spot where he had seen the black shape appear in the middle of the night.

*　　*　　*

Rory pulled the sheep carcass from the back of his truck and tossed it down on the ground in front of him. As usual when he came to this spot, he stood for some time and waited, staring into the distance where the water and horizon outran his eyes.

He wasn't the same man that had stood on that spot thirty years previous. Rory didn't think he'd even recognize that man anymore. What would he even say to a man like that? What would that man say to him? It was a conversation he was glad he'd never have to have.

No matter how long he stood, he knew he would remain to stand alone. He shoved the sheep forward with his foot until it lay on the shore with the water gently lapping at the carcass. Rory got back into his truck and started the engine.

Giving one last look out at the water, he smiled as moisture filled his eyes. "Happy Anniversary, Nessie."

– 7 –

Some reporters could find a story anywhere. The simple sight of a fruit stand or a group of children playing would end up a front-page story with poetic, flowing prose that was worthy of being nominated for a Pulitzer.

Some stories found reporters. Pure luck could elevate a reporter's career to levels that would take most others years to achieve. Inevitably, these reporters would fall back down with time unless their luck continued or they developed some talent while riding that luck.

Alex Stafford was somewhere in between those two types. He certainly had abilities beyond luck, but he didn't see a story in everything he looked at. When he was determined, he could find a story, but the result wouldn't be worthy of any awards. Anything could be interesting if you looked at it from the right angle. His job was finding that angle.

He was nervous driving back out to the loch to find Rory again. He couldn't escape the image of the old man cutting that sheep's throat. He also couldn't help imagining his own throat being sliced open if the old man grew tired of a reporter hanging around.

I think it would be best if I left the old man alone, Alex thought. He could always fill in the details by talking to some more of the people that lived and worked nearby. If the story wasn't coming together by midday then he'd go back and talk to Rory. Maybe.

The first person Alex found was the captain of a tour boat. The captain laughed when Alex asked about the old man. They had had dozens of run-ins in the past. Most of them ending with the stubborn old man forcing the group back to the docks.

"I don't really care, to be honest with you. I get paid by the trip. Doesn't matter whether it's five hours or five minutes."

The captain explained that he owned the boat and worked for Mythical Tours as an independent contractor. The company had taken to watching Rory and recording his weekly schedule. Once they saw a pattern they would plan their excursions around the times he was away from the loch.

"He comes back once in a while unexpectedly." The captain chuckled. "The tour girls get quite cross with him. It's hard not to laugh sometimes."

The captain told Alex some of the more amusing stories about his run-ins with Rory.

He went back to a few fisherman he had spoken to the previous day to ask a few follow-up questions. They didn't have much to say. It seemed as if they appreciated reporters as much as Rory did. At least none of them had killed anything in front of him.

"Never actually saw him bother anyone," one of the fishermen admitted. "I'm not here every day, though." He began checking over one of his fishing poles when his head snapped back up. "Oh! There was this one time I saw him get rid of a bunch of university kids. They were doing some research project. Heard one of them say something about sonar something-or-other. Rory waited until they were standing away from their equipment and crushed it all with his truck."

The man laughed heartily as he cast his rod out again.

"You should have seen the faces on those kids. The most beautiful part is he got out of the truck, right there in front of them, acting like some kind of senile old fool. He had them so convinced that they brought him and his truck home. Walked him right into the house. Even made him a cup of tea."

The man was still laughing as Alex thanked him for his time and walked away. Alex read over his notes and wondered where to go next when he looked up and saw Rory marching toward him like an angry bull.

A slight panic set in and Alex's hands rose up in front of him.

"Whoa. Rory? Are you angry?"

"Of course I'm angry, you fool idiot!" Rory yelled. "You think I haven't seen you wandering all around here all morning bothering people?"

"I'm just asking a few questions. It's my job!"

"We don't like questions around here." Rory turned and began to stalk away.

"So I hear," Alex spat back. "You going to run me over with your truck?"

Alex had expected Rory to turn around and retaliate, embarrassed, or to deny that he ever did anything of the sort.

Instead, without slowing or looking back, he called out, "Maybe!"

After a few more marching steps Rory did stop, but instead of looking back at Alex he looked up and to the east.

Alex looked in the same direction, but didn't see anything. After a few seconds, a noise became clear. A helicopter was approaching.

Both Rory and Alex stood as still as statues, watching the aircraft approach. Alex was sure it would smoothly pass over the loch on its way to Inverness or possibly even as far as Iceland.

Instead, the helicopter slowed almost directly over their heads and began to descend. Painted on the side of the helicopter was a logo that Rory may not have been familiar with, but in London it was a household name; a corporate superpower.

"What is Chase Industries doing here?" Alex said in surprise, though the roar of the descending helicopter rendered his words completely inaudible.

Both Rory and Alex walked toward the spot where the helicopter was about to touch down. The grass bent under the power of the spinning blades.

As soon as the helicopter landed, and the blades stopped spinning, two men in dark suits got out and began surveying the area. A third man, dressed in a much more expensive suit, jumped out of the helicopter with a big smile on his face.

"Sir, we haven't done our sweep," one of the dark-suited men said.

"Nonsense, there's no need." The third man looked at Rory and Alex and held his arms out wide. "Gentlemen!"

He walked over and continued to smile at them as if he alone knew the world's greatest joke.

Alex pointed at him, dumbfounded. "You're Harvey Chase."

The man's smile widened, but he still said nothing.

"Aren't you?"

"I am, I am!" Chase finally admitted. "And this . . ." He stepped forward, beyond Rory and Alex, looking out at the water, his arms held wide. ". . . is the Loch Ness! It's beautiful!" Chase exclaimed.

Rory sneered at the man. Alex flipped to a fresh page in his notebook and stepped beside Chase.

"What brings you to the Loch Ness, Mr. Chase?" he asked.

"My friends tell me it's a sight you have to see with your own eyes, and I'd have to agree. Maybe I should take a ride on one of those little tour boats. What do you think?"

"I, uh . . ."

Chase burst out into a hearty, possibly fake, laugh. "Obviously, I'm joking. I love a challenge. But in the business world, I've dominated every goal I've ever set for myself. Now I've set my eyes on . . ." He paused, choosing his words carefully, "more challenging endeavors."

Alex looked at him with wide eyes. "You're here looking for the Loch Ness Monster."

Rory's face twisted into a mask of disgust.

"The Loch Ness Monster," Chase said, once again extending his arms wide, as if welcoming the beast out of the water. "Nessie, as she's more commonly known. Been around for centuries as far as the legend goes. Forty years at least by recent accounts."

"Are you an expert in aquatic life?" Alex asked.

"No," Chase answered, still smiling, "not at all."

"Then hunting is your expertise."

"I would say business is my expertise, but I'm picking up new skills all the time."

"So many people have already tried. Experts. What makes you think you'll be the man to do it?"

"A brilliant mind, a willingness to try things that have never been tried before. That, and resources, my friend. I know, I know. That sounds conceited, but there's no point in being coy. There are a lot of experts, but few of them have resources. So, I hire the experts and give them access to my resources. Best of everything."

Alex glanced toward Rory to find he was gone.

"In fact," Chase continued, "I've already built an entire team that will be arriving here on site in the next day or so. We'll set up a camp right here on the shore of Loch Ness and get to work. In fact, I've already conferred with several of the experts I spoke of, and we've come up with a plan."

- 8 -

Rory tried to busy himself with housework and forget all about Harvey Chase, but every few moments he found himself drawn to the window. While an army of men arrived in vans, trampled the grass, and started setting up a city of tents, that fool reporter stood talking with Chase the entire time. They were probably becoming good friends, laughing about how Chase would kill the Loch Ness Monster and turn her into a pair of boots and a matching belt.

They probably thought he didn't know anything about Harvey Chase or his family, but he'd read enough newspapers on his visits into town. The man's family owned the most profitable companies in all of the United Kingdom. Investors consistently poured their money into Chase Industries' various interests and almost always saw a lucrative gain. Chase's resources were almost without limit. Rory and the loch had never faced such a dangerous opponent.

Rory went to his shed and began organizing his storage to make space. He worked his way toward the back corner of the shed, where his target sat underneath a large canvas tarp. Pulling the cover to the ground, Rory revealed the large construct.

It was a sculpture of sorts. Made up of a series of logs and driftwood, it roughly resembled the shape of the fabled Loch Ness Monster. Not even he knew how authentic it looked, but the average person who saw it at a distance might believe it to be the beast of legend. It didn't need to be authentic. It only needed to work.

On its own, the decoy would float across the loch. Upon first sight, it would cause a panic, but anyone who watched it for more than a few seconds would see its statuesque swim pattern and realize it was fake. Rory had a slightly more convincing plan in mind.

He set about checking the decoy's durability. Rory hadn't needed it in some time and it had been sitting under a tarp for years. Rory positioned himself behind the decoy to push it away from the wall. He crouched down and pushed with his shoulder. The decoy wouldn't move.

He tied a rope around the front of the decoy and pulled. Again, the decoy didn't budge. Placing a 2x4 between the decoy and the wall, as a lever, he pulled until he was red in the face and beads of sweat formed on his forehead. The decoy slid a few inches away from the wall before Rory's strength gave out and he collapsed on top of the fake Nessie.

For a moment, he wanted nothing more than to grab his axe and turn the decoy into kindling. Fortunately for the decoy, he had a hold of his temper by the time he caught his breath.

He stood in the shed with his arms folded looking at the

decoy and waiting for a solution to become apparent. His shoulders sagged and Rory left his shed.

Chase and Alex were still standing a short distance away. Chase was telling some exaggerated story with dramatic flailing of his arms, no doubt making himself to be a great hero.

Rory marched over to them and jabbed Alex on the shoulder.

Alex turned to him slowly, a look of bewilderment on his face.

"I need to talk to you," Rory said.

"I don't believe we've met," Chase said before Alex could reply.

"You're right. We haven't met." He turned to Alex once again. "I need to talk to you."

"It'll have to wait a few minutes." The man was acting like Rory was making an unreasonable request.

Rory looked at Alex for a moment longer, hoping the uncomfortable silence would make him change his mind, then glared at Chase. "You know where to find me," he told Alex.

Before another word was said, Rory was stomping back toward the shed. He heard Chase call after him.

"It was nice to meet you."

Rory refused to acknowledge Chase had said anything.

Rory covered his decoy back up in case Chase decided to walk over with the reporter. He seemed like the kind of man that went wherever and did whatever he wanted without seeing a problem to it.

Rory prepared a series of sandbags while he waited. Two hours later, Alex finally showed up. Alone.

"What was so important that you needed to talk to me right away?" Alex asked.

"What was so important that you couldn't step away for a minute?" Rory replied.

"I'm a reporter. He's a billionaire. People are interested in the things he does. No one else knows he's out here. That's called a scoop. In my profession, this situation is what you might call a jackpot."

Rory grew quiet. He knew the next thing he needed to say, but he wasn't sure he'd be able to say the actual words. Thirty years living by the loch and he never once had to say to someone what he said to Alex. "I need help with something."

A smug smile appeared on the reporters face. "Do you?"

"Now don't go getting all righteous on me. I need your help, but I also need to know I can trust you. You have to promise you're not going to tell anyone what you're about to see," Rory said in a very serious tone.

"Why should I promise that?"

"Because you're a reporter. Reporters are curious. And there's something in here that I think you'll find amazing. But unless you promise not to tell anyone you're never going to see it."

"Fine," Alex said with a sigh. It was clear he didn't think Rory had anything worth seeing.

Rory walked over and pulled the cover from his decoy. Alex stared, letting his eyes grow and his mouth fall open.

"Is that what I think it is?"

"What do you think it is?" Rory asked.

"Is this the reason everyone thinks the monster exists?"

"Not quite," Rory admitted. "But I'm flattered you might think that. Help me move it away from the wall."

Together they pushed the decoy into the center of the shed. Rory went to work checking it over. He tightened a few bindings, and replaced others. For a moment he considered replacing a cross beam, but decided it wasn't necessary.

Rory glanced over at Alex, who was staring at the decoy

with a grin on his face. He could only imagine what the reporter was thinking. Hoping Alex wouldn't ask all the questions going through his mind was, without doubt, useless.

"So, if this isn't for some kind of hoax, what are you doing?" Alex asked.

"Chase wants to find a monster. I'm going to let him."

"So, this is for Chase. Why? He's not bothering you. Are you just bored? Is this entertainment for you?"

"Not bothering me? Did you see how many people he has out there? A brand new city popped up in the last few hours. You don't think that's going to create a lot of noise?"

"There has to be something else." Alex motioned to the decoy. "No one would go to all of this trouble over a noise complaint."

"No. It's . . ." Rory hesitated, shuffling around the decoy a little, "it's complicated." He retightened a few of the ties, desperate for a reason to avoid eye contact with Alex.

"What if I told you I wouldn't help you with . . . whatever the hell this thing is?" He thrust his hands at the decoy.

"Then I would keep working at it on my own, and probably die of a heart attack, or a stroke, or something else just as horrible and you'd feel guilty for letting it happen."

Alex barked a laugh.

"When I met you yesterday, you acted like the toughest man alive. Now you need my help like you've got a foot in the grave."

Rory stopped shuffling around the decoy and stared at his hands for a long time. He kept hoping the young man would change subjects in the uncomfortable air of silence. When it became obvious that that wasn't going to happen, he considered how much to reveal before looking up at the man.

"That monster that some believe lives in that loch? Well, maybe I believe in her too. And maybe I don't think someone like that Chase fellow should be able to come here and scoop her up and take her away. If she truly does exist, it means she's been here longer than any of us. That means she has a right to stay."

For a moment, Alex just stared at the old man. Rory squirmed under the gaze, waiting for the laughter that would inevitably follow. Without a word Alex grabbed a sandbag.

"Where do you want these?"

"Put them out by my dock. We'll tie them on out there."

They worked for a few hours with a rare word spoken between them. Although he wouldn't have admitted it to anyone, Rory felt a fragile bond forming between himself and the young reporter. The man had no obligation to help Rory in even the smallest way, and what they were doing was no small thing.

"Why?" Alex said in a near whisper. The word was such a sudden break of the thick silence around them it startled Rory.

"I told you. Chase wants a monster . . ."

"Not that. This obviously isn't the first time you've stopped someone from looking for her. You tend a few sheep, cut grass at a golf course and grow your own food to survive. You live in this small house all alone. Why? Why do you do it?"

"My life wasn't always like this."

For the first time in thirty years, Rory told another human being about his wife.

* * *

Before Rory found himself standing on the shores of Loch Ness, he lived in Glasgow with his wife, in a two-story house, and he had a drinking problem.

Over the span of a few months, Rory's drinking had increased from a daily drink to bringing home a bottle of whiskey each night for his supper. His wife, Mari, would beg him to eat the dinner she made for him every night, but he would rarely eat more than a mouthful. Even that was only so Mari would leave him alone.

She spent most nights crying in the bedroom. He usually fell asleep in the living room listening to the radio, though passed out was probably a more accurate description.

Once or twice a week, Mari would confront him about his drinking. She would tell him that he was going to drink himself to death. Her lectures were mostly ignored. He refused to hear about it. The nights when she pressed him, he shouted at her until she ran into the bedroom with fresh tears on her cheeks.

On the night that he left, she had pressed him more than usual.

"You're going to drink that whole bottle, aren't you?" she asked, standing in the doorway to the kitchen.

He was sitting in his favorite chair, with his feet up, listening to news reports on the radio. He picked up the half-empty bottle on the end table next to him and studied the contents.

"Yes, I believe I will. In fact, my only regret is that I only brought home one bottle."

"One? That's your second one. Tonight. One morning I'm going to come out here to find a corpse sitting in that chair. You know that, don't you?"

"Mari," he said in a warning tone.

"Are you that desperate for death? Because there are much faster ways to go about it. Ways that are easier for me to live with."

Earlier in their marriage, when Mari mentioned she thought he was drinking too much, he would finish his glass and put the remainder of the bottle in the kitchen cupboard.

On that night, he quickly stood and grabbed for Mari's arm but missed when she took a step back. Rory lost his balance and ended up sprawled out on the floor.

When Rory got up, he expected her to be smiling and laughing at him. She wasn't. Instead, she looked at him with a sincere sadness in her eyes. It was a sadness for herself, for what her life had become, but it was also a sadness for what he had become. A sadness for the man she had married, who had been killed by this alcoholic doppelganger.

That sadness spread from her eyes into his, but was quickly replaced with anger. He slapped her across the face, sending her stumbling. Mari collided with the end table beside Rory's chair. The small table fell over and its contents were thrown into the air.

"No!" Rory called out, with a hand stretched out. Time seemed to slow as he watched his bottle of whiskey fall onto the floor and the contents spill out onto the carpet. He scrambled over and snatched it off the floor, but it was too late. The bottle was nearly empty, half a mouthful remaining which he drank instantly.

He stared at the empty bottle and watched his wife cowering on the floor with a hand on her face.

"Look what you did!" he screamed at her, showing her the empty bottle.

"Then it was worth being slapped," she spat back.

Rory bared his teeth and pulled his arm back for another swing. This time he made contact just above her temple, and instead of his hand it was the empty whiskey bottle that hit his wife.

Mari was unconscious before she landed face first on the floor. Blood poured from the gash in her forehead and pooled on the floor beneath her face.

Rory couldn't bring himself to move. He hadn't meant to hit her with a bottle. He was so drunk he had forgotten he was still holding it. He shouldn't have hit her at all!

Mari wasn't moving. He tried to shake her, but she didn't respond. Too drunk to tell if she was still breathing, he called the paramedics. When they began asking questions he didn't feel like answering, he hung up on them.

They would still send someone and they'd arrive soon. Based on the call he made, they would probably send the police as well.

He took a look around his house, not knowing it would be his last. His humble home. Usually it was so clean. The table lying on the floor, along with its contents, was out of place. And his wife, lying on the reddening carpet.

Everything was a blur. Not only from the pressure of the situation, but from his mind swimming in alcohol.

He grabbed his car keys and ran to the front door. He spent another moment looking at his wife lying on the floor, bleeding, because of him. Tears came to his eyes and he resisted the urge to sink to his knees. He forced himself to open the door and step outside. He gave Mari one last look over his shoulder. Her life was about to get infinitely better.

* * *

"I haven't had a drop of alcohol since that night," Rory said.

"Oh, my God," Alex replied. "Did she die?"

"No!" Rory was offended at the thought. "I called a friend a few days later and asked after her."

"Where did you go?"

"Here. Haven't left since."

"What did Mari do after you left?"

"I don't know. I haven't spoken to anyone in Glasgow in decades."

"Why not?" Alex asked incredulously.

"You certainly always have a lot of questions, don't you? No matter how many questions I answer, you've always got another."

"I'm sorry. It's the reporter in me."

"When does he go off duty?"

Alex stopped and turned his attention back to the decoy. "What's next with this?"

"Let's see what Chase is up to first."

Rory walked out of the shed, with Alex close behind. The city of tents was growing darker with the setting sun. The white tents turned orange as they reflected light from the sun and from several campfires. There was no sign of Chase. Another man in a suit, much older than Chase, showed up and began directing people between the tents and campfires.

"When it gets a little darker, we'll put the decoy in the water."

Rory brought chairs out from his house and they watched the commotion of camp Chase. They tried to count how many people he had brought in, but they were constantly on the move and Rory kept losing his count. Alex mentioned it must have been close to a hundred.

When darkness fell, and Rory was fairly certain Chase's people wouldn't see them, Alex and Rory pushed the decoy from the shed to the water's edge.

Rory began stripping off his clothes.

"What are you doing?" Alex asked.

"Don't want to get my clothes wet," he stated as if it was obvious.

"Why not just roll up your pant legs?"

"We have to go out a little farther than that. You can swim, right?"

"Of course I can swim! Can't we just get it in the water and send it off?"

"This thing is going to sink at first. We need to take it out far enough that it's completely submerged."

"You couldn't have told me this a little sooner?"

Rory shrugged. "Seemed obvious. I thought a smart young man like you would—"

"All right, all right!" Alex said, waving his hands to cut off Rory's response.

Rory had to admit to himself that he enjoyed being the cause of the younger man's frustration, even if they were starting to like each other. 'Like' might have been too strong of a word.

Alex kicked his shoes and socks off and began to undo his belt. He looked over at Rory who was completely nude.

"Come on," Rory said. "Let's get this done so I can go to bed."

"I'm not taking my clothes off."

"You have an extra set in the car?" Rory asked.

"Why would I have a change of clothes in my car?"

Rory shrugged.

"Let's just do this," Alex said, sounding defeated.

Together, they pushed the decoy into the water and quickly found themselves up to their necks in the freezing water.

"This water is freezing!" Alex said. Whimpers kept escaping from his lips.

"Keep your voice down," Rory chided him. "I know it's cold. That's why we're going to do this quick before hypothermia sets in."

"Hypothermia!"

They worked as quickly as possible, tying the sandbags to the decoy's frame. Alex complained about it being hard to tie sand bags with numb fingertips. Rory smiled and continued his work.

They swam along with the decoy for a short while longer until the sandbags pulled it under the surface. Rory told Alex to head back to shore. Then he took a deep breath and swam underneath the water along the base of the decoy. Using a small knife he had brought out with him, he poked a small hole in each of the sandbags and made sure a little sand started to leak out. It took a few dives due to the combination of murky water and working at night. He had to do the whole thing by feel.

Alex was waiting impatiently on the shore when Rory came back in. "Finally! I thought you had died out there."

Rory was stiff from the cold and he was grateful to slip back into his dry clothes. Alex was hugging himself and shivering uncontrollably.

"Let's go inside. I'll start a fire," Rory said.

"What were you doing out there?" Alex asked once they were warming their bodies by the fireplace.

"I had to cut a hole in the sandbags. The sand will slowly leak out and when the bags are light enough, the whole thing will float to the surface."

"And Chase will think that's what people have been seeing," Alex concluded.

"Let's hope."

A long silence played out between them, filled only by the crackling of the fire.

"Thank you," Rory finally said, "for helping. I know you didn't have to do that."

"It was . . . interesting."

- 9 -

Alex woke in his hotel room the next morning with sore muscles in his legs, arms, and back. The simple act of getting out of bed caused more than a few involuntary grunts to escape his lips. He wondered how sore Rory would have been feeling at his age.

He sat on the edge of the bed and grabbed the phone to call his boss.

Yesterday, Alex wanted to come home but Edwards had asked him to wait for another day. For the first time Alex could remember, he was glad he followed his editor's advice. With the arrival of Harvey Chase, Alex had gone from having no story to having one of the biggest stories of the year. It wasn't the story Edwards had asked for, but he would be a fool not to print it.

The line rang a number of times before Edwards's secretary answered the phone.

"Observer."

"Hi, Doris. It's Alex. Is Martin available?"

"He's in a meeting. I'll have him call you when he's done."

Alex gave her the number to his hotel room and hung up the phone. The waiting caused him to pace around the small room a little. He wanted to get back to the loch and see what Chase and his team were doing. Having grown up reading stories about Chase Industries and the eccentricity of the Chases, he knew there would be some incredible stories coming from this situation.

Alex was still thinking about the headlines when the phone rang.

"Hello?"

"Hi!" said Loren. Her voice squeaked through the receiver.

"Loren. Hi. I meant to call you last night, but I got in so late."

"That's okay." Her pause said it wasn't. "It's good to hear your voice."

"Same," Alex agreed. "How is everything there?"

"Good. Did you get your story?"

"Yes. Well, no. Not exactly. I got a story. Did I ever get a story!" He gave her a quick recap of the previous day's events.

"A story's a story, I guess," she suggested. "Does that mean you'll be coming home tonight?"

"Tonight? This is a huge story. They're going to want to me to stay here and cover it.

"They could send someone else, couldn't they?"

"They'd better not! This might be the biggest story of my career. I want to wring every word I can out of the entire situation. But look, I've got to keep this line open. The boss is supposed to ring me soon."

He heard her signature noise of disapproval, a clicking of her tongue.

"I know you want to talk, but I've got to be available for his call. I'll call you right back. I love you. Bye!"

Alex hung the phone up before she could protest any farther, and checked his watch again.

*   *   *

For the fifth time in an hour, Martin Edwards jerked awake hoping none of his colleagues in the board room had noticed. The monthly meeting was centered around financial plans, advertising budgets, and spending goals for the future. All things he had very little to do with, in his opinion.

Truthfully, if they asked him, he could tell them how to fix the issues each department was having. He could tell them what the idiots in advertising sales should have been doing instead of whatever they did now. It should have been obvious to everyone, though apparently it was only to him, how to cut spending in half. And if he spent a little time, he could surely find suppliers that could provide materials at a fraction of the current price.

If Martin Edwards ran the *UK Observer*, they'd be the top paper in a matter of months! But as the editor, there wasn't any reason to pay attention to conversation on financial matters.

Doris walked into the room and headed straight for Edwards. He gave her a stern look, but she didn't slow. She leaned down to whisper into his ear.

"You said you wanted to know when Alex called. He just called a few moments ago."

She placed a slip of paper in front of him with a phone number and left the board room as quickly as she had come in. A smile crept onto his face. The timing couldn't have been better.

Edwards waited for a lull in the meeting and cleared his throat.

"Excuse my interruption, gentlemen, but one of my reporters is standing by with some exciting news." He tried to remain unreadable, but he had made the word exciting sound cryptic.

The others in the board room, eight in all, looked around at each other shrugging. It was highly unusual for a meeting like this to be interrupted for a reporter's story, but they would forget all about that once Edwards could put Alex Stafford's failure on display and spin it into incompetence.

Alex had certainly called to say there wasn't a story. Of course, he was right, but as long as he made sure the department managers he was meeting with only heard the information Edwards wanted them to hear, it would create an awful image of the *UK Observer's* star reporter.

Edwards quickly dialled the phone number to Alex's hotel room, keeping the call on speakerphone.

"Hello?" Alex said.

"Alex! It's Martin. I'm still in a meeting with the other heads here, but I wanted to—"

"Martin, this is incredible!"

"Incredible? What?" Edwards sputtered. The satisfied smile on his face was nowhere to be found, replaced with a look of confusion.

"Harvey Chase!" Alex said. "Harvey bloody Chase showed up yesterday afternoon. He's come to the loch to hunt the Loch Ness Monster! I've sent you an opening story. Should've been on your fax first thing this morning."

"That's impossible," Edwards whispered. He looked up to see everyone in the meeting waiting for an answer from him. He hadn't checked his fax that morning, as usual, but couldn't let everyone know that. The incompetence he intended this phone call to imply could end up on him. He put on the largest smile he could, it felt unnatural.

"I did, Alex. It was really great stuff!" He had sent Alex to a reporter's grave and the son-of-a-bitch gets possibly the story of the year dumped into his lap! Was there any justice left in the world?

"Alex, come on home. You've been gone long enough, we'll send someone else out to cover the remainder on this." There was no way to take this away from Alex completely, but at least he could minimize the effect.

"I'd like to stay," Alex responded. "I talked with Chase for some time yesterday. We have a good chemistry."

Edwards began to shake his head, but Gary Whitson spoke up. "Alex, it's Gary. I think it's a good idea for you to stay on this story."

Gary Whitson wasn't the owner of the *UK Observer*, but he was the next closest thing. Hired by the owner directly, they were not only colleagues, but friends. Gary and the owner played darts a few times a month over scotch. When he spoke, it was considered words from the owner's lips.

"I just thought," Edwards stammered, "we should send someone who can get pictures for us as well."

"You don't have a camera, Alex?" Gary asked.

"No, sir."

"Get one. Best one you can find. Ship the film daily. Overnight or faster. Cost is no object."

Edwards felt the control being yanked away from him. He wanted to go to his office and close the door for the rest of the day, but he had to sit there and pretend Alex Stafford was doing a great job.

"That's settled, then," Edwards spoke up, renewing his false smile. "Great job so far, Alex. Looking forward to reading the next article."

"Right," Alex replied. "Have a good one, all."

Everyone around the table echoed their goodbyes and a call-ending click sounded from the phone.

For the next half hour the department managers, along with Gary Whitson, did nothing but gush about Alex Stafford and Harvey Chase. Edwards prayed for the meeting to turn back to financial charts and budgeting concerns.

"What story did you send him for in the first place, Martin," Gary asked.

Everyone shifted their gaze to him, faces still wearing half smiles from their giddy conversations.

"Come again?" Edwards hadn't anticipated being questioned.

"What did you send him to the Loch Ness for?"

"There were reports of . . ." Reports of what? Everything he thought of sounded foolish. They were excited about Chase looking for the Loch Ness Monster. Maybe. ". . . sightings of the Loch Ness Monster."

"A monster sighting?" Gary asked, disgust evident in his voice. "That's not really the kind of thing we should be reporting on. We're a newspaper, not a rag." He turned his attention away from Edwards. "What's the trending delivery cost for the year so far?"

The meeting conversation shrunk to a gentle buzz in Edwards's ears. His thoughts were consumed by Alex Stafford who was probably wearing that smug, satisfied look he used whenever he found a horseshoe up his arse.

At least Alex would be far from the office for a while. Edwards would just have to think of another way to make Alex a liability.

- 10 -

Everyone at the Fort Augustus Golf Club was talking about Harvey Chase. They all spoke with the same excitement as if they had met their favorite movie star.

Rory attempted to avoid the conversation, but no matter where he went, Chase's name was on everyone's lips. His only escape was cutting the grass. With the rider's blades spinning, everyone was rendered into a mute only capable of making a buzzing noise.

"Morning, Rory," Claire said with a smile as he walked into the pro shop.

"Claire," he said, his eyes trained on the floor. There was still more work he could do for the day, but he didn't want to overhear one more conversation about Harvey Chase.

"Your fertilizer came in. Did you see?"

"Yes, thanks. It's away in the shed."

"The members have been all in a ruckus today about this Harvey Chase fellow. Have you heard?"

Along with the rest of his day, Rory found the best part of his day ruined.

"I heard. Heard he's some kind of fool. Looking for the Loch Ness Monster or some idiot thing."

"You don't think he exists?" Claire asked, leaning over the pro shop counter.

"I've been living on the loch for thirty years. You'd think I'd have seen her by now."

"Oh, so it's a she, is it?" Claire said with a wink.

"Most people say she, don't they?" Rory's face grew hot.

"I suppose they do," she admitted. "You keep telling me about this house on the edge of the loch. I love waterfront property. When are you going to invite me over to see your place?"

Rory couldn't figure out why anyone would want to see his little house. Maybe she didn't know how small and meager the house was, but he had never said anything to Claire to make it sound like anything special. The fact that it was on the water couldn't be that impressive.

"It's really nothing to see, Lass."

"You always say that, but I'd still like to see it."

If Rory had been a younger man, a more attractive man, he would have thought Claire was flirting with him. Though she wasn't much younger than him, Rory looked decades older than Claire. Even knowing all of that, the conversation stirred his desire.

"Have a good afternoon," Rory said with a nod.

Instead of going home, Rory drove to the city of Inverness. He parked out in front of a non-descript two-story building. The exterior was in decent repair, but it wasn't without its imperfections. A few chips of paint from the siding and the odd weed growing out of the cracks in the cement allowed the property to blend in with all those around it.

Inside the building was a thriving business. One of the world's oldest businesses. A business without a sign or advertising, but whose customers were some of the most loyal.

Rory approached the receptionist, avoiding eye contact and fiddling with his fingers.

"Mr. Stewart," the receptionist greeted, "we haven't see you in a while. How can we help you today?"

"Uh, hello," Rory replied. "Is she available?"

The receptionist flipped open a calendar book and traced a finger down to the day's date.

"Yes, she is. Shall I escort you upstairs?"

"Thank you, but no."

Rory knew the way. Floral perfume and strong incense filled his nostrils as he climbed the stairs to the second floor. The smells would have been even nicer without the knowledge that they existed to cover up the stench of sex and sweat.

In the upstairs hallway, with rows of doors on each side, the sounds of pleasure seemed to come from every direction. The long walk down the hallway was always the most disconcerting. A man might be able to lie to himself about being in a brothel, that he was different than the other men that patronized the place, but with the sounds of sex all around him the illusion was impossible to hold.

He counted until the fifth door on the right and gave it a knock.

The door opened to reveal a dream. Her name was Brandy. She was gorgeous to his old eyes, wearing only a bathrobe which displayed her curvaceous body.

"Rory," she said with a smile that gave him a fluttering in his stomach and a swelling in his underwear. "How are you?"

He smiled like a fool as he walked into the room. There was no question that Brandy could never love the old man, but that didn't stop him from loving her.

"It's been a while since you came to see me. I was starting to think you'd found another," she teased.

Rory had been coming to see Brandy for almost ten years. She started when she was twenty-three, and Rory had been one of her first clients. A lot of men who came to places like these liked to visit every girl, especially when there was a new arrival, but Rory had never visited anyone other than Brandy.

She took him by the hand and led him over to the bed. They talked for some time as they always did, lying beside each other.

Rory mainly listened. He liked the feeling of someone lying beside him. Someone warm, not just physically, but emotionally. She might not have been in love with him, but it was enough that he could fool himself into believing she might like him.

Brandy always knew when the conversation was over. She would then crawl on top of him and make love to him. Maybe it was the amount of time between visits or the fact that she was so young, but each time he came he felt like he might die, and he would have been fine with that.

Afterwards, they slept for a while. He paid a little extra for that time. Sleeping with another warm body in his arms seemed to be the only time he got any real rest. After their nap, he would get dressed while she continued to chat.

He paid in cash, and she'd walk him to the door giving him a kiss goodbye, as if he were leaving for work for the day.

That was it. There were no expectations that he couldn't fulfill, no questions that he didn't want to answer, no talk about Harvey Chase. It was how life should have been.

-11-

A commotion from outside of the tent roused Chase from his meditation session. He remained seated on the tent floor, with eyes closed and his feet resting on opposite knees, and listened, straining to hear a reason for the commotion.

People were shouting to one another, but they were far enough away from his tent that he couldn't make out any of the words. When the shouting didn't show signs of stopping, Chase pushed himself to his feet with the palms of his hands pushed together. When he was ready, he exhaled and opened his eyes feeling refreshed.

On the days he had time to meditate, he could afford to cut the night's sleep to four hours without feeling tired the next day. It was incredible how much work one could accomplish with four hours when the rest of the world slept.

Chase moved around his tent, retrieved his shoes, and sat

on the edge of his bed to put them on. When his team had set up camp, they had insisted he take one of the largest tents for himself. He disagreed. The largest tents needed to be used for equipment and planning, and the actual work that needed to be done. Most people who didn't yet know Chase assumed he required constant coddling, but that had never been true.

He allowed himself a medium-sized tent, though medium meant it was big enough to park two tanks side-by-side, as well as a few luxuries.

His bed was a queen-sized feather mattress raised off of the floor with an aluminum frame. In one corner of his tent, he had a small bistro table with a pair of chairs which came in handy when he wanted to sit and listen to his radio, or enjoy a glass of scotch and a book.

Chase's personal assistant, Jerry Triggs, popped his head into the tent.

"Harvey, I'm not exactly sure what's going on out here, but I think you should come and have a look."

Chase liked Jerry very much. He had been a long time employee of Chase Industries, originally serving as the assistant to Harvey's father, Harold, for three decades. When Harold died and Harvey took control, he inherited, among other things, Jerry Triggs.

Jerry was much more than the average personal assistant. Anyone who mistook Jerry for a secretary was a fool. In fact, Jerry had his own secretary, along with a business degree and more years of experience in business than most CEOs.

Jerry took a kid, who had just lost his father and gained a billion-dollar company, and turned him into a business machine. Whenever Chase decided to leave the office for an eccentric adventure, Jerry went along with him to assist in whatever way he could, whether he agreed with the reasoning or not.

They stepped outside of the tent together and saw people streaming toward the edge of the loch.

"Good afternoon, Mr. Chase," a few people said when they noticed him standing outside of his tent.

"Afternoon," he repeated back as he craned his neck trying to spot the source of the commotion. It appeared as though a team of his men were hauling something out of the water.

His heart began to race. They couldn't have caught her already. If they had caught her, someone would have come to fetch him. He broke into a jog, barely resisting the urge to sprint to the water's edge.

He was forced to push his way through a crowd of people. It seemed his entire camp was there waiting.

A large crane apparatus was set up at the edge of the loch. It looked like a large tripod with a boom that could be rotated to any angle. The boom was extended out over the water with a thick, metal cable plummeting straight into the loch.

The winch whined as the line retracted bringing with it a potential treasure. Something broke the water's surface. It looked like a log covered with moss and mud. As more was revealed, it was too oddly shaped to be a log. This was something else.

The boom swung the thing over land and lowered it to the ground. Men swarmed in, studying their discovery and talking to each other in hushed tones.

More experts, Chase thought, bitterly.

He watched them walk slow circles around their find, facial expressions dropping as they went. It became obvious that whatever they were hoping to find, this wasn't it.

"What is this?" Chase blurted out. "You all look like your childhood dog just died."

One of the so-called experts stepped forward. He must have

thought himself the leader, or at least the representative for the group, but Chase hadn't even bothered to learn his name.

"We spotted this thing this morning." He motioned toward the large object with his hands. "We were doing some initial studies and it just bobbed to the surface before sinking again. Some have believed for years that the fabled monster in this loch did exist, but died. When we saw this we considered that theory a possibility and the decaying process had brought it to the surface. But, now that we've had a close look, it's definitely not organic."

"Not organic? It looks like wood. Wood isn't organic?"

"That's not what I meant. I meant tissue. Flesh."

"I see. What do you know about it?"

"Not much. It may be a bit early to say this, but I think this, what would be best described as debris, is what people have been seeing. All the sightings, it's possible they were just seeing this."

"What's the next step?" Chase asked. He wasn't quite being impatient with the man, but his words were very direct.

"I would suggest we shut down for the day to analyze our findings."

"Shut down? No, no, no. My good man, we can't do that. Science is depending on us to push onward and find something that can benefit mankind. This here just looks like a bunch of old wood. Besides, there's enough of you here that we can have one team analyze what is clearly some old wood, and the other team can keep moving forward. Let's use the daylight and really get somewhere. What do you say?"

The man smiled, feeling inspired by Chase's mini-speech and marched off to likely try his best to replicate the speech, but would undoubtedly screw it up somehow.

"Is that the monster?" said Jerry from Chase's side.

"Can you believe these people? Not organic? Not organic!"

"Looks like wood," Jerry stated simply.

"Very astute, Jerry."

"Isn't wood organic?"

"Why do all the world's experts seem to have the least amount of expertise? Isn't that a requirement to be an expert?"

Jerry stood by as Chase began inspecting the object closer for himself. He poked and pulled, studying things from multiple angles all while complaining about whether his team would be able to find a goldfish in a fish bowl.

Chase stood up and watched his team. They seemed to be arguing with each other. If they spent half the amount of time working that they spent arguing, Chase would be on his way back to London with Nessie in a cage.

"I think we should get rid of these guys," Chase said in a low voice.

"Harvey," Jerry replied impatiently, "if you really plan on going through with this, you're going to need people that know this stuff. People who are—"

"Experts?" Chase offered.

"Yes."

"I want you to call Dr. Darin Schnabel. Tell him I'll double my last offer. If he still refuses, tell him I'll triple it. Keep going until he agrees to be here tomorrow."

Dr. Schnabel was a German scientist and considered to be the world's best in the field of aquatics. He was instrumental in the development of sonar recording equipment, underwater cameras, motion detectors, and other various technologies. He was also the man Chase had first asked to be head of the crew. Dr. Schnabel had laughed at the thought of hunting a myth. Chase had given up too easily then. Now he would have the doctor's acceptance, no matter what.

In the distance, he saw Rory watching as he pretended to

tend to his flock of sheep in his little field. He glanced back at the monster they had pulled out of the loch.

"One more thing, Jerry," Chase said, looking back out toward Rory. "Take a few men and have this non-organic thing loaded onto a flatbed truck."

Jerry shook his head as he walked to find some men. He'd been wondering why Chase wanted it loaded up but he knew better than to ask.

Chase went back to his tent to get a drink. The hunt was going to be difficult. He didn't feel in control of anything. He wasn't familiar enough with any of the equipment they were using and there wasn't much that he could do. He decided he would find a way to inject himself somewhere, even if that meant hindering progress a little.

When he took control of Chase Industries, he was in complete control of the company's finances and direction at all times. It turned out he had a mind for business and thrived under Jerry's tutelage. Inside of a year, he had a firm grasp of everything from the company budgets to its varied investments. It all came from his knowledge and his decisions.

This hunt forced him to strictly rely on other men's knowledge. That was a difficult thing to do. If he set his mind to learning the hunt, he could be just as good as any expert by the end.

"Mr. Chase?" a voice called just outside his tent.

Chase sighed and studied the scotch in his glass as he swirled it around. Draining the rest of the glass, he then put on a large smile and called out. "Come in!"

The reporter he had spoken to the previous day entered the tent. He wore a nervous smile and stared at the inside of Chase's tent the same way some would look at the Sistine Chapel.

"Is this a bad time?"

"Nonsense, my boy!" Chase called, motioning for him to come further into the tent and sit at the small table with him. "No such thing as a bad time."

Chase grabbed the man's hand in a firm handshake.

"Great to see you again. Always good to find oneself around another Englishman, isn't it?"

The reporter smiled. Chase stood and began pouring the man a scotch, as well as freshening his own drink.

"Please, forgive me, but I seem to have lost your name."

"Uh, Stafford, sir. Alex."

"Alex Stafford!" he said, as if it had been on the tip of his tongue all along. "I remember now. What brings you to my tent, Alex Stafford?"

Chase smiled and handed Alex the glass of scotch.

"My boss is fascinated by your . . ." His eyes darted around the tent, "goals. He thinks it's a great story."

"Does he?"

"I do too," Alex offered, a little too quickly to be true. "Can you imagine if you really did pull something out of this lake?"

Alex seemed to recognize his mistake and fell silent. He wouldn't be the last person to believe Chase was hunting a ghost story. People had been thinking that for years. Ever since he started taking time away from the company to make similar hunting trips, he had had many critics.

At first, people called him eccentric or thought he was pulling a publicity stunt. As if Chase Industries was in need of publicity! A few people in the beginning, and more every week, started claiming he was going insane and that his hunts were just the fancies of an unwell mind.

"I'm not crazy, you know," he said.

"No, no," Alex said, giving a nervous laugh. "I don't think that."

"It's okay if you do," Chase admitted with a smile. "But I'm not. Are you familiar with the term Cryptozoology?"

"Somewhat, yeah."

"A lot of people think it means the study of fictional creatures."

"That's not what it means?"

"Although that is part of the field, there's a lot more to it than that." Chase looked at Alex, waiting for a reaction. Alex took a large gulp of Scotch, just to break eye contact.

"Cryptozoology," Chase continued, "translated from Greek, means the study of hidden animals. It is the search for species whose existences have not been proven. If you were to spend your time searching for the dodo bird because you believed there were still some in existence, that would make you a cryptozoologist."

Alex nodded, but wore a bit of a blank expression. He wasn't convinced.

"Did you know that the Komodo dragon was considered a myth until 1912?"

"What? No." Alex smiled in disbelief.

"Truth. It was called the giant monitor and it was nothing more than a story."

"What happened? Why did it all of a sudden change?"

"They found one."

Chase watched the fact dawn on Alex: the slight widening of the eyes, the gentle curving of the corners of his mouth. He was getting it.

"You see, Alex, I'm not here believing that I'm going to catch some fairy tale creature. I'm here because what people have been calling the Loch Ness Monster is really a species that hasn't yet been proven to exist."

It was mostly true. Once he caught the beast he would tout it as the creature of legend, but that was all just marketing. Maybe the Komodo dragon would still be revered by large crowds if it had been spun as the giant monitor.

Alex fell silent and Chase basked in the moment. There was nothing better than making someone speechless with enlightenment. Most people didn't know enough to just enjoy that kind of silence. They'd jump to fill the quiet with an idiotic comment or some other kind of pointless noise.

Alex finally gave his head a small shake, and found words once again. "Have you made any progress since we talked yesterday?" he asked.

"Progress? Oh, yes. Allow me to show you our big find from today."

Chase led Alex out of the tent and over to the large object his team pulled from the loch. A small team of men had just finished putting it onto a flatbed truck.

Chase laughed when he saw Alex go a little white in the face.

"I assure you, friend. It is no danger to you. I'm told it's not organic." There was an edge of bitterness the last few words that he regretted having shown.

"What is it, then?" Alex asked.

"I'm glad you asked. After close consideration and inspection, I have deduced that this here is nothing but a decoy."

"A decoy?"

"Oh, yes," Chase said.

"What makes you think it's a decoy? It could just—"

"Happen to be shaped like a sea dragon?" Chase asked, smiling.

"Maybe," Alex replied, though he didn't sound like he believed his own argument.

"I thought it a possibility too, but come and look closer."

Chase waved him over and began to point things out to Alex.

"If this was really just a bunch of branches and things that had become entangled together, I'd be able to pull things apart quite easily. I tried and I couldn't. I wondered why, so I looked closer. If you look here, you'll see a small hollow. Easily overlooked by most. But if you feel around inside that hollow you'll feel a nut and a bolt. There's another over here. I'm sure there are at least a dozen more, all hidden very well. Even more blatant than that are the empty bags tied to it. I might believe this thing picked up some garbage while floating around the loch, but these things are tied on. You can see the knots.

"This is no natural happening, and it's not what people have been seeing for years. This, Mr. Stafford, was constructed."

"Who do you think would have made it?" Alex said after a moment.

"I have my suspicions. Would you like to take a ride with me?" Chase asked as he jumped into the driver's side of the flatbed truck. Alex walked around to the passenger side of the truck and climbed in.

"Where are we going?" Alex asked as Chase started the truck's engine.

Chase gave Alex another smile and said, "Not far."

-12-

Rory heard an engine approaching and looked out of his living room window. The sight of the flatbed truck bouncing across the grass toward his property made him feel like a mischievous child who knew he was caught. His eyesight wasn't as sharp as it once had been, but he was pretty sure his decoy was loaded on the back of that truck.

The truck came to a halt a few feet from the fence that contained Rory's flock of sheep. For a second, he had thought the driver didn't plan on stopping. The hydraulic engine that raised the truck's bed began to whine and the rear of the truck inclined until the decoy crashed onto the ground. After the fall, it would require some repairs if he ever had need of it again.

Chase got out of the truck, wearing that stupid smile that seemed to be stuck to his face, and leaned against the fence. He seemed content to wait until the end of the world if that was how long it took for him to get his way.

Rory's spot at the living room window wasn't hidden, but Chase wasn't looking in his direction. As the minutes went by, it became obvious that waiting Chase out wasn't an option. Instead he slipped from the house and grabbed his feed bucket from the shed. He walked into the sheep pen, with his head down, as if he was only outside to feed his livestock and hadn't even noticed Chase.

"Afternoon, Rory."

"What are you doing here?" Rory asked, still not looking in Chase's direction.

"Isn't it obvious? I've come to return your property." Chase motioned with both hands to the decoy now lying on the ground in a pile.

"That's not mine," Rory said. "I don't even know what that is."

"Oh, you don't?" Chase mocked.

"I could use it for firewood, I could, if you need someone to take it off your hands."

The flatbed's passenger door opened and Alex stepped down from the truck. He looked a little pale and was avoiding eye contact. Rory's own face must have been turning red from the heat of his boiling blood. He wondered what the reporter had told Chase and silently scolded himself for trusting a man he had just met.

"What do you think about all this, Alex?" Chase asked. "You think this decoy belongs to Rory?"

Alex looked at Rory for the first time and then looked at the decoy.

"I don't know. There really isn't any way to prove it's his or anyone else's, for that matter."

What was this reporter up to now? Whose side was he on? Was he spinning some story? Maybe they were working together to try to get Rory to confess.

"But it could be his," Chase insisted.

Alex hesitated. "By that logic, it could be just about anyone's."

"But it could be his," Chase reiterated.

"I guess, it could be . . ."

"It could be yours," Rory said, cutting Alex off and pointing at Chase. "Or it could be yours." This time he pointed an accusatory finger at Alex. "It could belong to anyone from your team of lackeys there. It could be my dog's! He's running around with sheep there. Maybe you can accuse him for a while."

Chase observed Rory, wearing that same smile on his face.

"You don't think I've heard what the people around here say? You don't think I know all about you? I respect what you're trying to do here, what you've been doing here for years. However, whether you like it or not, and I'm guessing not, I'm here to catch your monster, and nothing's going to stop me."

Chase climbed back into the truck before Rory could reply. The tires spun on the slick ground, spitting grass and dirt into the air. Alex stood abandoned with only a small fence separating him from Rory. The two men just looked at the ground, occasionally glancing at each other. When Alex finally opened his mouth Rory cut him off.

"Don't even say it!" Rory said. "I don't know why you're even still standing here. It's clear where your allegiance lies. I won't forget again."

Rory turned to go back to his sheep.

"Rory, come on! He left me here."

"Don't care," Rory called without turning around.

"I was just interviewing him and he asked me to go for a drive. I didn't know we were coming here."

Alex swung a leg over the short fence and Rory spun around. "You step one foot on my land, I'm going to get my gun!"

"Come on, Rory. You don't have a gun," Alex said. "Do you?"

"You want to find out?" Rory turned back to his sheep.

As Rory worked, he noticed Alex still standing on the other side of the fence, waiting. He pretended not to notice the younger man as he fed and checked the sheep. It was over a half hour before the reporter gave up and starting walking back toward Chase's camp.

Yeah, go back to your friends, Rory thought.

Once he was certain no one was around, Rory came back out and looked at the decoy sitting in the field just beyond his property. It was in worse shape than he originally thought. Repair wasn't completely out of the question, but he didn't want someone from Chase's camp to see him drag the decoy back into his shed. He had told the rich bastard he'd use it for firewood, so that's what he'd do.

He spent the next few hours cutting the thing to pieces with a gas-powered chainsaw and ended up using a few of the dryer pieces that night in his fireplace. As the wood cracked and popped, he thought about the failure of his plan. It was a fairly simple plan designed to fool simple people. Thinking back on the plan, he wasn't surprised that it hadn't fooled Chase. Any plan was worth the attempt, though.

Chase was an opponent unlike any other he had faced before. Even beyond the unmeasurable resources he flaunted, he was intelligent, and would be suspicious of Rory from now on. If Rory was going to get rid of Chase, his plans were going to have to be a lot more cunning.

-13-

"Making friends again?" Jerry said as he strode into Chase's tent.

Stretched out on his bed, Chase lowered his novel to look at Jerry with a raised eyebrow.

"I saw your little altercation with that elderly fellow. He didn't look too happy with whatever you had to say."

Chase sat up and smiled. It was a rarest of his smiles. Genuine. "I was just returning the man's property."

Jerry busied himself tidying up the various things Chase had left lying around his tent. He'd have to make sure someone in the camp was assigned cleaning duties or bring in a few more people for it.

"How's everything going out there?" Chase asked.

"As well as I expected it to," Jerry stated.

"Which is to say they haven't found anything."

Jerry didn't respond which, for him, was the same as agreeing.

"Is that because you think the beast won't be found or because you don't think it exists?" Chase sat up, his words brimming with intrigue.

Jerry sighed and turned to Chase. "It doesn't really matter what I think, does it? I'm here, doing my job, as usual."

"Oh, but it does, Jerry," Chase said, standing from the bed. "It impacts my morale."

"Your morale? I didn't think anything could dampen your spirit. Is this because I didn't go with you to Pennsylvania? I told you that wasn't because of your . . ." He paused, choosing his words carefully, "goals. I had a family matter that required my attention."

"And you missed my biggest success so far. I had proof!"

"I wouldn't call that proof, Harvey."

"Bah!" He waved dismissively at Jerry. "You should have seen it before we got on the plane. Something happened to it. Accelerated decomposition, or maybe it was the pressure of the cargo hold. I should have had it in the cabin with me." Chase lost himself for a few minutes, considering what he could have done to change the past.

"No matter, Jerry, no matter. This hunt is going to be far bigger, and you're going to be here to see the whole thing!"

It wasn't about proving anything to Jerry, and Jerry knew that. Chase was trying to prove to the world that he wasn't insane.

When Chase took an interest in all things paranormal, he aspired to prove the existence of things the world thought were nothing but stories. He started attending ghost hunts and planning hunting trips.

The interest didn't stop at ghosts. Every time Chase heard about another myth or fable, he poured himself into researching the new legend. He had piles of notebooks and scrapbooks filled with newspaper articles, sighting reports, and hand-written notes for each creature.

It wasn't long before the media found out about Chase's new hobby. Stories ran for months. They claimed that running the company without his father had sent Chase into a downward spiral of mental instability.

With every newspaper in the UK printing similar stories, members of the board started accusing Chase of squandering the company's profits on these ridiculous trips and hunts. The company released a statement, and financial reports backing it up, proving that not a single pound of company funds had been used for the eccentric trips, but it wasn't the financial perception of Chase that became the problem.

People began taking him less seriously in both public and private matters. A lot of businesses that held contracts with Chase Industries began to question their relationship with the company. Chase had no choice but to step away from day-to-day operations and let men of good reputation run the business. There were still some partners that insisted on dealing directly with Chase, some of them just as eccentric as he was, but most preferred businessmen with a reputation that was a little more professional.

Even though Chase had been bored with running the company, he didn't like being forced out of his responsibilities under those circumstances. He would have rather it had been his own decision.

Jerry struggled a little with the decision as well. He could have shifted into a different role and been in the office full-time as acting CEO of Chase Industries if that was what he wanted. Chase would always be the true CEO, no matter who was acting. Instead he decided to be wherever Chase was at any time. His devotion was too strong and his relationship was beyond that of employer-employee.

"What time is she going to call?" Chase asked.

"Who?"

"My mother. I can see you brought that mobile phone contraption of yours. You'd need a whole other tent to hide that thing. You only bring it with you when you and my mother have conspired to force me into talking to her."

Jerry smiled. Though Chase was nearly forty, at that moment Jerry saw him as a teenager.

Back then, Jerry would show up at the Chase household at night, instead of Chase's father, several times a month. Jerry would bring dinner home for his boss's wife and son and try to explain why their father and husband wouldn't be coming home on that particular night.

They were always very gracious when he visited. They would invite him in to have dinner with them and Chase would question Jerry on what deal his father was negotiating. Even though Jerry always gave vague answers, Chase would put it together quickly. He always was a smart boy.

After the teenaged Chase had gone to bed for the night, Jerry would spend a little time talking with Chase's mother, Mona, over a glass of wine or two. Occasionally it would turn into a bottle or two.

In a similar way, when Chase was on an excursion and his mother called, Jerry would spend a little time talking to her once she was done with Chase.

"She should be calling any minute now."

As if the phone had been waiting for Jerry to speak the words, it began to ring. Chase reached his hand out, for once not putting up much of a fight.

Jerry brought the phone over and placed the cradle in his palm.

"Hello, Mother," Chase said into the phone.

"Hello, Darling! How are you?"

"Fine, Mother. I'm fine. How is everything in London?"

"Dreadful."

"Really, Mother? Dreadful?"

"That's right. It never seems to stop raining. I'm a lonely widow and my only son is always half way around the world on one adventure or another."

"I'm not vacationing, Mother. It's a lot of work taking on these ventures."

"It's work now, is it?" she asked.

"More than you'll ever know."

"Aren't people usually paid for the work they do? Your work only seems to cost me money."

"Goodbye, Mother. It was nice talking to you."

"Wait! I'm sorry. Don't hang up. I just want to talk to my son. I miss you. When are you coming home?"

"Soon. This is something I need to do. But I can't return until I can bring something back with me."

"I need you here. I need someone to take me out when I need to go somewhere. I need someone to help with a mess of things around the house."

"You've got maids for that."

"Not those kinds of messes. I need someone to move my furniture around."

Mona Chase had a series of annoying hobbies. The most annoying of the set was her constant desire to rearrange a room. She could rearrange a different room in her house every day for a month. By the end of that month, she would already be thinking of new ways to lay the rooms out.

"Fine, Mother. Hire an assistant to help with whatever you need. Once you've got your candidate I'll have Jerry approve a monthly payment."

"That's not quite what I was hoping for, but I guess it'll have to do until you can come home. What kind of assistant should I hire?"

"Hire anyone you want, Mother. You can even have Jerry if you want." Chase gave Jerry a smile and wink. Jerry only rolled his eyes. "This is completely your choice. Just make sure you have someone at the office run a background check. You don't want to end up hiring a bloody crook."

"Yes, of course."

"I've got to go now, Mother. I've enjoyed talking to you."

"No, you haven't, but I appreciate that you took the time anyway. Is Jerry there? I'd like to ask him something."

"Mother would like a word," Chase said holding the phone out to Jerry.

"All right," Jerry said. "The team has prepared a presentation of their plan for you. If you would like to go on ahead, I'll join you in a moment."

Jerry watched Chase leave the tent. The hair at the back of Chase's neck was growing a little long and was beginning to curl. Absently, he raised a hand and felt the hair at the back of his own neck.

*   *   *

Chase walked into his team's main tent and everyone stopped talking at once. A long table sat in the center of the tent covered with print-outs and reports, several large boards on wheels, also covered in various reports, lined a few of the tent walls, and a few cots that looked like they had yet to be used were tucked away in one corner.

Everyone called this tent the War Room. Chase thought it a ridiculous name, but if it made everyone else happy he wasn't going to ruin the fun.

"Good evening, team!" Chase said, putting on his trademark smile. "Did we catch any logs today?"

Polite laughter filled the tent. Chase still didn't think there was anything amusing about the wooden decoy, but his joke had broken the awkwardness in the room and that was worth making light of their progress.

"I hear you have a plan?" he asked, plopping down in a chair.

"Well, I've only just arrived," said a man with a German accent, rising from his chair. "But, yes, I think we have a solid plan."

Chase smiled, pleasantly surprised. Jerry hadn't told him that Dr. Darin Schnabel had arrived. In the back of his mind, he wondered how much money Jerry had to offer before the man agreed to come.

"Dr. Schnabel," Chase said, stretching a hand out toward the doctor. "I'm delighted that you've finally seen the light and decided to join us."

The German doctor left Chase's hand hanging in mid-air. "I wouldn't say I've seen any kind of light, Mr. Chase. I stand by my original thoughts on this. You're on a fool's errand that will only end in disappointment, but I'd be a very foolish man to turn you down when you've generously offered to buy me a new home."

Chase's smile faded and he slowly pulled back his hand.

"In 1954, a fishing boat made sonar contact with something very large, keeping pace with the craft, nearly 150 meters below the surface. It didn't last long before it disappeared." Dr. Schnabel spoke without enthusiasm while handing Chase print outs on SONAR technology.

The man's lack of energy made Chase regret authorizing Jerry to offer the German doctor so much money.

"We're going to use several submersible sonar scanners. Other studies have been done with them in the past, and more often than not there's some kind of contact even if it is fleeting."

"Fleeting contact," Chase spoke up. "That doesn't sound like anything I'm interested in. We've got to do better than fleeting contact."

"I can't guarantee that," Dr. Schnabel retorted. "However, we have altered the sonar units that we'll be using. If something large is detected, the unit will fire a small tracking device. Something the size of what your monster is believed to be wouldn't even notice the tracker. At that point, we simply follow its movements until the opportune moment to retrieve it from the water."

Chase had to admit, whether the man believed in it or not, it was a solid plan. He stood and handed the sonar reports back to Dr. Schnabel.

"I like it. I like it very much. Good work, everyone."

"So you consider the plan to be adequate?" Dr. Schnabel asked.

"Personally, I don't care if we have to drain the whole bloody loch. I just want that monster."

-14-

The drive from the hotel in Inverness to Chase's camp was turning into a morning tarter for Alex. It was only fifteen minutes, twenty if traffic was heavy, and the scenery was beautiful, but it was still annoying him.

Maybe it was the repetition or because the drive meant dealing with an eccentric, rich mogul or a cranky, old man. Maybe it was because he wasn't driving home. Would being home actually have made him happier? Last night, when he had phoned Loren she seemed distant. All of her responses and conversation came two or three words at a time. She had still asked him to come home, still unable to respect that he had to stay and do his job.

Just before hanging up the phone he told her he loved her, as he usually did, but instead of returning the sentiment, all Alex got back was the soft click of the phone hanging up. He wanted to call her straight back and ask if she did in fact still love him. Truthfully, he had wanted to call her back and yell at her for hanging up on him. The thought of it made him feel foolish and he had gone to bed instead.

Alex parked his car near Chase's camp and tried to look casual as he wandered into the area. He wasn't sure how Chase felt about a reporter hanging around his camp. The man easily shifted between acting like Alex's best friend, and abandoning him. Alex wondered if Chase suspected he had been involved with the decoy.

As Alex got closer to the camp, he noticed a small group of men that all seemed to be craning their necks for a better view. A small barrier sat in front of them, along with a guard wearing a Chase Industries patch on the shoulder of his security uniform.

Among the men, he found the familiar face of Grant Huxley. Huxley was one of the senior reporters for the *UK Observer*'s biggest competitive newspaper, *Daily UK*.

Alex didn't consider Grant Huxley to be his enemy, but the man was his biggest rival in the world of journalism. Readers loved Huxley's columns, he had a good public reputation, and he had almost as much experience as Alex.

In the course of the average year, Alex and Huxley found themselves covering the same story at least a dozen times. They always acted with professional courtesy, even when they were lacking in personal courtesy.

"A little late to the party," Huxley sneered, still attempting to get a glimpse of something, anything. "They're not letting any of us past this little baby gate, are you Larry?"

The guard standing behind the gate smirked at Huxley, but said nothing.

It was good while it lasted, Alex thought. He knew Chase

would eventually shut him out, but he had hoped his scoop would have lasted a little longer.

"Any sign of Chase today?" Alex asked. "Did he say anything?"

"No. I haven't seen any sign of him. Doesn't seem like there's much story left here. You should probably just run along and head home, Stafford."

He was tempted to do just that. It was easy for Alex to write stories when he could talk with Harvey Chase whenever he wanted. Stuck behind a barrier, with several other reporters, any stories would prove to be a grind, and even then, similar to every other reporter's story.

"Your name is Stafford?" the guard asked, looking at Alex. "Alex Stafford?"

Alex nodded and showed the guard his press ID.

"Mr. Chase told me you'd be coming. You're welcome to come into the camp."

Huxley's mouth fell open and his face turned red.

"Well, Huxley, there doesn't seem to be much story left here, you might just want to run along home now."

He patted Huxley on the back, a little harder than he should have, and stepped beyond the barrier.

Alex strolled around the camp with a bounce in his step and a smile on his face. He nodded and gave a polite greeting to each person he passed, as though he were part of Chase's team.

Near the shoreline, men loaded boats, many of them were carrying odd-looking orbs. They looked somewhat futuristic to his eyes.

"Excuse me," he said as one of the men passed near him. "My name's Alex Stafford, I'm with the *UK Observer*. Do you mind if I ask what that thing your carrying is?"

"Sonar receiver," the man said as if it was common knowledge.

Before Alex could ask another question the man continued on his way toward the boats.

"You must be the reporter Harvey was talking about," a voice said from behind him.

Alex turned to see an older, well-dressed man. If Alex didn't already know him to be dead, he would have thought it was Chase's father.

"He was talking about me?" Alex asked. "What did he say?"

"He said he had been talking with a reporter and his name was Alex," the man stated.

"Oh, I see."

"I'm Jerry Triggs. I'm Harvey's—"

"Personal assistant," Alex finished, shaking Jerry's hand. "Sure. I've heard of you. I am from London, after all."

Jerry smiled warmly. "You had some questions about the sonar receivers?"

"I suppose I did. I didn't even know what they were called until about ten seconds ago. What do they do?"

"Our teams are going to take them all around the loch and submerse them. They'll be tied down with varying weights to cover different depths. They send out a continual sonar signal, and we've got a team of men monitoring those signals. If something large swims past one of them, we'll know about it."

"If something large did swim by, how would you know which receiver it came from?"

Jerry smiled and shrugged. "I'm merely repeating things that more educated men have been telling me."

Alex let out an appreciative laugh.

"How's Chase, I mean Harvey, doing with the hunt so far?"

"What do you mean?"

"I imagine a man of his stature is used to nearly instant

gratification in everything he does. He's been here more than a few days with little to show."

"He is used to quick results, but he knows how to be patient, when the need is there. He knows this hunt may take weeks or even months."

"Is he getting personally involved?"

Jerry opened his mouth to answer, then closed it and sighed. "Listen, I'm fine with answering these questions for you, but please, don't go off and write an article making Harvey out to be some lunatic. He may be a bit eccentric, but a lot of billionaires are."

"I assure you, Mr. Triggs, I'm not one of those reporters."

"There he is!" Chase's voice rang out from across the camp.

Alex looked to see Chase strolling from the tents with that large smile on his face.

"Good morning, Mr. Chase," Alex replied.

"Mr. Chase passed away some time ago. Please, call me Harvey."

Chase warmly shook Alex's hand.

"I need to apologize for yesterday. I didn't mean to leave you stranded over at the old man's place. My mind was in a different place. I hope he didn't give you any trouble as a result?"

"He had a few choice words for me," Alex said, nodding.

Chase chuckled. "Unfortunate, but you of all people know that words can't really hurt a man."

Alex shrugged. *Not something anyone should say to a reporter,* he thought.

"While we're on the subject of words," Chase continued, "you're not the first reporter to wander over here today. I've seen at least a dozen of them around today."

"Yeah," Alex said with a wicked smile. "I ran into them a few moments ago. I'll bet they're cursing my name right about now."

Chase laughed again. "That's not going to change anytime soon." Chase put an arm around Alex and gave him a hearty squeeze. "I've decided that we're only talking to you on everything that happens here. You are our man."

"Exclusive rights?" Alex laughed.

"Call it what you like. I can't stop other reporters from hanging around and writing about what they see, but they won't get a word from me or anyone on my team."

"That's exceptionally kind. Thank you."

"And, here's your next story. 'Today I got onto a boat with Harvey Chase and helped him capture the beast.'"

"Sounds great," Alex said. He didn't believe any beasts would be captured that day, if ever, but being able to stand beside Chase for an entire day was an enormous opportunity.

"Jerry?" Chase asked. "Will you be joining us?"

"I don't think so," Jerry replied with a smirk. "I find dry land a bit more preferable."

A little over an hour later, after the crew had made all their preparations, Chase and Alex stood on the deck of one of the boats, watching the shore grow distant.

*　　*　　*

Rory had been watching the activity around Chase's camp for hours. He didn't have Chase's plan completely figured out, but he knew a little. Men had been loading devices onto boats all the morning.

He watched a few of the men stop to discuss the devices. In most of those interaction it seemed like one man was explaining something to the other. One man would gesture at the device and then point out at the loch.

If Rory was going to figure out anything else about Chase's plans, he was going to have to get a look at those devices.

He walked over to the camp and snooped along the shoreline, hoping a device had been left behind. When Rory got close to the camp someone spotted him and called out. He scurried away before anyone could confront him. If Rory was going to get a good look at Chase's equipment, he'd have to go see it in action.

Rory grabbed his fishing pole and shoved off in his little motorboat. He followed one of Chase's boats, trying to stay far enough away to remain inconspicuous. He watched the men on deck struggling with one of the devices, attaching a weight to the bottom and then wrestling it over the boat's railing. With a splash, the device disappeared under the loch's surface. One of the men on deck was looking at a small monitor. After a few seconds he nodded to the others and the boat started moving again.

Every time the boat stopped, they repeated the same steps. Fiddling with some kind of orb-like device, attaching a weight, throwing it into the water and moving on to the next spot.

After making a mental note of the locations where Chase's men had dropped a device, he decided to head for home and prepare for his next move.

He looked through several boxes in his spare room before he found his old diving gear. Like the decoy, he hadn't had to use it in a long time, and found it to be in rough condition.

The glass in his mask was scratched and the rubber had several pinhole leaks. The oxygen tank was working, but he'd need to get it filled. Much like the mask, the diver's suit had several holes in it. Unlike the mask, the suit didn't need to be in perfect condition, but if water was able to leak in, it could cause him problems with hypothermia if he was diving for an extended amount of time. His flippers were the only part he couldn't find a problem with.

He sighed and tossed the half-useless equipment back into its box.

Chase's vessels were returning from their various areas of the loch, heading back for the camp. Rory watched the boats and wondered, *What kind of equipment would they have on board?*

*   *   *

Nausea twisted Alex's stomach into one large knot. He didn't know he was sea sick, but he had never spent any time on the water before.

He had been aboard a large yacht once, to interview a media mogul. The man had just bought another Ferrari making him the largest collector of Ferraris in the United Kingdom. It hadn't been like being on a boat at all. There was no rocking back and forth and no feeling like his stomach was moving separately from his body. Being on a yacht that size was more like being in a house; a really big, expensive house.

One of the crew members must have recognized the look on his face and placed a large, but gentle, hand on Alex's shoulder.

"Pick a spot on shore and stare at it. Land is the only thing you can look at that isn't going to move." He claimed it was an old trick that every sailor knew for beating seasickness. After staring at a tree for ten minutes, Alex started to think the trick was overrated.

"Beautiful, isn't it?" Chase beamed as he walked up beside Alex. Alex began to wonder if there was anything that didn't make the man smile.

Alex should have been watching the crew, making detailed notes on what they were doing, asking questions, but despite the failure of the old sailor's trick, he couldn't rip his eyes away from that little tree.

Whenever the boat's engines cut off, and it drifted to a stop, his stomach would settle a little. At that point, he would watch the crew work on one of the sonar receivers for a few minutes before dumping it into the water.

Each time they prepared a receiver, they would check a chart for the desired depth and attach the appropriate weight. Once it was in the water, someone would check the readout on a small screen while another radioed in to a crew member back at the camp. Once they received confirmation that the unit was transmitting back to base, they would move on to the next location, and Alex would find his little tree back on the shore.

As he watched the crew members work, he thought about getting the notepad from his pocket and making a few notes, but the gentle rocking of the boat was enough to keep his hands wrapped around the ship's railing.

All around the loch, Chase's boats were depositing receivers.

"How many of these things are you dropping?" Alex asked after one of the stops.

"Fifty-six, I'm told," Chase replied.

"That seems like a lot."

"This seems like a lot of water."

*　　*　　*

Rory sat waiting for all the lights in Chase's camp to go out. The last light went out at 2 a.m. and he crept toward the camp, watching for any movement. For an old man, he moved like a shadow when he needed to. The only difference his age made was the amount of pain he felt in his joints when he had to move so precisely.

When he reached the boats, he quickly climbed onto the one farthest from the camp. The deck was clean and, more importantly, empty. He found and checked all the storage compartments but didn't find anything of use. Moving on to the second boat, he found an oxygen tank. He didn't need the tank, but he took it anyway. It would save him from having to get his own filled.

After searching the last boat, he was disappointed that he didn't find a new diver's suit. He did find a new mask, which was the most important piece he needed. Dealing with holes in his suit would be annoying, but holes in his mask would prove to make a dive impossible.

Rory was about to climb out of the boat when he caught some movement in his peripheral vision. His head snapped around and he saw a flashlight beam bouncing between the tents and heading toward the boats.

Rory dropped to his hands and knees and listened.

Had he been sloppy while he searched, and been spotted? He hoped the flashlight belonged to some security guard who was just doing a perimeter check.

Rory's heart beat faster when the boat began to rock with the weight of a new passenger boarding. He considered standing up, giving himself up and begging for forgiveness, or dropping his found supplies and making a run for it. Unless the man with the flashlight was also in his seventies it wasn't likely that Rory would be able to outrun him. He could hop over the side and disappear into the black water.

The man was muttering as he got closer.

"All these tents and I end up in the one with three men that snore? How's a guy supposed to get any sleep?"

The man continued to mutter as he went down into the ship's galley and collapsed onto the small bed.

Rory continued to wait and listen. Ten minutes went by before he heard the man's breathing become rhythmic. Rory stood and gathered his equipment, attempting complete silence.

He looked over his shoulder every few steps until he was back inside his house. Nothing had happened, no one had moved, and there were no more flashlights that he could see.

Rory now had the equipment he needed to get a look at Chase's devices, and Chase was the one who had made it possible.

-15-

After his late night mission, Rory had only allowed himself a few hours of sleep. The rest of the time he spent familiarizing himself with his new equipment and waiting for the sun to rise. Night would be a better time to avoid being seen, but the loch was dark enough during the day. Diving at night meant diving completely blind.

Once the sun was high enough in the sky, he brought his scuba diving gear out to the edge of the water and hid it in his boat. He spent an hour watching the camp and battling his own paranoia. He dressed behind his boat, obscured from any potential viewers in Chase's camp.

Walking into the water, he dove under the surface and headed for one of Chase's devices. It was simple enough to find the spots where Rory had watched Chase's men make their drops. Finding those same spots under water was more difficult. Rory had to do it by feel, estimating how far to swim. His intimate knowledge of the loch, gained by decades of living there, was the only way he was able to find his way.

Cold water leaked into the suit through various holes. It felt like ice had come to life and was crawling over his entire body, climbing and squeezing into every crevice. *It can't be helped,* he told himself and kept his mind on the goal.

The first device was deeper than he had thought. Too deep to see much, he searched the surface of the orb with his hands. He couldn't find any switches or buttons that might turn the thing off. He found the metal loop where the weight was attached with a bit of rope.

Rory reached for his knife. Something bit him in the arm. He slapped a hand over the offending area, and the pain increased. There wasn't much he could do about it until he could see what was causing the pain. It felt similar to an eel bite, which he had experienced a number of times.

He turned his attention back to the rope that held down the orb. Rory wouldn't be able to find every device Chase and his people had dropped into the loch, but he cut it loose anyway. At least Chase would have one less device to assist with his plan.

When he finished sawing through the rope, the device shot up toward the surface. Rory headed for the next location he had seen one of the contraptions deposited. He wasn't surprised to find the same result. No buttons and nothing that could tell him anything about Chase's plan. As with the first one, Rory cut the device loose. As it shot up toward the surface he felt another sharp pain flare up in his leg. *Another eel?* he wondered. *What's got them so angry?*

On his way to the third location, Rory heard a strange sound and then felt something collapse around him. It held him tight, restricting the movement of his arms and legs. He pushed against it wildly, his primal instincts taking over. After a few seconds he realized it was a net. A large fishing net.

Rory's knife was out again and he started cutting at the net. He had only cut through a few of the cords when the net jerked upward. It was being pulled to the surface. The net squeezed tighter around him as it was pulled up. Rory's air supply got caught up in the web and was pulled from his mouth. He stopped trying to cut the net and desperately felt around for his regulator.

Between the murky water, the restriction of the net, and his oxygen supply sending bubbles into his face, he couldn't get a hold of the breathing apparatus. Panic began to take over. He could hold his breath for a while, but his lungs were already starting to feel tight.

With some effort, he reached over his head and grabbed the base of the oxygen tube. He felt along the hose from the top of the tank to the mouthpiece only to find it had become tangled in the net. With little choice, he tried to bring his mouth to the regulator, but the net was restricting him too much.

The air in his lungs burned to get out, but Rory refused to let it go. It was the only air he had left.

He renewed his efforts with the knife, sawing quickly at the net around his source of oxygen. Even if he couldn't free his regulator, if he could squeeze out of the net in the next minute, he was confident he could make it to surface.

Lungs ready to burst, Rory's body refused to obey any longer. He exhaled what was left in his lungs and sucked in a mouthful of water. As his lungs took in the water, he tried to cough. The act of coughing only brought in more water. He could feel his lungs and stomach filling. His stomach heaved and he vomited into the surrounding water.

He thrashed about but, beyond the net, the only thing he

could reach in any direction was water. It was all around him, but his fingers found no purchase in it.

All of Rory's strength seemed to be leaving his body. The knife slipped from his hand. He breathed in some more water. He was drowning, but he was feeling okay about it. Would she come? Would she save him? It was ironic, he thought, for a man who lived at the edge of the loch for so many years to drown in it. His watery grave turned white around him.

*   *   *

He was coughing. A series of coughs, followed by a big gasp of air. Air! He had been underwater, drowning, when he passed out.

Rory continued to cough until he rolled onto his hands and knees and vomited a few liters of water. Under his hands was a hard surface, slick with water, and Rory's vomit. That combined with the gentle swaying underneath of him told him he was on the deck of a boat.

"That's right. Get it all out," said a familiar voice.

Rory's eyes began to adjust. His vision had been blurred since he opened his eyes, but things were starting to come back into focus.

Chase and a small team of men all stood on the deck of the boat looking at him. Some faces looked confused, several were angry, while a few even seemed amused.

Chase grabbed Rory by the straps of his oxygen tank and yanked him to his feet. Chase was angry, but he somehow kept that damn smile on his face.

Rory felt uneasy. He wondered if Chase, or any of his crew members, would recognize that Rory was wearing some of their equipment.

Another crew member walked over with a hand-held device and began waving it over Rory's body. The device beeped and the man yanked something out of Rory's arm.

"Ouch!" Rory yelped.

"Here it is," the man said, handing the small item to Chase.

Chase held it up in front of Rory's face. It looked similar to a thumb tack.

"It's a tracking device," Chase revealed. "And here's another."

Chase reached down and pulled another out of Rory's leg. Rory kept from letting out another cry as it was yanked out.

"How the hell did they get there?" Rory demanded.

"I'll tell you exactly how they got there," Chase shot back. "You swam past a few of my sonar receivers, and since you're bigger than a bloody fish it tagged you with these." He held the tiny tracking devices up again. "We got the signal, jumped into the boat and rushed out to capture what we thought could have been the monster. Instead, we just got an old fool."

Once back on shore, Rory pulled his flippers off and began walking toward his house.

"Wait," Chase commanded. Rory kept walking as if he hadn't heard. "Bring him back."

Four men from the boat caught up with Rory and escorted him back to face Chase.

"What am I supposed to do with you?" Chase asked.

Rory pretended to think seriously about the question. "Well, I suppose you could clean me and make a nice old fool stew, but I don't think it'd taste too good."

"I could have you brought up on charges, you know."

"For what?" Rory asked with a laugh.

"Damaging my property."

"I didn't damage anything of yours," Rory said defensively.

"I was just doing some scuba diving. Is it illegal to have hobbies now?"

"My men found two sonar devices bobbing on top of the water, their weights had been cut."

"I have no idea how that happened," Rory said, trying to sound sincere. "I think you must have done that with your nets or your trackers or something. By the way, I almost drowned getting caught up in your net. I could have you brought up on charges for attempted murder!"

A few spectators let out a quiet titter. The titters turned to giggles and the giggles into laughter. Even Chase brought back his trademark smile and laughed.

"A man like me would never simply attempt anything. If you do something, you do it all the way."

That brought another round of laughter, though it was quieter and had an edge of discomfort.

"That is what you have in mind, isn't it? Murder? Maybe not for me, but you're planning on killing something, aren't you?"

"If I didn't know any better, Rory, I'd swear I just heard you admit to the existence of the Loch Ness Monster."

Rory didn't respond. He had already said too much.

"I'd like to go home now," he said, with his eyes cast down at the ground.

Chase looked at him for some time without saying anything.

Alex stepped from the crowd of people. Rory hadn't even noticed the young reporter, but he walked over to Rory and stood at his side.

"I think that's a good idea," Alex said. "Gentlemen, if you would let him go."

Alex looked at the men surrounding Rory. They didn't move an inch.

"I said, let him go." Alex did his best to sound stern, but the men still didn't move.

Alex and Rory both looked to Chase, who was watching everything with an odd smirk.

"Let him go," came a voice from the back of the crowd.

Rory had seen the man talking with Chase several times, but Rory didn't know who the man was.

"Yes, Jerry. Of course," Chase said with a dismissive flourish.

Chase, the four men surrounding Rory, and the mystery man all dispersed, heading toward various tents.

"Who was that man?" Rory asked Alex.

"Chase's assistant."

"Seems to me he could find himself a much better job."

*   *   *

"Why were you holding that old man? What were you going to do with him?" Jerry demanded once he and Chase were back in Chase's tent. "Tie him up? Put him in a cage?"

"The thought had crossed my mind, along with several others."

Jerry closed his eyes and shook his head.

"Relax, Jerry. I was joking. I only had my men holding him while I was deciding whether to call the police or not. It didn't seem worth the trouble."

"Good. After all, he's just an old man."

"Maybe so, but he's becoming a nuisance. If he's going to keep getting in my way, something's going to have to be done about him."

"Getting in the way? His bumbling has done nothing but bring a few laughs for the crew. If anything, he's helped morale.

If he truly becomes an issue I will take care of it. For now, I think it would be best to just ignore him."

Chase poured himself a glass of Scotch and nodded. "We'll see."

Jerry smiled to himself. Chase could never end a discussion by admitting someone else was right. Jerry was much the same way.

"Either way, knowing that the tracking system worked, I don't think we should consider this morning a total loss."

"Oh, I don't consider this morning a total loss at all," Chase replied.

"Is that so?" Jerry replied cautiously.

"Yes. Before I came into my tent I was informed that a third tracking device was deployed. We've tagged something else."

-16-

"I don't cook or clean. I don't run frivolous errands. I prefer not to drive unless it's absolutely necessary."

"Is there anything else that you don't do?" asked Mona Chase, sitting behind the desk in her study. Across from her sat the eleventh applicant she had interviewed in less than a week.

"I've attached a list to my resume."

"So, you have," Mona said flipping to the page. "Cooking, long periods of standing, long periods of sitting. Tell me, is there anything that you do?"

Twenty exhausting minutes later she saw *Mr. Don't* out of her study, promising she would let him know.

She collapsed into her chair and threw an arm over her eyes. Eleven applicants and not a single one of them were even close to her employment standards. If she was being honest with herself, she didn't need someone who met all of her standards.

The things she wanted help with were simple tasks that anyone could do. The applicant she was looking for didn't need to be an efficient multi-tasker, or someone with unrivalled work ethic. She just needed someone who was dependable, someone who put in an honest effort and, most importantly, she needed someone who she would enjoy spending time with.

She wasn't hiring a friend, but being a friend might be considered one of the responsibilities. That fact always made her feel a little embarrassed. Most people didn't need to buy friends.

One of Mona's housekeepers appeared at the study door, knocking gently on the door frame.

"Mrs. Chase?"

"Yes?"

"There's an American man here. He says he wants to apply for the job."

"Oh, God!" she blurted. "I can't take another interview today. Just tell him the position has been filled."

"Yes, ma'am," she said in return.

"Wait a second," she called.

"Ma'am?"

"Did you say he was an American?"

"I'm pretty sure. He sounds like an American."

Mona sat back in her chair and smiled. She rather liked the idea of having an American assistant. The thought had never occurred to her before, but the idea grew on her as she sat and considered it. The North American culture was a fascinating one. So similar to her own, yet foreign at the same time. Her son would absolutely hate it if she had an American assistant.

"Should I tell him we're not taking any more applicants today?" Chelsea asked.

"No. I've changed my mind. Please show him up."

A moment later, a man appeared at the study door, led by the housekeeper.

Mona stood as he entered and shook his hand, a big smile on her face.

"Good to meet you. I'm Mona Chase."

"The pleasure is mine, Mrs. Chase. My name is John Lasorda."

"I must be honest with you, Mr. Lasorda," she said once they sat down. "I'm very curious why an American man would be applying for this position."

"Uh," Lasorda laughed, cheeks turning a light shade of pink, "I ended up in England after following love, but that didn't end too well for me. But, I like it here, so I've decided to stay."

"Ah, love. It'll be the end of us all one day," she mused.

"I'm sure you're right about that."

Mona smiled as the man continued to talk. He was charming and easy to talk to. Anyone who could move his life to another country could certainly handle any task she would ask of him. He was also rather good-looking, which wasn't a requirement, but it did fall in the benefit column.

The interview hadn't even officially started and Mona already knew she was going to give this man the job.

-17-

"Sir, we have movement on the other tracker," a man said, poking his head into Chase's tent.

"Truly?" he asked sitting up on his bed.

It was late, but Chase had always been a light sleeper. A man of his position had to be ready to jump out of bed at any moment and be prepared for whatever situation he was being thrown into.

"Yes, sir. Dr. Schnabel thought you would want to know."

The second target had been tagged during the commotion created by Rory. It moved for an hour after that, but by the time the crew had another boat ready to go, the movement had stopped. Dr. Schnabel had approached Chase on the subject with the cold separation he was becoming known for around the camp.

"We'll keep monitoring for movement, but we have to consider the possibility that the tracker fell off of the second target or that it was merely some debris that was tagged, which has stopped moving since."

The entire team had agreed that unless the tracker started moving again retrieving it would be a waste of time. Everyone except Chase. He wanted to go back into the loch and find that tracker, whether it was attached to something or not. The contract Dr. Schnabel had signed gave him certain freedoms, including that of running his own team. If Chase felt something was imperative, he would impose his authority, but he had to be careful about what he took a stand on. If Chase was too overbearing the doctor might decide to leave the operation.

Chase entered a new tent that had been set up beside the War Room. The new tent housed all the sonar monitoring equipment. Inside, there were more screens than a television store. The displays were mainly black with green circles. A line rotated from the center of the circles, like a clock running extremely fast. As the line moved, it revealed an array of green dots in various configurations and intensity. None of it made any sense to Chase, but the other men in the tent were gathered around the screens, staring like the secret of life was about to be revealed.

Dr. Schnabel stepped back from the group and turned his attention on Chase.

"We can't tell exactly how big it is, but it's been moving for the last twenty minutes. Nothing out of the ordinary for aquatic life, so far."

"All right," Chase said, clapping his hands together. "Let's get a boat loaded up and get out there."

"We can't right now," Dr. Schnabel said. "There's a big storm heading this way. It's already raining."

"Bah. Rain. I'm from England. If I stopped what I was doing

every time it rained I'd never have left my house. I'll bet we can get out there and get a net on it before that storm gets here."

"I would recommend against that," Dr. Schnabel said.

"You would?"

"Yes."

"What would you recommend we do?"

"Keep an eye on its pattern for now and head out as soon as the storm passes. We should be on the water by late tomorrow morning."

"Late tomorrow morning? What if we lose the signal, or the tracking device falls off? I can't take that risk."

"Again, I very seriously recommend—"

"Well, I recommend," Chase said, cutting the man off, "that you keep monitoring for movement here while I get a team ready and head out onto the loch."

Dr. Schnabel nodded, but didn't appear to be happy about being bullied. Chase realized that that could have been enough to make the man quit, but it was worth the risk. They could be tracking the monster.

An hour later, Chase had a boat ready to go and a team to man it. Most of the team volunteered when Chase announced in a loud voice that they had a target on the move. He had to inspire a few additional men by suggesting they could be sent home if they didn't like the weather. When the boat pulled away from the shoreline, they were only contending with a light rain.

Dr. Schnabel was in constant contact with the man captaining the boat. Updates were coming in by the moment about the location and movement of the tracker. The captain kept showing Chase on a map the locations they received.

Chase looked out at the water, feeling close to his goal. He pictured the fantastic beast jumping out of the water and landing on the deck of the boat as he stood over it, victorious.

The lights were on at Rory's house, Chase noticed. That was a good thing. He'd hate to see anymore interference from the old man, especially when Chase was so close.

He noticed that the boat changed directions again.

"She's running scared," one of the men on deck mocked. Another man laughed as they readied the nets.

Much like the sonar receivers they were using, the netting system was highly customized by Dr. Schnabel.

Instead of throwing it on the surface, letting it submerge, and relying on your target to swim into the net, Dr. Schnabel's system fired a tightly packed net, almost like a bullet. The gun used to fire the net had a small dial to indicate the intended depth. When the net reached its desired depth, it would expand and ensnare the target.

Two men each grabbed a gun and stood on opposite sides of the boat, waiting for a signal from the captain, who listened carefully to Dr. Schnabel's radio instructions. Chase felt like a firecracker with a short fuse. The anticipation was torturous.

The humming of the engines cut and the boat drifted. The captain came away from the boat's controls and stood between the two men holding the net-launching guns. He held the walkie-talkie close to his ear.

"What's going on?" Chase demanded. "Are we having engine trouble?"

The captain shushed him. At any other time Chase would have embarrassed the man for his insubordination, but he could forgive it in a moment as important as this.

Everyone waited. The only sounds that could be heard were the gentle falling of rain, small waves lapping against the side of the boat, and the gentle static coming from the walkie-talkie in the captain's hand.

The captain tilted his head, waiting for some word.

Though the rainfall still wasn't heavy, Chase was soaked from the elongated exposure. A big drop of rain dripped from his nose every few seconds.

"I think we lost it," said Dr. Schnabel through the walkie-talkie.

Chase's heart sank. They had missed their chance.

No one else seemed to feel discouraged. In fact, no one moved. Chase felt a small flutter of hope. It might not have been over yet.

They stood frozen for several minutes. Periodically the walkie-talkie would crackle and a voice would say, "nothing yet."

Twenty minutes had passed when Chase noticed the rain was getting heavier. The captain relaxed in his stance and looked at Chase with disappointment in his eyes.

"Maybe we should try again in the morning," suggested Dr. Schnabel.

"Will you give it another five minutes?" Chase was shocked to hear he was almost begging the captain for more time. The man nodded and they continued to wait. The rain grew heavier.

Finally, the captain looked to Chase again. The men could barely hear each other over the rain hammering on the deck. "Sir, we've got to go."

"I've got movement," came Dr. Schnabel's voice from the walkie-talkie. Everyone froze and the captain held the speaker to his ear. Chase stepped in close just in time to hear, "It's right under you. Port side."

"Fire! Port!" the captain yelled.

The man to the captain's left pulled the trigger and the loaded net disappeared into the water, though a steel cable remained as a tether between the net and the gun. In one fluid motion, the man placed the gun into a winch, secured it, and fed the extra line into the roller.

"We've got rapid movement," said the voice from the walkie-talkie. "I think you've got it."

"Bring it in!" called the captain.

The man who had fired the net hit a button on the winch and the line began rolling in. Chase watched, unable to blink. As the line came up, the boat started to rock. Chase looked at the boat nervously. He had never considered what would happen if the beast was bigger than the boat.

The captain must have had the same thought, because he was on his walkie-talkie telling someone to get another boat ready.

Cold rain pounded at them and a deep rumble sounded in the distance. As the pressure on the winch increased, it began to whine loudly. Chase wondered if it would be able to handle their catch.

As the net got closer to the surface, the boat rocked harder. The experienced sailors, with seasoned sea legs, didn't have much trouble staying on their feet, suffering a single stumbling step at worst. Chase struggled to keep himself from falling to his knees. He fell into the starboard railing and wrapped his arms around it.

Something broke the surface. Chase pushed himself to his feet, trying to get a glimpse of their catch, but fell back into the railing.

Several men ran over to the winch and grabbed the net wherever they could get a grip. Every man on the net grunted and strained in the attempt to bring it on deck. Chase squinted at the net, waiting to see any kind of indicator of what they had caught: a head, a fin, anything.

The men continued to wrestle with the net, calling out suggestions to each other. With a final unified effort, they brought the net up over the railing and dumped it onto the deck.

Chase felt the sharp stab of disappointment. It wasn't a

monster. The thing was no bigger than a man. It was just some kind of fish.

The boat continued to rock from the swelling waves. Chase was now able to push himself to his feet and lurch over for a closer look at their catch.

"It may not be the monster, but that's probably the biggest pike I've ever seen," said one of the men.

Chase looked at the man with disgust. The look wasn't intended for the man specifically. Once he had time to think about it, Chase would realize that all the men did their best, and performed very well under the conditions. Chase was disgusted with his luck. With the situation.

Another rumble sounded, closer this time.

"All right, boys, we're heading back. Now!" the captain called and the engines came to life.

"Captain!" Chase called.

All the other men went to work readying the boat for docking. The captain took a step closer to share a word.

"Is it possible this isn't what we were tracking?" Chase asked motioning to the fish.

"What do you mean?"

"Is it possible that this fish was swimming close by the beast we were actually tracking and we caught this instead?"

Chase had to explain his thought again. He was grasping at the hope that the monster he was seeking was still somewhere just below them.

The captain thrust the walkie-talkie into Chase's chest and walked away to join his crew in getting the boat back to shore.

Chase didn't bother to radio in. He wasn't thinking straight, so he just stood on the deck and stared at the bass flopping around the deck.

Once the boat's engines were working at full power, they

moved noticeably faster back toward the camp than they had moved away from it. Even the wind seemed to be urging them back to shore.

A moment later, Chase found out why.

Lightning cracked down on the boat so loud and so bright that it turned his vision white and muffled all sound. There was shouting all around him; at least he thought it was shouting.

The boat lurched, and with his senses dulled, Chase couldn't stop himself from falling backwards. His arms flailed, hoping to find something to hold onto. A hand grabbed his arm for a brief second before slipping off. Then Chase collided with a railing, his ribcage exploding in pain. The world seemed to spin around him and then he was completely submerged in freezing water.

He still couldn't see much. The muffled sound of the boat's engines, and the men aboard her, seemed to grow more distant by the second. Either his hearing was getting worse, or he was being left behind.

Treading water proved to be difficult. Not only was he disoriented from being blind and deaf, the pain in his ribs made it difficult to breath, and his clothes and shoes hindered his movements. With great effort Chase worked at shedding his coat and shoes. Each time he used his hands to remove a piece of clothing, Chase sank beneath the water. His ribs wouldn't allow him to hold his breath for long. He had to let himself sink a few times before he was done.

He tried to look around. His vision was mostly useless. He thought he saw some lights in the distance, but couldn't be sure. There was no time to wait for his vision to clear. Being idle in his situation would be the death of him. He swam for the lights. The Loch Ness was 37km long and between 1 and 3km wide, he had a fifty percent chance that he was swimming in the right direction.

Chase thought about his personal trainer, back in London, and how she was constantly trying to get him to do more cardiovascular exercise in his workout routine. He wished he had listened.

His skin was starting to burn. Not a good sign. He wanted to curl up in a ball and sleep. Instead of swimming with open hands, he kept his numb fingers in a fist. It may have slowed him down a little, but he couldn't have opened his hands even with his life depending on it.

His feet were so numb that he wondered if they were still there. Perhaps the monster had sneaked up behind him and bit them off. His strokes were slowing with each passing second. His arms and legs were sluggish to respond to his brain.

Chase became lethargic about the entire situation. He actually made peace with sinking to the bottom of the loch and told his entire body to relax. Taking one last breath of the chilly night air, he slipped beneath the surface of the water. He looked back up at the surface as he descended. His vision had cleared enough that he recognized the moon in the sky. It was a beautiful thing to have as his last sight, even if it was a little blurry.

He was a foot under the surface of the water when his foot touched down on the bottom of the loch. Shore was closer than he thought. Lethargy was thrown aside and Chase forced his legs to propel himself upward and forward with the little strength he had left. His face barely made it out of the water as Chase stole a gasp of air. He didn't sink as far the second time, but he didn't have enough energy to push off from the bottom of the loch. Instead, he began walking forward as quickly as he could manage under water.

After a dozen hard-fought steps, Chase could keep his nose and mouth out of the water if he stood on his toes. His vision was still a little blurry, but there were definitely lights in front of him. Those lights meant he wasn't far from a warm bed and he was so tired.

Each step seemed to cut his energy in half. He collapsed and barely felt the splash as he hit the water's edge. Now that he was mostly out of the water, he was much more aware of the rain which continued to beat down on him.

Lying with his face half in the water, each breath was a mixture of water and air. Chase tried to push himself up with his hands. The weight was too much. Instead, he clawed at the stony sand, pulling himself out of the water an inch at a time.

He knew he had to get out of the water and onto some land to even have a chance at escaping hypothermia, but his muscles wouldn't work anymore. *I just need to rest for a second,* he thought. Lying his cheek down in the water, he exhaled heavily, trying to keep water from filling his mouth.

A door slammed somewhere nearby. He raised his head and tried to find the source. A blurry little figure was running toward him.

It's about time, he thought. Chase felt hands grab him underneath the arms, and then everything went black.

-18-

Derek McGivern shivered on the shore of Loch Ness wearing nothing but his underwear while six of his friends stood behind him, all red faced and short of breath from laughing. He turned to them and pleaded.

"Come on, fellas? Do I really have to do this?"

Finlay, the oldest of the group, stepped forward. "Damn right you do!"

"Come on, ya baby," another of his friends added. "We all had to do it. You ain't getting out of it either."

Derek turned back to the loch. His initiation was to swim from the shore to Cherry Island and back again. The entire swim was a mere 300 yards, but in the middle of winter even the most seasoned swimmers wouldn't do it in their underwear.

"Get on with it," someone shouted from behind him.

He knew the whole experience would be worse if he waded

into the water. Instead, he took a deep breath, a few running steps, and plunged his entire body into the loch. It was hard to believe that water so cold was still liquid. He heard his friends laughing loudly every time an ear rose above the surface as he swam.

Halfway to the small crannog, Derek's body started to adapt to the temperature. The swim felt more refreshing than any pool he had ever been in. He felt alert and full of energy.

Climbing up onto the island, he turned back to his friends and gave a victory cry as he raised his arms high above his head. On shore his friends came alive, shouting back and raising their own arms in celebration.

Filled with adrenaline, Derek wanted to keep swimming out instead of heading back to shore. The responsible part of his brain knew that, no matter how he felt, swimming too long in this water would cause problems.

He ran circles around the small island a few times, continuing his battle cry. A gentle breeze turned his wet skin into ice. He dove back into the water. It actually felt warm compared to the air. On the way back, each time his ear broke the surface he could hear his friends cheering him on, instead of laughing at him.

Again he found himself at the halfway point and smiled. He kicked something solid with his foot. It didn't hurt, but Derek couldn't swim any further. His foot was stuck.

The guys on shore noticed he had stopped swimming and fell silent.

"I'm okay," Derek called, giving a wave with his hand.

Something pulled on his foot, and he found himself under the surface. He thrashed wildly with his arms and kicked at whatever had hold of his foot. His foot slid out of its trap and he clawed for the surface.

The swim to the surface seemed to take a long time. How

far had he been pulled down? He finally broke the surface with a violent gasp. His friends looked on wide-eyed, a few of them were pulling clothes off and stepping into the water.

"Something grabbed," was all he could say between gasps when he was pulled down again. This time he struggled and managed to keep his face above the surface. Randomly, his leg received an extra tug and he dipped below the surface, but he fought his way back above the water each time.

In the corner of his eye, Derek saw a man in a boat rowing toward him. No one had seen or heard the man approach, but there he was. The man reached out and took Derek's hand in a steely grip. Derek kicked while the man in the boat pulled. Derek felt like he was being stretched.

Derek's foot slipped free again and he quickly climbed into the boat, with the man's help. The man sat down at the oars.

"You okay?" the man asked.

"Something grabbed me!" His heart was pounding in his ears. He shook violently from shock and the temperature of the water. He couldn't stop staring at the water, waiting for something to attack the boat.

"Aye, it can seem like that sometimes."

"What can seem like that?"

The man started to row back toward the shore with a slight smile on his face.

"Oh, there's lots of logs that float around in here. Just under the surface. Sometimes you hit one and get your foot stuck. The log sinks a little and pulls you down. Good thing you got your foot out."

"No," Derek insisted. "This wasn't a log. It let go and grabbed me again."

"Like I said, these logs, they rise and fall below the surface.

Bad luck to get your foot caught once. Not likely for it to happen twice, but it's possible, isn't it?"

"It wasn't a log," Derek said, pouting like a young boy.

When they reached shore, Derek's friends wrapped a towel around him and sat him down on the ground.

"What happened out there?" Finlay demanded.

"Don't rightly know," said the man with the boat.

"My foot got caught on something," Derek said from the ground, sounding embarrassed. "I have no idea what. Doesn't matter." He shut down, not saying anymore.

Derek rubbed his ankle and examined the skin. He expected to see some teeth marks, but all he saw was some reddened skin that could have been the result of friction.

"Well, thanks for coming along when you did," Finlay said, shaking Rory's hand.

"What was this all about, anyhow?" the man asked, motioning to Derek sitting on the ground.

"Oh," Finlay's face turned a little red and he rubbed the back of his neck. "I guess it's a little silly, but it's our initiation. Derek is the newest addition to the police force."

The man got back into the boat and wore that slight smile again.

"I see," the man said, using an oar to push himself away from the shore. "Seems to me you would have more important things to do."

*   *   *

How long ago had it been that he saved that young man?

Rory relived the memory as he watched the rain pound against his windows and pulled his cardigan tighter around him. It was rare to see a storm of that ferocity around the loch. They were in one of the little spots in the world where everything was usually constant.

He threw a few more logs into the fireplace and pushed the coals around. Normally he would have already been in bed on a night like tonight. But tonight he had to stay up. He had to keep the fire burning.

It was still hard to believe that Harvey Chase was asleep on Rory's couch. When he had pulled the man from the water's edge, Chase was unconscious and shivering violently. Rory had brought him into the house as quickly as he could, though Chase was a heavier man and it took some time.

The old man already had a small fire lit for himself, but he threw on several more logs once Chase was inside. He had then gone to work undressing Chase and wrapping him in dry blankets before laying him out on the couch. His skin had been cold to the touch and his breathing shallow.

After Rory had done everything he could, Graham hopped up on the couch and snuggled up to Chase. Rory called for him to get down, but when Graham didn't move he let the dog stay. As long as he didn't lay on top of Chase he was only providing additional body heat, which would only help.

Rory hung Chase's clothes on the back of a chair near the fire. Then he had nothing left to do but wait.

He passed the time by reading a book in his comfortable chair near the fire, where he could also keep an eye on Chase. Every hour he would put his book down, stoke the fire, and add more wood when it was needed.

Every once in a while, when he glanced at Chase, he wondered to himself why he didn't just leave the man in the water. After all the time Rory had spent trying to stop the man from hunting, a permanent solution was presented to him and he had turned it away.

He supposed letting the man die wasn't much different than killing him.

Rory jolted awake in his chair, still holding his book in one hand. Light flooded into the room, meaning the sun was up. Rory had been asleep for hours. He jumped up to check on Chase. He was surprised to realize he had been worried about Chase.

The man was fine. His breathing was a little deeper and his skin nearly felt normal. Graham raised his head and whined quietly. Rory smiled and patted him on the head.

"You've done well, boy."

Even with things looking better, Rory reignited the fire, which, except for a few glowing coals, had gone out.

At Chase's camp, every boat they had was out on the water, searching.

Let them search, Rory thought. He'd rather they spent their time on something pointless. Less time for them to spend hunting.

Rory briefly entertained the idea of locking Chase up, or tying him to a chair. If his men couldn't find him they might pack up their whole operation and go back to London, believing their boss to be dead. And once Chase agreed not to return, Rory would let him go.

Even if Rory was willing to go forward with a kidnapping, Alex's nosey reporter nature would bring him over to the house before long.

Rory made some oatmeal over the fire, making plenty of extra in case he needed breakfast for two. When Chase didn't wake up, Rory gave the extra to Graham, who gobbled it up with his tail wagging.

Later that day, while preparing some lunch for himself, Rory heard Chase grunt.

His eyes were still closed, but he was squirming and grunting as though he was having a nightmare. Graham ran over and licked Chase's face. His hands came up to his face, gently fending the dog off.

When Graham backed up and sat with his tail wagging, Chase's eyes opened. Small slits at first, but they opened wider after having a moment to adjust to the light. He looked around the house and gave a weak smile to the dog. And then his eyes fell on Rory.

Rory half expected the man to start smiling like a fool again. Instead, he closed his eyes, gave his head a shake, and then opened them again. He tried to sit up, but Rory pushed him back down by the shoulders with ease.

"Rest," Rory commanded.

"Wha . . ." Chase tried to say, "Wha . . . water."

Rory got a cup of water and held it to Chase's lips. He drank slowly, only a sip or two. His eyes darted around, taking in his surroundings. Rory pressed the cup into Chase's hand and went back to the kitchen.

His famous fish stew was almost ready, though it was only famous between himself and his dog. The next time he looked, Chase was sitting up on the couch, patting Graham's head. Rory had no idea what to say to the man.

Rory carried two bowls from the kitchen over to the couch.

"Fish stew," Rory stated. "Though yours is mostly broth. Might be better to start with that."

He placed the bowl of broth on a little table beside Chase.

"That's okay," Chase said, his voice hoarse. "Don't think I'm ready for anything with fish."

They ate in complete silence, beyond the sounds of spoons scraping bowls and the occasional whine from Graham. Chase finished half of his broth before putting the bowl down.

"Would you mind passing me my clothes?" Chase asked. It was the first thing Rory had ever heard him say with any degree of humility.

Rory felt the clothes and found they were dry. He handed them to Chase without a word. Chase dressed and re-wrapped himself in the blanket.

"Obviously," Chase said after another uncomfortable silence, "there's no way I could thank you for what you've done."

Rory said nothing. He couldn't believe he was having lunch with a humble version of Harvey Chase.

"Simply put, I owe you my life. If there's ever anything you need, just say it, it's yours."

Rory sat in his chair staring at the bowl in his hands. After some time, he looked at Chase and said, "Go home." There was no anger in his words. Just honesty.

"I'm sorry?" Chase asked.

"Pack up your stuff, take your men and go home. Stop this crazy hunt."

"That's probably the only thing in this entire world that I just can't do," Chase said.

"That's the only thing I want."

"I'm sorry," Chase said. He shrugged off the blanket and pushed himself to his feet. "Again, I can't thank you enough. It's just not possible. I should really go and let my people know that I'm all right. And my offer still stands. Anything you want."

"Except that one thing," Rory shot back.

"Yes, well . . ."

Chase took a few steps forward and staggered, nearly losing his balance. Rory put a hand on his shoulder. "Maybe you should sit back down. Just for a bit."

"No, no. I'm fine," Chase said as the corners of his mouth perked up. The smile was back.

"Fine. If you won't sit back down, I'll walk you over there."

It hurt to be so accommodating to the man. It was an odd feeling. Rory had saved Chase's life, and now he felt somewhat responsible for him. The thought of him passing out halfway back to his camp actually worried Rory.

"There's something else I should thank you for," Chase said as they walked toward his camp.

"What's that?" Rory asked.

"While I lay on your couch, unconscious, I had a dream." Chase looked at Rory with a sly smile. "My dream was a near parallel to my waking world. I stood in front of this very loch and tried to figure out a way to capture the Loch Ness Monster.

"Before long, I found myself beginning to float. It all seemed completely natural, being in a dream and all. I flew higher and higher until I could see the entire loch. Until you see it all at once, it's really hard to grasp just how massive it is. That's when I saw her."

Rory's head snapped around to look at Chase.

"I also saw myself, somehow. I was in a boat chasing her around like some mad man. The version of me that was flying high above the loch thought, *It would be a lot easier if the damn loch wasn't so big!*"

Chase stopped and turned to Rory with his arms out.

"I'm going to make the loch smaller!"

Rory took a step away from Chase. "How the hell do you suppose you're going to do that?"

"Harvey?!" someone called out.

Rory didn't even realize how far they had walked. They were standing on the edge of Chase's camp. Chase's assistant was jogging toward them. A look of relief mixed with shock was on his face.

"Oh, my God! You're alive!" Jerry called.

"Of course I am! Why wouldn't I be?"

"You . . . you . . . you disappeared. No one noticed you were gone until the men docked. We thought for sure you'd drowned."

"I came close," Chase said with a chuckle, and slapped Rory on the back. "Thanks to this man, it was not to be my fate."

"Him?" Jerry asked.

"That's right," Chase confirmed.

Jerry sprung forward and grabbed Rory's hand, shaking it vigorously. "How can we thank you, sir?"

Chase raised his hands into a calming motion. "It's already been taken care of, Jerry."

"What were you saying about your plan?" Rory interjected.

"Oh, right. My plan." Chase's eyes narrowed as he studied Rory, and then the corners of his mouth slid into a grin. "Well, I don't really have all the details figured out, but I promise you'll find out all about it before I'm done here."

Chase wasn't lying when he told Rory he would give him nearly anything. But he didn't feel the need to let the old man know about his new plan. Rory had already tried to sabotage his previous efforts. There was no reason to give him advanced notice to plan his next attack.

When Chase turned to go to his tent, he was surprised to see that Rory wasn't trying to follow him. He wasn't surprised to see Jerry two steps behind. Jerry wasn't saying anything, which meant Chase would hear that much more once they got back to the tent.

When they were inside the tent, Chase faced Jerry and prepared himself for a lengthy rant. Instead, Jerry grabbed Chase in a tight hug and held it. This was a line in the employee-employer relationship that Jerry very rarely crossed. It was unprofessional, Jerry would say in most situations, despite the lengthy relationship between himself and Chase, and the entire Chase family.

It was a hug that said Jerry hadn't been worried about his job or what would happen to the company. It was a hug that said he had been worried about Chase.

"I'm okay, Jerry," Chase said.

Jerry took a long step back, with an unchecked smile on his face, still holding onto Chase's shoulders. Were there tears in his eyes?

"Of course you are, my boy." Jerry dropped his hands to his sides and the momentary lapse of his professional demeanour was over. "What happened, exactly?"

Chase told his assistant the whole story. He knew most of the story, though he also told Jerry about the parts that Rory had had to tell Chase about. He left out the parts that made him seem the most vulnerable.

Chase poured himself a glass of scotch as he finished the story and motioned toward Jerry with the glass. "Can I temp you to join me?" he asked.

"You just woke up from nearly dying," Jerry commented.

Chase shrugged and took a drink.

-19-

"He wants to do what?"

"Dams," Alex said into the phone, on the verge of laughter. "He wants to use dams to divide the whole loch into sections. Can you believe it?"

"That's ridiculous," said Loren. He could hear her holding back laughter. She still wasn't happy that Alex had been away from home for so long, but she was entertained and intrigued by the story. Alex had been making a real effort lately, calling Loren multiple times a day. She didn't seem to appreciate his attempt, but she always accepted the calls.

"I know! He came up to me yesterday, after everyone thought he had drowned, and invited me to sit in on his team meeting. Let me tell you, when Harvey Chase puts on a meeting, it's like a show."

* * *

Alex stood near the back of the War Room waiting for Chase. Every team member was packed into the tent, except for a few security guards. In the middle of the tent were two long tables side by side. On each table were several pitchers filled with a black liquid and a long, thin, plastic container filled with water.

Chase walked into the tent, tossing the flaps with a flourish, wearing that goofy grin he always seemed to wear.

"Good evening, everyone! I've brought you all here tonight to find out if anyone has come up with a better plan to capture the Loch Ness Monster."

Everyone began muttering to each other. The collective whispers were quickly rising to a din. Dr. Schnabel stepped forward, apart from the crowd and raised his hands until everyone stopped talking.

"The SONAR plan hasn't been given enough time to abandon it already."

"It has produced two failures already, one resulting in me being all wet." That brought a bit of nervous laughter from Chase's audience. "And it seems to me no one has a new plan, but that's all right, because I have one." His smile revealed his excitement.

He stood between the two tables, at the very center of the tent. Chase pulled a small plastic lizard from his pocket and dropped it into one of the long containers filled with water.

"Could I have a volunteer come up here and get this little lizard out of the water for me? You there. Come on up here."

A man took a step forward looking intimidated. He reached into the water, pulled the lizard out and handed it to Chase.

Chase began applauding loudly with a big smile on his face and kept clapping until everyone else had joined in. Chase put an arm around the man and announced, "This man just caught the beast!"

Everyone clapped and laughed, a few people even gave hoots. Chase knew how to play to an audience.

"I'm going to ask you to do it one more time." Chase picked up one of the pitchers of black liquid and added it to the large container. He then tossed the plastic lizard back in.

When Chase's volunteer reached to put his hand into the black water, Chase stopped him.

"As most of you can figure out, this is meant to be a representation. In keeping with that, to get the lizard out you can't just reach in and feel around until you get him. If it were that simple, we'd have been done days ago."

The crowd laughed. They were much more relaxed.

"Instead of using your hand, you'll be using these chopsticks. So, now I ask you again, get the lizard out."

The man took the chopsticks from Chase's hand and stuck them in the water. It was clear he wasn't very practiced with chopsticks. The man even resorted to holding one stick in each hand and he searched the mini loch. Everyone watched in silence for minutes while the man kept bringing the chopsticks out of the water without the lizard.

"Anyone able to help him out?" Chase asked the group. "Who's got a suggestion?"

"Dump the water," someone called out.

Chase smiled. "Drain the loch, eh? Not a terrible idea, but all that water has to go somewhere. We're talking about more than seven cubic kilometers of water. Where are we going to put all that?"

Silence.

Chase patted his volunteer on the back and gently took the chopsticks from him.

"Thank you for your assistance."

Chase turned to the other table as the man returned to the crowd.

"Now imagine we took this great big, long loch we're camped on the shore of, and started building walls."

Everyone noticed that the second container was actually a series of smaller containers as Chase pulled them apart. He grabbed another pitcher of black liquid and poured a little into each container. Then he produced a similar little lizard and dropped it in one of the center containers.

Chase picked up the two end containers and poured a little liquid into each of the others. All of the remaining sections were full, but when Chase was done pouring, he had an empty container in each hand. He put the empty sections back on the ends and picked up the next two full containers in line and emptied them.

Chase repeated these steps, working his way from the outside in. Each time he emptied two containers, he would pause to show his audience, and to inject a dramatic effect.

Finally, Chase emptied one of the middle containers, revealing the little plastic lizard. Using the chopsticks, he plucked the toy lizard out of the container and held it up for everyone to see. Applause erupted from everywhere at once. Almost everywhere. Dr. Schnabel watched Chase with a blank look. Chase was too busy basking in the applause and adoration of his crew.

*   *   *

"It still seems . . ." Loren searched for the right word.

"Insane?" Alex suggested.

Loren giggled in that way Alex liked. He could see the way her face looked in his mind. Her nose crinkling up, making her even cuter than she already was. Her teeth sticking out just a little, a feature that some would say was unappealing, making her striking in his eyes.

"I miss you," he said.

"Does that mean you're coming home?"

"I can't now," Alex said. "Harvey Chase is about to start one of the most ambitious, yet ludicrous, projects that has ever happened in the entire United Kingdom!"

"Not even for a day or two?"

"A day or two from now, I will have missed a big part of this story."

"Fine. Can we just talk about something unrelated to your work?"

Alex could hear the frustration in her voice. She tried to hide it, but after knowing her for so many years there wasn't much she could hide from him.

"Sure," Alex replied, a little too willingly. "I was thinking the other day, maybe you could come here for a few days. We can take a short vacation or something. I mean, I know it's Scotland, but I'll bet we could still find something to do."

"I'm pretty sure that still has to do with your work," she spat.

"I guess, depending how you look at it."

For the next few minutes, they shared an uncomfortable silence peppered with awkward conversation, small talk that two strangers might share on a bus. Alex tried to think of something to say, but everything that came to his mind either involved his job or could be misconstrued that way. With the amount he had been working, nothing else had happened to him that was worthy of conversation.

"That's why I won't come to Scotland, Alex. We have absolutely nothing to say to each other." Loren slammed the phone down so hard that Alex had a ringing in his right ear for the next half hour.

-20-

Rory grumbled to himself as he trimmed the grass on the ninth hole. Years of maintaining the course meant he could cut every hole in pitch black, which was useful since Rory's entire focus was spent hating Chase.

Rory had saved Chase's life. Without Rory stepping in, the water would have pulled Chase back out into the loch. It was common decency that moved Rory to help the man. The same type of decency that would never allow man to offer someone anything they wanted and then refuse to give what was asked for.

For hours after Chase had gone back to his camp, Rory paced around his house projecting his hatred for the man on everything. He hated his house and how small it was. He hated all of his furniture and how old and broken down it was. He hated that he didn't have any nice things. In fact, the things he did have were covered in dust.

With his mind focused on the wrong thing, Rory didn't hear the golfers on the ninth hole calling out to him. But he did hear the sound of something being hit with the lawn mower blade, the same thing bouncing around in the mower's deck, and then finally, he watched a mangled golf ball fly out of the mower's chute.

"Ya bastard!"

A fat golfer was marching toward the mower, pointing his driver at Rory.

"What have you done?" the golfer demanded. "I was having the game of my life! It probably would have been the club record!"

Rory thought of several replies, but any one of them would have made the situation worse. He spotted Claire, and one of the fat golfer's friends, heading their way from the pro shop. It was better to let Claire handle the situation.

He turned off the lawn mower, which he regretted since it allowed the fat golfer to throw more insults at him.

As the fat golfer turned his complaints from Rory to Claire, Rory allowed his mind to wander. He thought of what it would be like to run the fat man over instead of just his ball. As he imagined the scene, the fat golfer turned into Chase. The fantasy continued, and Rory took the large chunks of Chase, dripping with rich blood, and threw them into the loch so the hunted could become the prey.

"Rory!" Claire called.

He was pulled from his fantasy and back to the ninth hole. The fat man was gone and Claire had a concerned look on her face.

"Where did you go?" she asked. "I called your name a dozen times."

"I'm sorry, Claire. I've got a lot on my mind today."

"Are you not feeling well? In all the years you've been here, you've never run over a player's ball before. And on the fairway, no less. Should you go see a doctor about this?"

"His ball wasn't on the fairway," Rory replied.

Worry pulled at the outside of Claire's eyebrows and her mouth. Rory could tell what she was thinking. He wasn't senile though, just distracted.

"Thanks for the concern, Claire, but I'm fine. Just haven't been sleeping is all. That man out by the loch, and his team, make an awful lot of noise."

"I want you to go home and get some rest."

"I will, Claire. I'll just finish the last 3 holes and head home."

"No. Go now. Someone else will take care of the grass."

"I can do it," he assured her.

"Rory, I just had to give away five rounds of golf. As your manager, I'm telling you to go home. And if this happens again—"

"I'm fired?" Rory said. His voice had an edge that he hadn't intended.

"Rory," she said, placing a hand on his arm. "I was going to say if this happens again, I'll take you to the doctor, myself. I may be your boss, but I'm your friend first. Go home. Rest."

He agreed to go home, but he wasn't going to rest. He was going to use his anger as fuel and find out what Chase had planned. Then he'd find a way to stop it.

-21-

"It's an interesting idea. I'm just not sure it's going to work," Dr. Schnabel explained to Chase.

Chase poured a scotch for himself and one for the doctor. "It's something that's never been done before, but that doesn't make it impossible."

"Perhaps I don't fully understand," the doctor said.

Dr. Schnabel stood there grimacing at the idea as Chase searched through a pile of papers on a small desk. When he found what he was looking for, a map of the Loch Ness, he flattened it out on the small table.

"According to this, the loch is nearly forty square kilometers. It's long and thin, two kilometers wide in most places. Therefore, we divide it into twenty sections. Four square kilometers to a section."

He studied the map closely, tracing a finger along all the waterways that connected to the loch.

"See? If we get all the incoming sources dammed, it should bring the water level down far enough that we can empty one, maybe even two sections at a time."

The doctor said nothing, but his silence revealed a lot.

"I know you're thinking it's insane, and that maybe I am too, but I'm asking you to give this plan a chance. Once the loch is divided, one or two sections will be completely empty. Then we transfer water from full sections into empty ones.

"With the loch sectioned off, every creature will be contained to a smaller area. One by one we empty each and every section, until we've done the entire loch. There will be nowhere for anything to hide. We will see every living thing in that loch."

"That works in theory, but in the real world, you can't do that," Dr. Schnabel protested.

"Why can't I?" Chase argued.

"You'll be altering people's daily lives. People fish here, and what about the tourists? Those tour boats have been out on the water every day since I've been here."

"Anyone troubled by my plan will be generously compensated. If anything, tourism will be stronger. Who wouldn't want to say they were here when the monster was captured? People will pay a premium to see our operation. I'll even allow tours through approved areas of the camp."

"Have you thought about the trouble you'll be causing beyond the loch? Damming off all incoming water won't be good for natural ecosystems. I can't imagine government officials will allow it."

Chase chuckled. "I love officials, and officials love me. A man of my stature and resources can get past a couple of officials with a single conversation and a few cheques."

"What are you going to use as dividers? Some kind of cofferdam, I assume?"

Chase smiled at the doctor.

"Cofferdams are a very good idea, and they would serve our purpose. However, a cofferdam the size we would need has never been made. Not to mention the amount of time each dam would take to create, install, and take down afterward. Multiply all that by twenty. I have deep pockets, but even my resources aren't infinite."

Dr. Schnabel shook his head. "So what then?"

Chase led the doctor out of the tent and to the edge of the camp. A large fish tank was set up on the back of a flatbed truck. Chase had another display planned. He needed everyone to see his plan worked, even if it was a miniature version.

Curiosity brought people to gather around the large tank. Chase noticed Alex was among them, scribbling the occasional note. He excused himself from Dr. Schnabel and walked over to the reporter. "I'm glad you're here. Do you have your camera?"

"Of course. What's that all about?" he asked, motioning toward the tank.

"A test."

"What kind of a test?"

"Wait and see. It'll be worth seeing, I promise you that."

Alex tried to ask more questions, but Chase deflected him with promises of answers to come. The reporter finally gave up and went to inspect the large tank, snapping a few pictures.

A transport truck arrived an hour later filled with hundreds of crates marked *Chase Industries*. A few men from Chase's crew grabbed a crate and took it over to the tank. One of the men began lining the bottom of the tank with small packets from the box.

Chase watched the faces of those around the tank as the

experiment was set up. The looks of intrigue and confusion were enough to give Chase a genuine smile.

"What are those?" Alex asked. "They look like flower boxes."

"You'll see."

When they were finished in the tank, Chase's team handed him a small remote. They spoke for a moment in hushed tones.

Everyone watched Chase closely as he paced in front of the large fish tank, remote in hand.

"Since I revealed my plan, a lot of people have been asking how we're going to construct such huge walls in such a short amount of time. You might also be wondering why I have a big fish tank set up and if I've lost my mind."

Laughter arose from the crowd.

"Let me answer those questions right now."

Chase stepped away from the tank, making sure everyone could see where the small packets had been set up. He held the remote high in his hand and pressed the button.

Several muted pops came from inside the tank. Heavy streams of bubbles, that seemed unnaturally white, streamed out of the packets. Droplets of water bubbled out of the tank.

From the time Chase had pressed the button to the time the bubbles had completely dissipated, only ten seconds had passed. Gasps came from the crowd as the tank cleared and they saw the result of Chase's test. In the middle of the tank was a white wall, dividing the tank in half.

The wall looked like it could have been made up of chewing gum or Styrofoam. Chase knew from experience that the wall was smooth like plastic, but stronger than cement.

People applauded the demonstration and began to crowd around the tank. They leaned close to the glass for a look and reached out, touching the wall to see what it felt like. A few people pushed or pulled on the wall to test its strength.

"I have another big surprise for everyone. For lunch today, we'll be feasting on none other than the very bass that threw me off of my own boat."

That prompted another round of laughter from the crowd and they began to disperse, heading for the mess tent.

Chase walked over to where Dr. Schnabel stood staring at the large tank. Questions were forming in the doctor's head. He opened his mouth to start asking his questions, but Chase cut him off.

"Come have some fish, doctor," Chase said, patting the man on the back.

"Your demonstration was impressive. What is it made of?"

Chase chuckled. "Like a lot of great inventions in the world, it was a complete mistake. Come have some lunch and I'll tell you more about it."

Chase looked at his plate for some time before he took a bite of the fish. It was strange to eat the creature that had, indirectly, almost killed him. He took a bite, not really wanting the fish to touch his tongue. Once in his mouth, it tasted more flavorful than any seafood he could remember eating.

He didn't know if it was the preparation of the food or something in the situation that made the meat taste so savory, but he went back up for a second serving.

Dr. Schnabel had fixed himself a plate, but it sat untouched in front of him as he fired continuous questions at Chase.

"So this," the doctor paused, sputtering. "I don't even know what to call it. You said it was a mistake?"

"We were trying to make a high quality foam sealant. We took the concept of an aerosol can and your standard foam sealer and tried to get the best properties of each. Our initial testing in the lab seemed successful, but when we went to test it on a construction site, the sealant expanded so rapidly that it tore apart sheets of drywall. It cracked two-by-fours in half, broke panes of glass. A real disaster. A contractor on site grabbed a hose, thinking he could wash some of it away before it hardened. Water made it expand further and faster, and increased the density exponentially. It destroyed the house we were testing it on. It had to be knocked down and rebuilt from the foundation."

"So it's a chemical reaction. Incredible," Dr. Schnabel said.

Chase was pleased to see the doctor so interested. Perhaps it would be enough to convince him to stay until they captured the beast.

"At that point, I had the project locked away, labeled as a huge failure. I didn't have it destroyed though. Something like that had to have a use, I just had to find the application. What I had shipped in today is all that was ever made."

"Will it be enough?"

"No. But I've had a factory in England repurposed and a team of men are producing as much of it as they can, around the clock. As soon as it's produced, it goes to another facility where it's customized."

"Customized?"

"It's manufactured in a can. So part one is putting in a controlled explosion that creates a tear in the can."

"What were the wooden boxes for?"

"They did a test at the factory, much like we did here. When they blew the first can open, instead of making a wall, it just made a deformed sphere. They came up with the box to act like the barrel of a gun. It directs the expansion into a long, flat shape."

"Incredible," Dr. Schnabel commented. "But I still can't see how you're going to make this whole plan work. You made a small divider. To do that in the loch you need to make walls two kilometers wide, several hundred feet tall."

"You're right. We'll need to make much bigger walls. Even with enough boxes lined up they won't reach all the way to the top." he said. "But we'll figure something out. Maybe a timing system where one can detonates and ten seconds later another one goes."

"You could use a net," Dr. Schnabel offered.

"How so?"

"You string a net across the loch to act as a skeleton for the wall. Attach the boxes to the net, spaced properly for full coverage."

Chase was amazed at how differently Dr. Schnabel was acting after Chase's little display. "Brilliant, doctor."

"What are your plans for water displacement?"

"Industrial pumps," Chase said.

"That'll take months."

"Not so. The Loch Ness holds about sixteen and half million gallons of water. Over in America they're pumping more than that out of Lake Michigan on a daily basis. Daily. Each section is going to have anywhere from a million to five-hundred thousand liters. I think we can handle it."

Dr. Schnabel smiled, perhaps for the first time since he arrived in Scotland. The man was excited about the technology that Chase had brought, and perhaps about studying some of the aquatic life in such a controlled manner. The doctor was too skeptical to suddenly believe in the Loch Ness Monster. Belief would come later. For now, it was enough that the doctor was showing signs of passion.

"Are you ready to help me make history?"

-22-

Alex scribbled notes as he watched Chase's team prepare for the first divider. The first to go up was the southern-most wall, quartering off the first 2km. Chase had told him that he planned on draining that section almost immediately once the first divider was in place.

The process was astounding to watch.

A semi truck arrived, which appeared to have its trailer filled with fishing nets. Instead of hundreds of nets, it was just one big net that had been put together before it arrived at the camp.

A boat carried the net across the loch and fed it to men in scuba gear in the water. The divers then embedded the edges of the net into the sides and bottom of the loch.

The men on the boat handed the divers the boxes that, when deployed, would become a wall just like in Chase's miniature demo. The divers periodically disappeared and reappeared, making several dives to attach the boxes to various points in the net.

With nothing to watch while the divers were under water, Alex took the time to arrange his thoughts. Figuring he had some time before anything exciting happened, he paced around the camp and read over his notes.

"Hey, big shot," a voice called out. It was Grant Huxley, standing behind the security barricade. He was one of the few remaining, most of the other reporters either had gone home or attempted other ways to get their story. Every tour boat in the loch likely had at least one reporter on it, hoping it would get close to Chase's camp.

Alex turned and smiled. "Hey there, Huxley. How're things at the edge of camp?"

"Very funny. What's going on? You gotta give me something."

"I don't have to give you anything." To illustrate his point, Alex put his notebook into his jacket and patted the pocket.

"Alex, please. My editor is up my ass. I know you know how that is. They don't care that we have to go through hell to get a story."

Alex thought about Edwards, sitting back at the office, probably saying horrible things about him to anyone who would listen. He only found himself as Chase's exclusive reporter because Edwards had tried to send him on a dead end story.

"Okay," Alex said, stepping in close to Huxley and lowering his voice. The other reporters tried to watch them without staring. "You might find there's a little more to see on the west side of the loch, about two kilometers from the southern tip."

Huxley gave Alex a skeptical look. "You're just trying to get me away from this area."

"Huxley, no. I'm not."

"Yeah, yeah. I'm not going anywhere."

Alex shrugged and grinned before walking back toward the edge of the loch. Divers were climbing out of the water. Alex walked to find a good vantage to observe the next step.

Dr. Schnabel was close by as well. The divers all made their way over to him to exchange a few words. The doctor nodded and made a few scribbles on a notepad as he spoke with each diver. Alex wasn't close enough to hear any of the conversation, but he imagined each diver was going over a technical checklist with the doctor.

Alex felt the excitement building in his stomach, and among the other members of Chase's team who had started to gather around. The final diver exited the loch and took his turn with Dr. Schnabel. When the conversation was over, the doctor spoke into his walkie-talkie.

A moment later, Chase made his appearance, acting strangely. Instead of commanding the room's attention, the way he normally would, he stood off to the side with his arms crossed. There was a glint in his eye and a grin on his lips as he looked out at the water.

Dr. Schnabel picked up a megaphone and announced, "Detonation in ten seconds."

Just like with Chase's fish tank demo, everything began with bubbles on the surface, millions instead of hundreds this time. It looked like a 2km row of hot tub jets just under the surface of the loch.

After a moment, the bubbles tapered off. Once they cleared, the top of the very first divider was visible. Everyone broke into applause. The faces of those clapping were in shock. Eyes were a little wider, mouths slightly parted. Alex was sure their faces reflected his own. The fish tank demo was impressive, but the scale of what had just been done was massive.

On average, nearly a foot of the milky structure stood above the water. It wasn't perfect. It was quite lumpy all the way across, dipping down below the surface in some spots and sticking three feet out of the water in others. Some of the onlookers waded into the water to feel the new wall. Some even sat on it, laughing at the incredible success.

"It worked," Alex said aloud.

"You sound surprised," said Chase, walking up behind Alex.

Divers headed back into the water with fresh oxygen tanks, each carrying a few of the boxes. They would search for holes in the divider that required a patch.

"I guess I am," Alex admitted.

Chased smiled. "I thought you knew enough about me by now. If I want something to happen, it happens."

"I know, but that stuff is unreal. How did you ever come up with it?"

"Isn't it obvious?" Chase said, chuckling to himself. "The aliens gave it to me."

- 23 -

For three days, Rory had done little more than glance toward Chase and his camp. After hearing about Chase's plan to divide the loch into sections, Rory assumed the man would find failure all on his own. He choked on his own doubt as he stood on his rickety dock and stared at the wall running from the western shore to the eastern shore.

Not only had Chase succeeded in putting in a divider, he did it in a single day. Rory shook his head and walked over to the wall for a closer look.

He reached down and felt the wall with his hands. It felt solid, despite its spongy appearance. He even stood on it. It bared his weight easily, as if the wall was cement. Rory started walking the length of the wall and saw it was rather uneven, rising and falling the way the rolling hills of Scotland did.

He had to look twice at the southern side of the wall. The

water level was lower than the rest of the loch. It was already low enough that Rory wouldn't be able to get his boat in the water. Not without trucking it further up the loch.

Rory kept walking toward the eastern shore. If it wasn't for Chase's plan and the part the wall he stood on would play in it, he'd actually be enjoying his walk. It was the closest he would ever get to walking on water. It was also being surrounded by his beloved loch without needing a boat.

Just under an hour later, he arrived on the eastern shore where he found a large pump drawing water from the south side of the wall and dumping it on the north side, which explained the varying water levels.

Two of Chase's men stood near the pump, but seemed preoccupied. They hadn't noticed him or even looked in his direction even though he had walked the divider from one side of the loch to the other.

Rory stepped off of the wall and over to the pump. It was gas powered. He didn't know how much water it could pump, but it seemed to be spitting a small waterfall over the divider. With a flick of his finger, the pump was off. He watched Chase's men, expecting them to come running, but they were looking off to the north.

He crept closer until he could hear what they were saying.

"Another one already?" one of the men asked.

"That's what they just said. No point in wasting time, I guess."

"I still can't believe it worked," the first man said, peering across the loch. A message came through the first man's walkie-talkie. There was too much static for Rory to understand.

"Okay," said the first man. "You're clear to go."

Seconds later, water bubbled on the surface of the loch, about 2km north of their location. Rory watched with mounting interest as the bubbling grew more intense by the second. He was watching so closely that it made him jump when water exploded upward.

The water misted back to the surface of the loch, which was showing its annoyance in waves. The water slapped against the second wall. A second wall! Rory stared in disbelief. The walls were hard enough to believe on their own, but the speed that one could go up was unthinkable!

Chase's men looked at the wall and began laughing and shaking each other's hands.

"Three down!" the second man said.

Three? Rory thought. They must have put one of the monstrosities at the north point of the loch. He felt the back of his neck get hot. When he first heard about Chase's plan, he didn't fully understand it. Then he chose not to believe that it would work. But if he was honest with himself, what made him the angriest was that he was afraid it was going to work.

A voice called out from behind Rory. "How did I know I'd find you here?"

He spun quickly and came face to face with Jerry Triggs.

"What is this crap you're putting in the water?" Rory demanded. "You're polluting the loch!"

"I don't know too much about that. I do know that Harvey has received all the required clearances for this project."

"You don't sound like you believe in this much," Rory commented.

"It's not my job to believe in it. It's my job to assist however I can. Regardless of what I believe, at least if he goes through with it, it'll prove what many of us already know."

"The monster doesn't exist," Rory finished.

Jerry studied him. "I can't quite figure you out. Seems like you don't believe, then it seems like you do, then you don't again. Can't make up your mind?"

"What I believe doesn't really make a difference, does it?"

"Not really. But you've made a difference in the way we've been doing things around here."

Rory looked the assistant in the eye, attempting to read the man's meaning. Two men appeared on either side of Triggs, each with a handgun in a hip holster.

"These are the newest additions to our security team. Harvey just brought them in last night. Their only job is to watch for you. Personally, I think it's a waste of money, but for some reason Harvey really wants to make sure you don't try to interfere anymore."

Jerry seemed to be waiting for a response. Rory wasn't going to bother giving one. The fact that Chase had hired extra security made him want to smile, but more security meant things were going to get harder.

"Gentlemen, could you show Rory back to his house?"

"Don't make it sound like I don't know how to get to my own house. I'll go myself!"

Rory spun and walked away. Behind him he heard Jerry say, "Make sure he goes all the way there. And turn the pump back on as you go by."

-24-

Martin Edwards slammed several copies of the *UK Observer* down on his desk, most of them crumpled or torn by his overweight fists.

That son of a bitch was supposed to go out and have his career murdered, he thought. *Now he's more popular than ever!*

There was a knock on his door and, before Edwards had time to give the knocker permission to come in, Gary Whitson strode into the office.

"Afternoon, Gary," Edwards said, a fresh layer of sweat coating his skin. "What can I do for you?"

Gary sat down in Edwards's chair, shuffling through the papers on his desk.

"We get anything from Alex today?"

"Of course," Edwards said, unable to keep the disappointment from his voice.

"All laid out for print, is it?"

"Front page." Again the displeasure in his voice was more obvious than he intended.

"You don't like him, do you, Martin?"

"What? Of course I like Alex. He's one of our best."

Gary studied Edwards. He seemed to be looking beyond the agreeable facade Edwards usually wore, beyond the excuses and the lies to see the man underneath. A man who didn't do his job to the best of his ability and instead of making himself look better through performance, he did it by trying to make others look worse. And men like Alex Stafford made men like Martin Edwards look bad without really trying at all.

"Yes," Gary agreed. "That Alex does good work." He emphasized the last two words with a wrap of his knuckles on the desk.

"Do you want to see the latest story?"

Edwards searched through the papers on his desk and found Alex's story.

"I like to read it off the newsstand," Gary replied, standing from Edwards's chair, and buttoning his suit jacket. "But the next time you talk to Alex, I want you to tell him that he's doing a good job."

"He knows that. I tell him all the time!"

Gary walked to the office door and looked back at Edwards.

"Tell him again."

Edwards closed the door behind Gary and felt ready to explode. He held his breath and trembled as his face turned red. He didn't dare let go of his breath just yet since the release would be followed by a string of vulgarity.

Alex bloody Stafford. Harvey bloody Chase. The man probably didn't even read the *UK Observer*. He gasped. Maybe he did read the paper. If not him, someone Chase knew must read the paper.

Edwards grabbed Alex's story and his red pen. He began making notes on the fax paper, and laughing to himself. He sent the corrections down to the fellows on the press and smiled for the rest of the day.

-25-

Rory already had his supper in the boat. It was the biggest fish he had caught in a month, but Rory stayed in his boat with an empty hook in the water.

Chase had four of his walls completed, two at each end of the loch. The section farthest south was completely empty, and after a drive around the loch, Rory knew they had already drained half of the north section.

Not only were they moving a lot faster than Rory guessed, they were getting more efficient with the setup.

Without an idea to stop them completely, Rory was resorting to plans just to slow them down until he could think of a better plan. Assuming he could come up with a better plan.

Rory had spent a few moments watching Chase's crew inspect the emptied section at the southern end of the loch. It was a sad sight. It wasn't enough for them to look. They went wading through the mud in diving suits with lifelines for a closer look at any clump bigger than the average fish.

Hundreds, if not thousands, of fish were lying in the mud, gasping and trying to swim away from the intruders. Chase's new security team had stood watching Rory the entire time.

It looked as though they were putting a barrier up every 2km. Rory picked a spot 2km from the last divider and floated there in his boat. If he stayed there fishing, they wouldn't be able to set up that divider. At least that was what he thought.

Despite his presence, Chase's team had worked around him, installing the massive fishing net under the water, diving with the small boxes. Rory tried to get in the way, and stay in the way, but they didn't seem bothered by him.

Once they seemed to be done with the net, however, they all just stood in a small group on the shore looking at him. That made Rory want to smile.

"Sir?" a voice called from the shore. Rory was close enough to shore that he heard the man, but pretended not to. "Sir?"

The shouting carried on for a few minutes before Rory finally turned and looked at the man, who started waving Rory to come closer.

Rory did as the man requested, taking care to stay in line with where the next divider was set up.

"What do you want?" Rory demanded.

The man forced a friendly laugh. "I was hoping I could convince you to fish a little farther down the loch."

"Sorry. Can't do it. This is my lucky fishing spot. Never seem to catch fish anywhere else."

"Well," the man forced another nervous laugh. "I kind of need you to move."

"Don't worry," Rory said with a grin. "I won't be long."

Rory moved a little farther away from shore again before the man could say anything more.

For the next two hours Rory sat in his boat pretending to fish. Occasionally, the man would try to call out to him, and Rory would give him a friendly wave that suggested he would be out of their way soon.

In his boat he muttered to himself, "You want me gone, you're going to have to move me yourself."

*   *   *

"They finished searching section one, nothing found," Jerry reported to Chase in his tent.

"That's okay," Chase reasoned. "I really didn't expect to find anything in the very first section. It'll probably be in the deeper sections where things get interesting."

"Have you thought about what to do with the aquatic life we're finding? We really should leave something alive in this loch by the time we're done."

Chase turned his back on Jerry, pouring himself a glass of scotch.

"This really isn't my area of expertise, Jerry. What do you recommend I do?"

"This might sound a little too simplistic, but how about picking up the fish and putting them into some water."

"Excellent suggestion, Jerry! I knew there was a reason I paid you so well." Sarcasm was rare for Chase. He took a pull from his scotch glass and gave a sigh of relief. "Still, sometimes the simplest solution is the best. Do we have the manpower for that, without slowing down progress?"

"No, but it might be in our best interest to bring in some more people."

"Bah." Chase waved a hand dismissively.

Jerry gave him a look so potent with disappointment that Chase actually had to look away. "I'll give it some thought. What else is happening?"

"Your mother called."

"Christ," Chase said. "When can I expect to have to talk to her?"

"Soon. She's coming for a visit. With her new assistant." The words came out peppered with disgust. "I really wish you had sent me to help with the interviewing process. She hired an American."

Chase began laughing heartily. "An American? Oh, Mother. She must be trying to get back at me for being away so much." He continued laughing.

"From what she said, they're getting along very well so far," Jerry explained, though his voice revealed his doubts.

"Well, I'm glad for that," Chase said. "Anything else?"

"Nothing at the moment."

"Excellent. I think I'll let my scotch have a bit of night air," Chase said. After topping his glass off, he left the tent with a parting nod.

The sun was sinking into the horizon, giving the loch a rare orange glow as if it was just waking up. No photograph, no painting, would ever match the sight he took in. Insects chirped nearby, lulling Chase into an even more relaxed state. A bird cooed overhead, possibly on its way to settle in for the night with her hatchlings. A gentle breeze blew, cool and refreshing without giving him a chill. She had been a formidable opponent thus far, the loch and the beast, but she was revealing her innermost beauty to Chase so he paused to share the moment with her.

When he entered the camp's communications tent, no one took any notice of him, as usual. Most of the men there were wearing headphones and communicating with someone at another part of the loch or listening to one of the SONAR feeds.

Chase wandered around a bit, trying to make sense of whatever he could. A large map hung on a nearby cork board. There were several small colored pins in the map near the northern end of the loch.

One of the technicians had told Chase a few days earlier that the pins indicated where their divers were. If they were at the north end, the way this map indicated, that meant they were working on the sixth wall. A genuine smile grew on Chase's face.

Dr. Schnabel finally noticed Chase's presence and sidled up to him.

"Good evening, Mr. Chase."

"Good evening. I see we're working on the sixth wall. That's excellent. Five walls up, fourteen to go, hey?"

"Yes, they are working on number six, but we don't have number five up just yet."

"What's the problem?" Chase asked.

"The team says there's an obstruction that they're trying to clear," the doctor said.

Chase didn't trust something about the doctor's response. The words were chosen too carefully. He was hiding something.

"Get them on the radio," he demanded.

Dr. Schnabel pulled the walkie-talkie from his belt and brought it up to his mouth.

"Team three, come back."

"This is team three," the walkie-talkie quickly replied.

Chase snatched the walkie-talkie away from Dr. Schnabel. "Team three, it's Harvey Chase. What's this obstruction I'm hearing about?" Chase made his voice sound friendly and non-threatening. He didn't want the man on the other end of the walkie-talkie trying to hide something like the doctor had tried to do.

"It's that old man in his boat. He won't move."

Dr. Schnabel's face turned a unique shade of pink as he looked at Chase like he expected to be slapped. Chase couldn't blame the man. He was running his team the way he saw fit. Yet the old man's latest distraction had cost them hours of daylight. The doctor should have called in for some help.

"Son of a bitch," Chase said. "Team three, I'm on my way."

Chase hopped into the nearest truck and drove along the edge of the loch until he saw a team of his men . . . and an old bastard in a boat.

"What is this?" Chase demanded.

One of the men spoke up. "Uh, we've been asking him to leave for hours. He keeps saying he's about to leave."

Chase walked to the very edge of the loch.

"Oi!" he bellowed out at the man.

Rory turned in his boat and gave Chase an overly friendly wave.

"Fuck off!" Chase yelled.

Rory gave one more wave and went back to staring at his fishing pole.

"All right, old man. That's the way you want it." Chase looked at the man who had spoken up. "Trigger the wall."

"Sir, I can't. That man—"

"Has had plenty of time to move. Trigger it. Now."

The man pulled a remote out of his pocket, but it might as well have been in the hand of a statue. He kept looking from Rory, to the remote, to Chase, and back to the boat again.

Chase snatched the remote out of the man's hands and poised his thumb over the button.

"Aren't you going to give him one last chance?" one of the men said.

"That was his last chance."

Chase hit the button and watched as bubbles rose all around Rory and his boat. The old man started to panic, which brought a smile to Chase's face.

Rory frantically pulled on his motor's ripcord, but on the third pull the motor, the boat, and Rory were all knocked two feet into the air. The boat spun, along with Rory, as it headed back toward the water's surface. With a splash, he disappeared under the water and the boat bobbed on the surface, capsized.

Chase began to laugh while his men watched, horrified. The laughter died out when he realized Rory hadn't resurfaced yet.

His first thought was to have one of his men call someone, but they wouldn't get there in time. Chase felt the need to jump in and pull the old man to shore, but he was frozen by memories of nearly drowning.

The surface of the water broke and Rory flailed to grab a hold of his boat. A non-stop torrent of curses came from the old man's mouth and Chase found himself laughing once again.

Chase tossed the remote back to the man he had taken it from and then grinned. "Was that so hard?"

-26-

Chase left his tent at the sound of an approaching helicopter. He recognized the pattern of the Chase Industries bird before it began its descent. With both him and Jerry already on the ground, and the rest of his high-level associates trying to stay distanced from the hunt, there was only one person that could have ordered a company helicopter to bring her here.

Jerry appeared beside him, calmly watching the helicopter descend.

"Why didn't you tell me my mother was coming for a visit?" Chase shouted above the din of spinning blades.

"I did."

"But you didn't say it was today."

"If I had, you would have disappeared," Jerry yelled back, a smirk growing from the corners of his mouth.

The helicopter lowered to the ground, forcing the

surrounding grass to lay flat. Chase laughed at Jerry's futile efforts to keep his hair from getting messed up. When the helicopter blades stopped spinning, they both looked like they had just got out of bed.

Mona Chase stepped off of the helicopter, looking at her surroundings as though she had landed on an alien planet instead of another country. Chase walked to meet her, arms spread wide and a smile pasted on his face. He stopped mid-stride when a young man stepped out of the helicopter behind her, placing his hands on her shoulders and leading her away from the helicopter.

Chase looked from Mona to the man. The confusion on his face must have been obvious, because Mona broke into a laugh when she looked at him.

"Son, this is John Lasorda, my assistant."

"Right," Chase said, remembering the phone call. "The American." He extended a hand toward John who took it in a grip Chase would call too firm.

"It's a pleasure to meet you, Harvey," John said.

"Likewise."

"No. I really mean it. I hope we get some time to talk privately. I have a few ideas I'd love to discuss with you."

Great! Chase thought, though the smile never left his face. John Lasorda wouldn't be the first man who thought he could attain a low-level job close to Chase and try to impress him with some half-cooked, not-so-brilliant idea. He usually avoided such meetings, but he would likely end up entertaining Mr. Lasorda to appease his mother.

Jerry and John eyed each other, silently judging. They couldn't have been much different. Nationalities and age aside, Jerry had always seemed like he was born in a three-piece suit where John wore jeans and a golf shirt. Jerry felt it was only appropriate to smile in public when good manners required it, but John had been smiling since he stepped off of the helicopter.

"Come, son," Mona said, slapping Chase on the shoulder. "Show me around. I want to see what the big deal is about Loch Ness and this monster."

*   *   *

They walked through the camp, arm in arm, while Chase pointed out the tents housing various teams and equipment and explained the plans that had been tried without success. He took her close to one of the completed dividers and explained his current plan.

Mona smiled and nodded without asking any questions as her son spoke. She understood little of what she was told, but she didn't care to know about it. She was only there to spend a little time with her son. A dinner back in London, or some time at home would have been preferable, but if he was determined to stay by this loch she would come to him.

He was suffering through the visit, she knew. Not because he didn't love his mother, but because he wanted to be out there continuing his hunt. His ambitions had to be put aside while she was there, and she loved him even more because he was willing to put them aside, if only temporarily.

"What will you do when you catch it?" Mona asked.

"I'll put on the most spectacular show London has ever seen."

He continued on about the attention the Loch Ness Monster would bring, and again she just smiled and listened. She didn't believe in the Loch Ness Monster, but that didn't matter. There was no need for her to spoil his attempts by forcing her views on him.

John and Jerry followed closely behind them, each making an effort to pretend the other didn't exist. It was strange to think that in a way she was being followed around by her past and future.

"It'll be time for tea soon, Mother. Shall we head to the mess tent for a bite?"

Mona did not want to see the kind of food that was available in a tent. She found it hard to believe anything would meet her standards.

"All right," she agreed. "And then John and I must be on our way."

"Leaving? But I've arranged a tent for you both."

Mona laughed and patted her son's cheek. She didn't plan on spending a single night in a tent. Her son knew that, which is why he had so enthusiastically made the offer. The time with her son was good, but it was almost at an end.

"Why don't you and Jerry go ahead, Mona," John suggested. "Maybe Harvey and I can have that talk now."

Mona smiled and took Jerry's arm, but when they turned to go, an elderly man was standing close by smiling at her. Before she could say anything Chase was back at her side, giving the old man a challenging stare.

"You must be Ms. Chase," the old man said. He approached slowly, with a kind smile on his face. When he reached for her hand, she reluctantly gave it to him, hoping he didn't kiss her.

He didn't. Instead, he dipped and bobbed in a bow and looked back up to her. "It's a pleasure to meet such a delightful lady of London. You grace this loch with your presence alone."

Mona couldn't stop the smile from appearing on her face and she felt her cheeks color.

"What a charming gentleman," Mona beamed.

"Good evening," the man said, giving another bow before turning to walk away.

"My, my," Mona said to Chase. "Such delightful neighbors you have here."

"Not really, Mother. If I told you half of the things that man—"

"Hey, Ms. Chase!" the older man called, now standing just outside of the camp. "I almost forgot to give you a little Scottish hospitality!"

The old man had turned his back on them and dropped his pants down to his ankles. He slapped his rear while shuffling around in tight circles.

"Bastard!" Chase swore.

"It's okay, son. John, let's prepare to leave. I've somehow lost my appetite."

-27-

"If it isn't my cheapest customer," Rob Morton said as Rory stalked into the store.

"I'm also the one in the worst mood," Rory grunted back as he began taking items off the shelves.

"Are there times you're in a good mood?"

"Any mail?" Rory called.

"Nope."

Rory slammed the majority of his groceries down on the counter and took out his wallet.

"You really are cross, aren't you? What's going on?"

"Nothing I'm wanting to talk about," Rory spat.

"It wouldn't have anything to do with one of UK's richest men having a camping trip in your backyard, would it?"

Rory made a sound of disgust. "It's a wonder how that man ever made a dime. He's so stupid."

"He's made much more than a dime."

"I don't want to talk about him. Tell me what's going on with you. I need to hear about some normal things. How's the family? Your wife come to her senses and kick you out of the house yet?"

"Not yet," Rob joked. "Down with a bit of a cold right now. I had to take home half the store's supply of chicken soup for her."

Rory smiled politely. He just wanted to pay for his groceries and go home, but Rob was one of the few people Rory could call a friend.

"My lazy, lay about son finally got himself a job."

"Did he?" Rory asked.

"Yeah. Some private security firm hired him to sit around and watch for suspicious people along the Caledonian Canal."

"Suspicious people?" Rory asked, his interest piqued.

"Yeah. I guess they've had some vandalism or something lately."

"I find that kind of stuff really interesting. Do you think he'd show me around the place?"

"I'm sure he wouldn't mind. From what he tells me, it's a pretty boring job. Does more reading and sleeping than anything else. When would you like to go?"

"Tonight is fine for me."

*   *   *

That night, Rory met up with Rob's son, Colin.

"My God," Rory said, shaking the boy's hand. "I haven't seen you since your daddy used to bring you to the store. How old are you now?"

"Nineteen," Colin said, looking a little embarrassed.

"Nineteen! Where does the time go?"

"Dad said you're really into all this water stuff?"

"Oh, yes! It's very interesting. It's a lot like plumbing, but on a much larger scale."

"You find plumbing interesting?"

"In its own way, I do."

Colin shrugged and led Rory on a tour of the canals in the immediate area. There wasn't much to see beyond docks and boats. Once he had seen one stretch, every other stretch looked the same.

They walked past some of the huge locks that would normally let traffic through. They were all closed now, turning the area into a marina.

"They tell me there isn't normally much traffic through this area, but right now nothing is coming through."

"Why is that?"

"You hear about that rich guy doing something by the loch?"

Typical teenager. A nuclear bomb could fall and all they would know is *something happened.*

"I heard something about him." Rory played dumb.

"Well, I guess he had the river dammed temporarily. Any boats moving past this point just have to turn around and go back, but most of them have an onboard radio and find out way before they get here."

"Interesting," Rory said, as if it was all new information.

Rory followed Colin up a short set of metal stairs into a small room overlooking the canal.

"This is the main control room," Colin said, opening a door and letting Rory poke his head in.

Colin moved to the close the door, but Rory slid past him into the control room. "Can I just look for a moment? This is the really interesting stuff."

The main console housed several monitors, all showing different areas of the canal. Below each monitor was a control panel that had more buttons and switches than Rory had ever seen.

Colin pointed to one of the monitors where they could see the locks they had just walked by.

"Normally there's an operator in here, but they don't bother with it at night. Watch this."

Colin pulled one of the levers and the locks on the monitor above the controls opened. He pushed the lever back into place and the locks closed.

"So," Rory said pointing, "that lever opens those locks?"

"That's right," Colin said with a proud smile.

"What's the monitor over there?"

Rory pointed to a monitor, different than all the rest. It wasn't built into the console, it didn't even appear to be a permanent fixture of the control room.

"That's the dam I mentioned earlier."

Rory stared at the dam. It wasn't a very clear picture on the monitor, but on the other side of that dam was a section of the Loch Ness void of water. The water from that section had been pumped into the remainder of the loch beyond the divider. The rest of the loch was brimming with water.

If the empty section was suddenly full, it would be days before Chase found something to do with the extra water. Like all of his plans so far, this wasn't a permanent solution, but something that would buy him a little time, something he sorely needed.

"One of the other guys told me the dam won't be here much longer," Colin said.

"I see. And which of these switches opens that?"

-28-

Seven dividers were completed and the eighth would be finished before the sun went down.

Jerry stood by the loch and watched the crew prepare to drain the second section on the southern end. The ends had both been drained, and at the northern side of the loch a team would be preparing to drain another section.

Jerry was glad to see the progress moving efficiently. Not because he was optimistic of the success of the hunt, just that it would end soon, regardless of the outcome. He was tired of the loch, tired of sleeping in a tent, and tired of hearing about the monster.

A commotion arose from the other side of the camp. Were people chanting?

Jerry walked through the tents, the chanting growing louder with every step. Behind the barrier, normally holding back a few desperate reporters, were dozens, maybe even a hundred people, all holding picket signs. Their signs said things like *Leave Our Loch, Go Back to London* and *Fish Killer* and had images of dead fish. They were chanting 'Chase is chasing the fish away.'

This was going to be trouble. It would be a lot of noise, that the press would love, and the police wouldn't be able to help. These people were exercising their right to protest and they probably weren't going to go away by throwing money at them. People like this were fundamentalists. They lived simple lives and no amount of money would shake them from their cause.

Chase wandered up behind Jerry, watching the picketers with interest.

"Well, well, well. What's going on here?" Chase asked.

"We should have known this would happen. They're not going to stop, either. Perhaps we can move the edge of the camp further out and keep them out of the way."

"Nonsense," Chase dismissed as he took a step toward the protestors.

Jerry grabbed his arm and locked eyes with Chase. "You can't buy these people."

Chase held the eye contact and replied, "I know."

The protestors had noticed Chase by that point and began chanting twice as loudly. They thrusted their signs up and down, and a few jabbed fingers at Chase.

"Good afternoon, everyone," he said with a big smile, holding his arms out wide.

They only chanted louder, putting extra hatred behind every word. Spittle flew from their mouths as they shook signs and fists at Chase.

"Enough of that," Chase raised his voice, yet held his friendly tone. "Enough of that. We won't solve anything by yelling at each other."

Slowly, the protestors fell silent. Chase shifted his gaze to the ones who were still trying to chant until they too stopped.

"Is there one among you who can speak for the group?" Chase asked.

They muttered among themselves until a woman, who was already at the front of the group, spoke up.

"I'll do it," she said. Some of her fellow protestors patted her on the back in support.

"Excellent. What is your name, my dear?"

"Helen." Her voice was cold. He would only get the facts from this one.

"It's nice to meet you, Helen. I'm Harvey."

"Don't you think we already know who you are?" she spat.

Chase continued, ignoring the rhetorical.

"And what is it that I can do for you people?"

"Leave. Leave our loch. Leave our country," Helen demanded. Her supporters gave a cheer of support behind her.

"You probably wouldn't be surprised to hear that you're not the first person to ask me to do that," he said, giving her a smile meant to share in the humor. Helen had no interest in sharing anything.

"I'd be surprised if I was the last," Helen replied.

"You've got a point there." Chase's smile remained, but Jerry could tell it was growing more difficult by the second for him to keep it there. "I'm guessing from your signs that you have an issue with our treatment of the aquatic life?"

"You call it treatment, we call it murder. We've seen the amount of fish dead at your hands. It's unacceptable."

The smile disappeared from Chase's face. "Yes. That is truly regrettable. Can I be honest with all of you for a moment? I'm embarrassed over this exact issue. I hired a team of individuals whose sole purpose was to protect the life in the loch. I paid top dollar for these people, who called themselves the authority in life preservation, but obviously, as we have both discovered, they're seriously unqualified."

Jerry was amazed. He had had a conversation with Chase where the man admitted to not caring about the dying fish, yet listening to him now Jerry almost believed him.

"That's why I'm glad to see all of you here," Chase said.

Faces among the picketers were starting to soften. Their signs, mostly forgotten, had been lowered, handles resting on the ground. They were paying close attention to his every word.

"You're here to save the fish, and I want them saved. I can't leave until I've seen this through, but we can work together. My team and I will focus on our search while you and your team can do a proper job of protecting aquatic life."

Murmurs rose from the crowd as the protestors turned to whisper to one another. Chase and Helen remained with eyes locked on one another.

"I have a chance at a pretty important victory, but you'll have one whether I succeed or not. You will save countless lives. You and your team will be left to your own form of leadership. You decide what the best course of action is and execute as you see fit. We'll cooperate where necessary, and of course, you'll have full access to our boats and whatever else you require."

Most of the protestors were now smiling. Helen's face still looked like a carving.

"Don't forget, Helen. This is also an opportunity to be a part of the team that discovers Scotland's biggest legend."

Jerry felt like laughing when Helen's face split into a smile and she stuck a hand out to shake Chase's. In the span of a few moments, Chase had pulled off one of the greatest acts of propitiation that Jerry had ever seen.

Chase and Jerry gave the protestors a quick tour of the camp and introduced Helen to several key members of Chase's crew. They had a few spare tents lying around that Chase told them they could use for as long as they were here. There weren't enough cots for all of the protestors, but no one voiced a complaint.

"Free reign of the camp, use of our resources. You're fairly trusting," Jerry said as they walked away from the protestor's tents.

"I believe they want to do a good job," Chase explained. "And I've asked our security team to pay them a little extra attention. I'm trusting, not stupid. And you may have noticed, they didn't ask for any kind of payment," Chase finished with a wink.

As the two men stood looking out at the loch, Jerry's mind returned to the efficiency of the project.

"I meant to tell you, it was smart of you to start draining as soon as a few dividers were up," Jerry said. "In fact, I think it would be best if we disposed of dividers as we no longer need them."

A loud buzzing sound rang out in the distance.

"What the hell is that?" Chase asked.

They looked around for the source of the noise, but it was echoing across the hills, seeming to come from everywhere at once.

"Oh, no," Jerry said as he spotted the source.

Jerry saw the dam that connected the south end of the loch to the River Oich beginning to lower. A waterfall appeared at the dam and began filling the empty section of the loch.

Other men had left their tents to investigate the noise. Chase grabbed the closest one by the scruff of his shirt. "Get that dam closed!"

Men scrambled, screaming into walkie-talkies, and climbing into vehicles to drive to the dam.

After a few moments, the dam rose into the closed position,

but it was too late. Section one was overfull. The water level of the entire loch had risen above the tops of all the dividers. On the surface, there was no evidence that the dividers existed at all.

Chase's face was already a deep pink, heading for red. The man he had grabbed jogged away as soon as Chase's grip loosened. He looked at Jerry with murder in his eyes.

"Jerry." His voice was deep. It was rare, even for Jerry, to see so much genuine emotion coming from Chase. "I want you to find out who was responsible for that dam coming down. Find out who it was and make sure they no longer have a job. And if I find out that old bastard had something to do with this, I swear . . ."

He couldn't blame Chase for feeling furious. Jerry himself felt frustrated and angry. The section they drained was full of water, and with the rest of the dividers under water, the part at the other end would have water spilling into it as well. They had an entire section worth of extra water with nowhere to put it. This would set them back days. Not to mention the possibility of aquatic life forms slipping into the previously checked area. Should they take the time to drain it again, or risk that nothing important slipped in and move on? The next few days were going to be very tense around camp.

Chase turned and stalked away. Jerry could remember a ten-year-old version of Chase throwing a similar temper tantrum.

With the incoming water dammed off again, the water level would gradually lower, as it had before. They still needed a solution for the extra water.

Jerry could have gone to talk to Chase, but the man needed to cool off on his own. Very likely, the next time Chase was seen outside of his tent his famous grin would be back in place and no one would know he was still furious.

– 29 –

Alex had spent the morning examining the dividers that had been put up so far and talking with members of Chase's crew. Everyone he spoke to told him that section one had to be re-drained because of a malfunctioning dam. Most of the team thought they should have moved on to the second section, but Chase was adamant that when the water level was raised again, something could have slipped into the first.

A few of Chase's men, ones that Alex had been seeing every day and was starting to develop a friendship with, told him that they believed the old man had something to do with it. There was no question of whom they were referring to. No evidence had been found to prove that Rory had anything to do with it, but everyone reported that Chase knew the old man was involved.

Getting rid of the extra water had been complicated.

They pumped water from the main part of the undivided loch and ran lines of hose to Loch Mohr, Loch Ruthven and Loch Duntelchaig. As the water level sank, they were able to pump water from sections one and twenty back into the main section. It was a long process just to get back to where they had already been.

Chase must have been furious.

When Alex turned around from talking with another of Chase's crew, Rory was there, with a satisfied smile on his face.

"Afternoon, Stafford," the old man said.

"Hello, Rory. I hear you're a dam operator now."

"Oh, I wouldn't know how to operate a dam, though I do find all of that stuff very interesting," Rory said.

"Damn. I was hoping to get a quote."

"It's well past noon, did you notice?"

"So?"

"Are you hungry?" Rory asked.

"I guess," Alex answered, confused.

"I was about to eat. Would you like to join me?"

Alex had no idea what would make Rory act so friendly. He didn't seem like the kind of man that would invite his best friend over for lunch, let alone a near stranger.

"Sure," Alex conceded.

Sitting at Rory's kitchen table was one of the most awkward experiences. The old man was still being overly friendly.

A plate of salmon and vegetables was served to Alex, along with a glass of water and a cup of coffee.

"Need anything else?" Rory asked.

"No, thank you. This looks great."

"All right. Let's dig in, then."

They ate for a number of moments in awkward silence.

"So, those walls are something else, hey?" Rory finally said.

"Yeah. They really are. You know, when Chase told me what he was planning I didn't think it was possible, but there they are."

"They have a unique feel. That texture, you know? What are they made of?"

It was strange that Rory was suddenly impressed by something that came from someone he despised. Alex began to sense the reason for all the unexplained kindness.

"I'm not sure. Chase said it was a sealant formula that went bad. Have you felt it up close?"

"Aye. It's as hard as a rock."

Alex nodded with a mouthful of food.

"It can't be that strong, though," Rory reasoned.

Alex shrugged. "I don't know. He said it was even better than concrete."

"But if it's just made of sealant materials, it must break down. Maybe paint thinner or something."

Alex chuckled a little. "You'd need a lot of paint thinner. Even then, I don't think it would do anything."

"What about those pumps of his?" Rory asked.

"What about them?"

Rory shrugged and Alex sighed.

"Let's just get to why I'm really here. I don't know anything that will help with your sabotage missions."

Rory and Alex stared at each other for some time, neither wanting to be the first man to speak or look away.

"You don't know or you won't tell?" Rory finally said.

"I don't know anything."

"And why should I believe you?"

"If you don't know whether or not to believe me, maybe you shouldn't have asked me in the first place."

Alex stood from his chair, tossing his napkin down on the plate.

"Thanks for lunch, but I really feel like I should be going."

"You shouldn't be helping him," Rory called out.

"What?"

"It's bad for you. Bad for the soul, it is. I know I'm not rich like he is, but helping me is the right thing to do."

"Look, I'm not helping either one of you. I'm an impartial reporter who just wants to cover the news."

"Sounds to me like you're looking to exploit this area, and anything living in it, to sell your newspapers. That puts you in his camp. Not mine."

"How many times do I have to repeat myself?"

"Unless you can tell me something that I don't already know, I have no reason to believe you're not his man."

Alex shook his head and headed for the door.

Rory met him at the door with a desperate look in his eyes.

"You tell me something!" he demanded, his voice breaking. The old man's fists were clenched at his sides. Rage and tears were in his eyes. "I'm trying to help her, but I can't unless someone helps me."

Rory walked over to the kitchen table and leaned on it for support, a hand covering his eyes.

"Rory, I'm really sorry that I can't help."

"You could, but you won't!" Rory yelled, hurling a plate at Alex's head. It missed him by a foot.

That was enough to eliminate the possibility of trying to talk any further with the old man. Alex had no interest in sticking around and taking more abuse from Rory.

He got in his car and headed for his hotel back in Inverness. He stewed about the old man as he drove, hearing his insults again and again in his head and picturing that dinner plate flying at his head. Working with Chase and his people was better, but he was sick of Scotland. When he got back to his hotel he would call the office and arrange for a replacement to be sent.

By the time he reached the small town of Inverness, he noticed Rory, in his beat up truck, right behind him. Alex rolled his eyes. Was there no way to escape this man? Even when Alex tried to walk away the old man was going to keep bringing the fight to him.

He pulled his can over to the side of the road while mentally preparing himself for another pointless argument. To his surprise, Rory drove right by without giving Alex a glance.

As strange as the old man was, something seemed odd.

Alex pulled his car back onto the road and followed Rory. He kept back as far as he could while keeping the old man's truck in sight.

After a series of turns, Alex saw Rory park the truck in front of a rather plain looking building. After Rory disappeared inside, Alex sat in his car for a few minutes trying to figure out what the old man was doing. The place looked a little like an apartment building, perhaps Rory had a friend who lived there. Or maybe Rory was just picking something up and would be leaving the building any moment.

After some time had passed, Alex got out of his car and approached the building. He was still a distance off when the front door swung open. Alex turned quickly on his heel, showing his back to the door and whoever was coming through it. A man Alex didn't know walked past him, heading away from the building.

Alex felt a little embarrassed, but crossed the rest of the distance to the door and entered the building. He was in a reception area of sorts. There was an odd smell in the air. It was somewhat familiar, but he couldn't think of what it was. The inside of the building was furnished more like a house than a business. A young, attractive woman sat behind a desk and looked at him expectantly.

"Hello," she said with a smile. "Do you have an appointment?"

"Uh, no. I'm afraid I don't. Could I make one?"

"Of course you can," she said and beckoned him to come over to the desk and placed a binder in front of him. "Some of our girls are available now, some you'll have to book an appointment for another day."

Alex felt his face get hot as he opened the binder to nude pictures of women. Everything suddenly made sense. A business with no sign out front, housing that had been turned into a business, and the familiar smell. He could place it now. It was sex masked by too much perfume.

"A friend of mine recommended the girl that he sees. Maybe you know him. Rory Stewart? He's an older fellow."

"Oh, we have so many clients. I wouldn't know any of them by name." She was a really bad liar. It was strange to see a woman in a brothel be so bad at lying.

Alex pulled his wallet out of his pocket and put a twenty pound note on the desk.

"Oh, you said Rory. Yes, I know him. He's here now, as a matter of fact."

"You don't say. Who's he with?"

"That's really not something that I should be telling anyone, you know?" she said, glancing from him to his wallet and back to him again.

"Uh huh," Alex said placing another twenty on the desk.

"He's with Brandy. It's always Brandy."

She flipped through the binder until she found the page with Brandy's picture.

"And how often would you say he comes to see Brandy?"

"Hey, you're not a cop, are you?" she asked, crinkling up her nose.

Alex sighed and placed another twenty down on the desk.

"Once a month, at most. Though tonight is the second time we've seen him so far this month."

"I see," Alex said with a vindictive smile.

You throw a plate at my head? he thought.

Alex went back to his hotel room to finally write the story he had been sent to Scotland to write. Putting a brand new sheet of paper into his typewriter, he typed out the article's title, *The Real Monster at Loch Ness.*

-30-

Upon heading to his tent, Chase noticed the majority of his team sitting and laughing around a campfire. Since the dam at the south end of the loch had set them back a few days, the team had been feeling a lot of extra pressure. A lot of it coming directly from him.

Chase had always preferred to have his employees' loyalty through respect, not fear. When he walked over to the campfire most people gave him a glance or a nod and went silent.

He put on a smile, one that was small and real instead of his usual practiced grin, and placed a hand on the nearest person's shoulder.

"What a beautiful night for a campfire." Looking around, he saw that small talk wasn't going to make anyone feel less uncomfortable around him. "I just wanted to come over here and thank everyone for the hard work they've been putting in to get us back on track. None of this would be possible without each one of you." A few people made eye contact with him and some even returned his smile. Most nodded with their eyes fixed on the ground.

"Would anyone like to hear about the time we captured the Kraken?" he asked.

A few voices called out, encouraging him to tell the story.

"It's fairly far-fetched, but there are a few men sitting around this very fire that can corroborate the story. Isn't that right, mates?"

A few men laughed and made confirming declarations.

Chase sat down next to a few other men on a log and got comfortable. Stories like this were seldom quick.

"It was three years ago. Historically, for hundreds of years, sailors claimed to see the Kraken somewhere in the Norwegian Sea. We plotted a course from Norway to Iceland. Long trip. I hired a Norwegian crew that had been sailing that water their entire lives. The captain was the prickly sort. Claimed it was a long enough trip without having to stop every time he read something big on the Fathometer. However, I hadn't paid the man upfront, so it was easy enough to convince him to stop.

"We used a three-stage system for identifying what was detected. Stage one, just look. Sometimes our target would be near the surface and we'd be able to see if it was just a whale. If we couldn't, the team diver would get into the water for a look. If our prey was deeper than 200 meters, we used a small submersible vessel that had small motors for propulsion, and a camera. The cost to get such a device was criminal, but it was an incredible little thing.

"When we arrived in Iceland, the first time, all we had found were whales and schools of fish. Disappointing, to say the least, but I don't give up easily. We turned right around and headed back to Norway. We arrived with the same results. The captain didn't want to turn around and go back, but I appealed to his inner adventurer."

"Does that mean you offered him more money?" someone called out.

"Am I that transparent?" Chase asked with a smile.

His audience laughed and he continued with the story.

"On the way to Iceland, the captain was less and less willing to stop when the Fathometer showed something. He claimed he had seen a whale surface moments before, or that something in his gut told him it was nothing.

"Well, we arrived in Iceland once again, and I asked the captain to turn around. He was furious with me. He only agreed to go back because it meant going home. He told me he wouldn't be making any stops. I kept asking, despite his claims. After the first day back, he wouldn't let me near the Fathometer.

"After a shouting match, I resolved to hire a new crew upon arriving in Norway, but when I told my men, none of them could look me in the eye. We had been sailing for almost three months. Everyone was exhausted and sick for home. My mind, my ambition, wanted to continue, but I had to admit my body needed rest. I changed my plan and told my men we were heading home. There would be another opportunity.

"I was standing on the bow a few days after that, trying to convince myself that I was just enjoying a cruise, when I saw what looked like a tentacle ahead of us. My heart started racing. I ran to the Fathometer, ignoring the captain's shouts. It showed something big. The captain held to his word, refusing to stop. But when I told him he wouldn't see another krona out of me, he cut the engines.

"To get even with me, he refused to let us use his diver. I didn't have one on my team, but I had done some recreational diving, so I geared up. Let me tell you, this was nothing like scuba diving in the islands."

"What was it like?" someone asked.

Chase stared off at the horizon, his mind travelling from Loch Ness to the Norwegian Sea.

"You know how it looks in pictures and movies of space? It's just black and looking at it, you get the feeling that it goes on forever. It's like that, but deep blue. And the deeper you go, the darker it gets.

"I dove as deep as I dared, but I didn't see anything. The pressure was getting uncomfortable, and as I said, it was just blue in every direction. I would have stayed down there until I found something, but I had a limited supply of air, and I didn't trust that the captain wouldn't leave without me.

"When I turned to go back to the boat, I saw it. It was in front of me with its tentacles spread around it. It was beautiful. Maybe the most beautiful thing I've ever seen. It looked . . . majestic; angelic, even . . . until I realized the tentacles were spread out because it was reaching them toward me. It was then that the size of the creature registered. It probably could have crushed me like a man would a beer can.

"My senses returned to me, and I levelled my spear gun and fired. The spear penetrated one of the tentacles, right where it met the body. It swam away, but my spear was attached to the gun I was holding. I wish I could tell you I held that thing in place, but it pulled me along like a child's toy."

Everyone around the fire was leaning forward, desperate to hear what came next.

"It dragged me deeper, and deeper, and deeper. I thought the pressure was uncomfortable before! It felt like my eyes were going to be pulled from my skull. Just when I was about to let go, it stops. It was quite a bit darker, but I could see a much larger spear had pierced its body. What I didn't know, was that the spear from my gun had a tracker in it, and once I fired it, the guys on the boat starting prepping the spear gun mounted on deck.

"They began to bring it in, and again I went along for the ride. I'll tell you, I haven't done any diving since."

"So what happened to the Kraken?" one of the men sitting around the campfire asked.

Chase smiled sadly. "Have you ever read *The Old Man and the Sea*? The beast was too big to bring onto the boat, so we towed it behind us. Even the Kraken is subject to predators when it's bleeding and can't fight back.

"We took the remains to a specialist along with the details of the capture. He believes there is an undiscovered species that people used to call the Kraken. For the time being, it's being called the giant squid. It's not as menacing as Kraken, but I'm not an expert."

Laughter circled around the campfire along with a bit of sporadic applause.

"Oh, that's nothing," Chase said. "Remind me sometime to tell you my Bigfoot story."

-31-

It had been a mistake for Alex to fax his story about Rory off on the same night he wrote it. By the morning, he regretted writing the first hot-headed word. Despite how Rory had acted the previous night, Alex had broken one of the most important rules of reporting. Never let your personal feelings do the writing. Use facts and quotes, and be impartial.

He would have called the office, but he knew if Edwards found out Alex wanted a story pulled, not only would it still be printed, the prick would move it to the front page. His only hope was that Edwards would think the story was garbage and dismiss it.

Alex needed a day off, so he took one. He didn't call it into the office, or even send a fax, he just didn't drive out to the loch that day.

Instead, he wandered around Inverness to see the town.

When he found there wasn't much to see, he caught a movie, and spent a few hours with a notepad in a little coffee shop, working on some fiction he hoped to someday turn into a novel.

"More coffee?" asked a waitress.

"Thank you," he said, pushing his cup toward the woman.

"What are you working on?" she asked. "You've been at it for some time."

He made a sound of disgust and pushed the notepad away from him.

"I don't know," he said. "I was thinking about maybe writing a book. But that's kind of stupid, right?"

"A book?" she asked. "Why would you think that's stupid? What's it about?"

She smiled and sat down across the table from him. The waitress, Betty, according to her name tag, was very pretty. She leaned forward, waiting for him to tell her about his book.

Alex cleared his throat nervously. "Well, it's about a man who wakes up and the entire world has gone insane. He wanders around trying to make sense of things, but every person he meets is crazier than the last."

She nodded thoughtfully.

"It's fiction," he added.

"You're kidding," she said with a wry look on her face. "Though I have had a few days that sound like that."

"Your accent," he said. "You're from England, aren't you?"

"Originally, yes."

"Why the change?"

She wore a sheepish smile and looked down at the table.

"I came out here with my fiancée at the time. He moved around a lot for his job, working his way up some stupid ladder. We moved to different places within the UK a half dozen times, and then the opportunity here came up. It wasn't long before he told me he had been promoted again. He was leaving for America and I wasn't going with him."

"What a bastard. Why didn't you go back home?"

"I don't know. Shame, I guess."

"Shame? It's not your fault, you know."

Betty went silent, staring at the table top. She glanced back at him, but broke eye contact again as quickly as it was made.

"I like talking to you," he said. As soon as the words were out of his mouth, he knew he shouldn't have said them.

She smiled and met his eyes again.

"I'm done at eight if you wanted to—"

"Get a coffee?" Alex suggested, holding up his cup and putting on a goofy smile.

"You know what I meant." She playfully slapped his hand.

They agreed to share a late meal and she gave him directions to a little restaurant close by. Alex was excited to have dinner with the young lady, but then he thought about Loren back home and how cold she had been lately.

He dismissed the thoughts. Nothing was going to happen. He didn't have to feel guilty for having dinner with someone just because they were the opposite sex—and extremely attractive.

The rest of the night was spent giving himself similar false reasoning.

Alex and Betty flirting all through dinner was nothing to be ashamed of. It was just a bit of conversation and fun. There was nothing wrong with her coming back to his room after dinner; they were just going to have another drink together. It was okay if they shared a kiss. It was only as friends.

It had never been his plan to sleep with Betty, though he had to admit seeing it a possibility. Once they were inside his room, he had just turned around and her lips were an inch from his.

He didn't know if she had cleared the last bit of distance or if it had been him.

Each time Loren came up in his mind, the alcohol in his system caused him to selfishly provide a reason why Betty was better than Loren.

Betty wore a sexy dress to dinner. The last time he took Loren out for dinner she had worn an old sweater. When Alex made a joke, Betty laughed. Loren scowled more than anything else. Betty had moved to Scotland to support her man. Loren wouldn't even come and visit hers.

Their kisses were gentle at first, but soon they pressed hard at each other's lips. Betty pulled Alex's shirt off and pushed him onto the bed. Straddling him, she gave him a wicked smile and pulled her sexy dress over her head and threw it on the floor.

A gorgeous woman was on top on him, wearing nothing but her underwear. A voice of reason in his mind warned that this was his last chance to turn back.

He didn't.

It had been a great day. Betty was asleep beside him, beautiful even in sleep. He imagined a possible future with her, seeing all the potential moments in their life together. Dating back in England, introducing her to his family, finding a new apartment together, marriage. Alex gave Betty a kiss on the forehead and stumbled to the bathroom for a shower.

He continued to think of possible futures as he showered. Betty was great, but he remembered that he would be back at Loch Ness the next day. Once again he'd be interviewing people that considered him to be a waste of time. He'd have to write another story about the exact same thing from a slightly different angle. He'd have to put up with Harvey Chase's annoying grin, and likely another attack from Rory.

Thoughts of the future returned, but this time they

surrounded Loren. He would have to break up with her. That would be a marathon of a conversation with lots of crying. All of his friends, those that didn't prefer to stay Loren's friend, would all have to be told. Would people need to know about his cheating? Maybe he could just tell people he didn't get together with Betty until after he and Loren were over.

When he exited the bathroom, Betty was gone. He rushed around the room checking for his wallet and watch and found they were both there. He was relieved at first, but then he almost wished she had been some kind of scamming thief. He was good enough to be used, which he really didn't mind, but that was all he was good for.

Until that moment, it had been a near perfect day. Then he glanced at the clock on the bedside table, and sighed. It was 12:01 AM and he felt a bit like Cinderella. His Princess Charming had disappeared, and in a matter of hours he'd be putting up with his evil step-sisters Rory and Chase.

*   *   *

When Alex arrived at Chase's camp the next morning, his head pounded from the alcohol which was only amplified by the shame. The memory of his indiscretion was bad enough, but he felt embarrassed when he remembered planning out a whole new life with a woman he barely knew.

Mervyn and Melvyn, the two guards Chase had hired to watch Rory, were the first people Alex saw when he entered the camp.

"Good morning, sir," one of them said. He had been told their names, but he couldn't remember which was which. Except for a two-inch difference in height, they were identical.

He mumbled 'good morning' ending with a 'vyn' sound,

hoping they would think he wasn't ignorant enough to forget their names.

"Hey, I'm curious," Alex said.

"About?" the taller one asked. He was Melvyn.

"Have either of you ever accompanied Mr. Chase on any of his other hunts?"

"Other hunts?" the shorter one asked.

Alex changed his mind and thought that one was Melvyn.

"Have you never heard of the other hunts or is this one of those 'I'm not talking' kind of things?"

"Neither. We hadn't ever worked for Mr. Chase until a week ago," said the shorter one.

"Oh, okay. Thanks, Melvyn."

The shorter one jammed a thumb in the direction of the taller one. "He's Melvyn."

"Sorry," Alex said, feeling his face get warm. He began to walk away, but turned back again. "This is going to sound strange, but was that Rory fellow looking for me yesterday?"

"The old man?" asked Mervyn. "No. He wasn't looking for anyone. We barely saw him at all."

"Yeah," Melvyn added in, "on slow days we see him out doing chores, but yesterday he didn't even do that. We almost went over to check for his body, but Mervyn spotted him moving around through one of his windows. Why?"

More shame. It wasn't Alex's responsibility to make sure the old man was okay, but having written the story he felt obligated in some way to do something.

"Nothing much. He was just a bit crossed with me the other day."

"We'll let you know if he asks for you."

"Thanks, Mervyn."

"Melvyn."

"Sorry."

Alex searched for an interviewee with a unique perspective on the Loch Ness hunt. Was there anyone he hadn't talked to? There had to be something he hadn't written about.

He kept stealing glances toward Rory's house. He expected to see the old man slowly, but deftly, moving around his property with one task or another. The sheep moved about in the pen, and the wind bent the grass over, but nothing else could be seen moving.

Alex thought about their last encounter and second-guessed every word he had said. He wondered about the different outcomes if he had changed an answer, or been a little more understanding or if he had stuck around to help the old man somehow. Even if he had been hit with a plate, it wouldn't have hurt very much.

I didn't do anything wrong, he reminded himself. He was justified in everything he had said. It was Rory that had crossed the line. Still, he couldn't shake the feeling. It was that damned story.

He felt the need to somehow make things right. Rory wanted information about Chase's plan, information Alex didn't have. He remembered something that Rory had told him before and began to wonder.

He hung around Chase's camp for another hour and put a story together of mainly recycled facts. It wasn't very good, but it would be good enough. With his work done, he jumped into his car with a plan in mind.

– 32 –

Rory was defeated.

The fight that had been bursting from him in the beginning left nothing but vapour in its absence. He had no energy or plan. Even if he had either, Chase's new security team seemed to be watching him at all hours of the day and night. Chase had won. His only hope now was that Nessie was smart enough to beat Chase on her own.

Graham lay on the couch wagging his tail as Rory shuffled from one end of the house to the other. All the wandering was pointless. He moved from his chair to the kitchen at lunch, only to realize he wasn't the slightest bit hungry. Sometimes he moved to his bedroom and forgot why he had gone in there. Once, he went to the kitchen to get a glass of water and found that he was already holding one.

After sitting and staring for such a long time, Rory stood

just to keep his legs from cramping up. He did a lap around his couch before he ended up in the kitchen. He began opening all the drawers and cupboards, telling himself he should reorganize but taking the first step to do so.

Behind one cupboard door he found a bottle of whiskey. He stared at the bottle for a while remembering when he had bought it. Another low point in his life. The bottle had never been opened. He had spent many nights staring at the bottle, the same way he stared at it now, but had finally put it away each time.

The bottle was covered in dust. Aged, some people might say. It probably wasn't a good enough whiskey to age well, but it might serve Rory's purpose.

He pulled the bottle from the cupboard and set it on the counter. Another cupboard produced a glass, which he set beside the bottle. His movements were slow, halfway between prolonging something unwanted and savoring a moment.

Hesitation. He had everything he needed: A bottle, a glass, and a reason to drink.

He quickly pulled the cap off the bottle and filled the glass. Little specks floated in the golden alcohol, further revealing its poor quality.

Holding the glass at eye level, he stared at it, nervously running his tongue over his lips. Was his mouth actually watering?

Outside, the crunch of stones announced a vehicle pulling into his lane-way. Even though he knew that was no reason to be mad, he got up from the table with the intent to verbally abuse his unwanted visitor.

He yanked his front door open and walked out onto the small porch. The glare on the windshield obscured the inside of the vehicle, but he recognized Alex Stafford's car.

"You've got some nerve coming back here, you do! You want me to throw something else at you? I got a whole house of things. I'll hit you sooner or later!"

The driver's side door opened and Alex stepped out of the car, looking calm, yet nervous. He held his hands up defensively.

"I know you don't want to see me right now."

"You or anyone else for that matter!"

Before he could bellow another word, the passenger door of Alex's car opened and a hallucination stepped out. No, not a hallucination. A memory. A dream.

Standing in his lane-way was a woman he hadn't seen in thirty years. In front of his house, nervously shifting from foot to foot, was Rory's wife, Mari.

He opened his mouth to say something, but could make no sound.

It was unbelievable, but Mari still had love in her eyes as she looked at him. Love, instead of hate and contempt.

Neither of them moved for some time, and no one said a word.

Mari took a step forward, her eyes locked on him. Rory abruptly turned and practically ran into his little greenhouse. He returned to his porch seconds later with a handful of lilies.

Mari took another couple of steps forward, her eyes locked on the flowers. They used to be her favorite. Rory hoped that hadn't changed.

"I always," Rory's words came out halted as though each was its own sentence, "grow some of these. The smell," Rory breathed in the scent, "reminds me of," he hesitated, "better times."

He extended his arm toward his wife. Her smile was slight but genuine and she accepted the bouquet from his hand.

"They're lovely," she said.

His stomach did a backflip at the sound of her voice. It was a bit deeper than he remembered it. It was more mature with a slightly smoky sound, but he would have been able to pick it out of a crowd. He felt more nervous than he had on their first date or the day he married her.

He slowly reached his hand out toward her face. She kept her eyes locked on his and didn't move away. His fingertips brushed her hair. It was mostly white now, instead of red, but it was still beautiful.

The edge of a scar near her temple peeked out from behind her bangs. He squinted and pushed her hair back further. The scar was two inches long. It had healed poorly. All these years, it had remained there as a constant reminder. It was a reminder of the mistakes he had made in his life. Despite all of it, she was still there, standing in front of him.

"Oh, my," he said, still staring at it.

Mari gently pulled his hand away from her face.

"You can still see it," she said, "but it only hurt for a short time."

Was she speaking of physical pain? Or was that her way of saying that she had forgotten about him after a time?

He stood staring at her until she pulled her jacket tighter around her shoulders.

"You're cold," he stated. "Come in, come in. I'll start a fire."

"That sounds nice."

Rory gave Alex the briefest of glances before holding the door open for his wife. He panicked when he saw the bottle of whiskey still sitting out on the counter. He rushed over and put the bottle back in the cupboard after dumping the glass into the sink. He hoped Mari hadn't seen it.

When he turned around, the look on her face suggested she had. That kind of appearance implied he had been sitting in his little house drinking the past thirty years away.

Mari took a seat on the couch while Rory brewed tea.

Graham, who had been sleeping on the couch, wormed his way over to Mari and put his head on her lap. He wagged his tail and rolled onto his back.

"What a sweet dog," she called to him. "What's his name?"

Rory pretended not to hear while he continued preparing the tea.

When he brought her a cup she asked again. "What's your dog's name?"

"What's that? Oh," he hesitated, "Nester."

"Nester?"

"Yeah. I got him from a friend." He shrugged and waved a hand. "He was already named."

They drank their tea in silence. Mari looked around at the house and Rory's belongings. Rory looked around as well, embarrassed of the meagre surroundings. His house was meant to be functional, not beautiful.

"So, you've been here all this time?" Mari said, breaking a long silence.

Rory nodded.

"I always thought you'd come home."

"After what I did? The man I had become? You deserved better than that."

"Being alone?" Mari's voice cracked. "It hardly seems to be what I deserved."

Rory stared at his hands.

"Let's not ruin this by talking about the past," she said, putting her hands on his. "I've waited thirty years to see you again."

He looked at her, eyes wide. "You've been waiting for me the entire time?"

She nodded quickly with a warm smile on her face.

His eyes welled up with tears. He didn't want his tears to fall—not in front of Mari—but they came. Only a few drops at first, but soon they rained onto the living room floor.

Mari wrapped her arms around him and gently pulled his head toward her to rest on her chest. Rory felt like a child who had just found safety after being alone and scared.

When she shifted and kissed his lips, he fell in love all over again. In an instant he remembered every quality he loved about her, and forgot all of the bad ones. Every good memory of her was in the front of his mind while all the bad ones sank into a subconscious cage. The feeling of her lips on his turned the last thirty years into nothing more than a terrible dream—a nightmare that he had finally woken up from.

Mari took his hand and pulled him into the bedroom, gently coercing him into the bed. They held each other and talked in hushed tones. They spoke of the past, when they had still been together, as well as the decades since they had been apart. Nothing was said with any animosity, neither of them was looking to assign blame. Rory was grateful for that since he knew that all of it belonged to him.

He was ashamed to think of the times he had gone to visit Brandy. It shamed him even more that he had even thought about Brandy as he lay with his wife. He had been convinced that he was a man with a man's needs, but it seemed he had just been lying to himself.

Rory hoped he'd forgive himself in time. He was looking ahead, and he was done betraying his wife.

* * *

A few times during the night he woke with a start. Fear overcame him. He whimpered at the thought of having dreamed of his wife's return, or worse, that she had been real and left while he was sleeping.

Each time, he found his beautiful wife asleep beside him. His fears were nothing but paranoia and insecurity.

Rory was up with the dawn, as was his norm, and he set about making a hearty breakfast. Once the smell of eggs and sausage was in the air, Mari emerged from the bedroom, yawning. Rory didn't want to stop looking at her, but he smelled the eggs starting to burn.

As they ate, Mari talked about everything she had been doing for the last thirty years. Jobs, friends, new and old hobbies, new foods she had tried, the odd vacation she took.

Rory was content to sit, eat, and listen to her talk. He could remember days when he wished she would stop talking, if only for a minute. Sitting at the breakfast table, he didn't care if she talked forever. He'd happily spend the rest of his life mute if it meant having her.

Every once in a while she'd stop and ask Rory a question about what he had been doing, but he'd just shrug and ask her about something else.

By the time Rory had finished two plates of breakfast, she hadn't begun to eat hers. When she looked down and realized she had been talking too much to even eat, she turned red and picked up her fork.

As Rory finished washing the dishes, a fully-dressed Mari walked to the door and slipped into her shoes.

He rushed over to her, with a hurt look on his face.

"Wait! Where are you going?" He felt his chest tighten, and his breathing didn't come as easily as it should have.

"I just have to go for a little while. There are some things I have to take care of." She hugged him and their lips met once again. "Don't worry. I will return to you, love."

Rory stood at the window and watched his wife, and his truck, disappear down the road. He started feeling miserable again, and wandered around the house. On the freshly made bed was a scrap of paper.

Rory picked it up and found a message from Mari. *I love you.*

All misery faded away. He tucked the note into his pocket and went to check on the sheep.

Once Rory was outside, instead of heading to the sheep pen he crossed the distance between his property and Chase's camp. Alex was standing near the edge and saw Rory approaching.

Alex took a cautious stance, wary of something flying at his head.

"Hello, Rory," he said. "How are you?"

Rory smiled at the man. "Better than I've been in a long time. You've done a good thing for me, you have."

"I didn't do much. Just made a few phone calls. When I told Mari that I knew where you were and that I could take her to you, she didn't hesitate. She really missed you, you know?"

Rory was embarrassed to let Alex see him grin like an idiot teenager, but he couldn't hold it in.

"I suppose I do. I have to ask though," Rory kicked at an imaginary rock on the ground, "I've been nothing but rotten to you. Why would you go and do something like that for me?"

Alex shrugged and looked out at the loch. "I don't know. It just seemed like something that I could do, being an investigative journalist and all, this wasn't the first time I had to find someone."

"But, still, why? Why would you help an old man like me?"

Alex considered his answer for quite some time. "Seems to me that a man who dedicated his whole life to helping someone else . . ." he nodded toward the loch, "it was about time someone helped the man."

"Do you happen to know where Mari went this morning?" Rory asked, after a moment of uncomfortable silence.

"I do, but I can't tell you anything about it. Except that it'll be something you'll really like."

Rory wanted to cry out, *she's really coming back?* Instead, he just grinned and tried not to look like too much of a fool.

"Can I ask you something, Rory?"

"Sure."

"When I brought Mari to your house yesterday I don't think I've ever seen two people happier to see each other."

"Well," Rory said, chuckling, "you might be right about that."

"Why'd you leave her? Why'd you start drinking so much? What made it all turn bad?"

"You might be the first person to ever hear this story," Rory said, shame filling his voice.

*   *   *

Rory's life had been perfect with Mari. Despite the fact that World War II was happening around them, Rory was completely content to chase his wife around the house for kisses. The day the bombs fell around Glasgow, they held each other tightly in their bed, and when the bombing stopped they laughed and cried for joy together.

One night, while Mari was getting ready for bed, the phone rang and the caller was about to bear the worst news that could ever befall Rory and Mari.

It was a Lieutenant Colonel in the British army, and the gravity in his voice told Rory everything before the man could say the words. Graham Stewart, Rory and Mari's son, was killed in action, serving his country.

Rory immediately lost touch with the world as his senses left him. His knees gave first, dropping Rory to floor. His hands went next and the phone fell to the floor, its rattle muffled to Rory's ears. His vision went white. A voice came through the phone, but it was nothing more than a buzzing noise that sounded far off.

For twenty minutes, he lay on the kitchen floor wrapped up in the fetal position. He wanted to scream his grief, but he couldn't seem to collect enough air in his lungs for anything beyond the sobs that silently shook his entire body.

Colors began to bleed through the white blanket of his vision and turned into the ugly pattern of his kitchen floor. The phone was still on the floor, beeping near his head. Rory pushed himself to his feet, wiping his eyes as he rose. He hung the phone up and sat down at the kitchen table with his face in his hands.

His son had been only twenty years old. When the war had started, he was anxious to go and fight. Scotland was joining their forces with the British army to fight the Nazis. It had all seemed so noble at the time, but boys of that age never considered dying to be a possibility.

Graham had written them every week to let his parents know he was still all right. They had just received one of his letters two days previous. By the time that letter had been put in their mailbox, his sweet boy was probably bleeding out from a gunshot wound, stuck on some German bayonet, or blown apart by a land mine.

Graham was their only child. In an effort to shelter the boy, Rory had tried to convince him he was wasting his time as a cadet on the front lines. He was much smarter than that. There were other ways that he could help, things that weren't even directly related to the war. Graham always used to tell him, *Dad, I'll do those things after we win the war.*

Until that night, Rory had supported the war efforts as much as any other Scot. He would marvel with his co-workers about how brave the soldiers were to go and defend their country. From that night forward the whole thing just seemed stupid and pointless.

A soldier being killed, whether he was English, German, or Scottish, was denying this world a young life with so much potential. No one knew what some of those men could have accomplished in their lifetimes. Inventions, cures, political leaderships. The possibilities went from infinite to zero in the time it took to pull a trigger.

Rory stood from the table, but he hesitated to move any further. He had been trying to figure out how to tell his wife, but it was quite obvious there was only one way. As he had experienced himself, nothing could soften the blow of losing a child.

When he walked into the bedroom, she was lying in bed listening to the radio. They did that most nights, hoping to hear anything that might tell them how the war was going, and how their son was.

"Mari?" His voice was a gravelly whisper, vocal chords still strained from the crying.

"There you are," she said. "I thought you'd fallen asleep out there."

"Turn off the radio."

Slowly, choking on each word, he told her about the phone call. The tears were instant. She shook uncontrollably, trying to hold a hand over her mouth.

Rory was only a few feet away, standing in the bedroom doorway, but at that moment he was miles away. He should have crawled into bed with his wife and cried with her. He should have told her it was okay to cry, to grieve. He should have grieved with her and held her until they had both cried themselves to sleep.

He shouldn't have left the bedroom and grabbed a bottle of whiskey from the cupboard, but that's what he did.

*　　*　　*

Alex stood with his mouth open. "I am so sorry."

Rory waved a hand to imply there was no apology needed, and before his hand fell back to his side he wiped a tear from his eye.

"You brought me my wife back. Thank you, Alex. Truly, thank you."

Rory could have imagined it, but he thought he saw a look of guilt cross Alex's face. It was probably just an old man's imagination.

Rory gave Alex a pat on the shoulder and walked past him into Chase's camp. He smiled as he noticed the private security team fall in behind him.

"At ease, fellows," he called over his shoulder. "I'm on a peace mission."

It took him a few minutes to locate Chase's tent. He had to ask several people walking around the camp. Each one gave Rory an uncertain look, glancing at the security guards close behind. After a few directions, he finally found the tent he was looking for.

He stopped, wondering about the etiquette for entering a tent. There wasn't a door to knock on, but it would be rude to walk in unannounced and uninvited.

"Uh, hello?" he called.

"Who's that?" came a voice from inside the tent.

"It's Rory Stewart, Mr. Chase."

Chase ripped back one of the tent flaps and looked out with a smile that expected a practical joke. Upon seeing Rory, the smile changed, the corners of his mouth drawing back in disgust.

"I have nothing to say to you," Chase said.

"Well, I have something to say to you, if you'll listen."

Chase hastily motioned for Rory to come in and then disappeared. Rory stepped into the tent, with the security guards right behind him.

"I assure you, you won't need them," Rory said, pointing at the two men.

Chase dismissed them with a wave and the men slipped out of the tent.

"So?" Chase demanded. "What's this all about?"

"I just wanted to stand face to face with you to say you win."

"I do?" he said. Chase expected that Rory was lying. Rory couldn't blame him after the battling they had done.

"Every plan I've come up with to stop you has failed. I can't think of another and I don't think I care to."

Chase grinned. "You're giving up." It wasn't a question. Chase was stating a fact that brought him great pleasure.

"Let's just say," Rory replied, "that I found something better to put my energy into."

Chase laughed. "Oh, that's brilliant!" He walked over and threw an arm around Rory, hugging him tightly. "You know, I don't know why we were ever fighting in the first place. We should have been working together. With the experience a man like you has after being around this loch for so long, we probably could have used you on the team."

"Don't get carried away," Rory said.

"No, no, no! I'll bet with you and me working together we

could have caught that beast within a few days. You practically have a relationship with her, am I right? I mean, the man that protects it. I'll bet you could have led us right to it, or it to us."

Chase was talking so fast and enthusiastically that he didn't hear Rory claiming that he wouldn't have been any help.

"How about giving me some information? What part of the loch does the beast spend most of its time? What bait would bring it to me? What can you tell me . . ."

"I've never seen her."

". . . that could be really helpful—" Chase stopped mid-sentence. "What did you just say?"

Rory sighed. "I've never actually seen her."

"Never seen it?" Chase's words teemed with disgust. "I find that hard to believe."

"It's true," Rory said without a bit of pride. "I thought I saw her once. To tell you the truth, I'm not even sure."

The grin was only gone from Chase's face for a minute. When it returned, he grabbed Rory by both shoulders. "Despite all that, we know it exists. Don't we?"

Rory didn't know what to say. He had spent a lifetime believing in her existence, and at his core he really did believe. Another part of him hoped that she didn't exist, if only for the reason that Chase wouldn't catch her and exploit her.

Chase was staring at him with such hope and enthusiasm in his eyes. Rory was jealous of the man's ability to feel that much hope. He couldn't even remember the last time he felt that way.

"Well, I know we haven't caught it yet." Chase dragged a crate of scotch out from under his bed and pulled out one of the bottles. "This is quite possibly the best scotch in all of the UK. I'd like to toast to our truce. What do you say?"

Rory eyed the bottle Chase held in his hands. Less than a day had gone by since he nearly gave in to the temptation of cheap whiskey. As he looked at a bottle of scotch that cost more than his house, the temptation was gone.

"I thank you, Mr. Chase, but I don't drink."

Rory forced himself to shake the man's hand and then left.

* * *

Mervyn and Melvyn entered the tent after Rory had left. Chase knew that they had heard every word of the conversation from outside of the tent.

"Should we follow, sir?" asked Melvyn.

"Just keep an eye on what he does over the next couple days, just to make sure he isn't trying some kind of new trick."

"You don't believe he's really done?" asked Mervyn.

"Truthfully, I believe him." Chase took a long drink of scotch. "But it never hurts to be cautious, does it?"

– 33 –

Rory clipped the last of the lilies from his greenhouse. There were just enough to fill a small vase for the kitchen table. He brought the flowers to his nose and breathed the sweet smell, which still reminded him of Mari. It always had, though until the previous day the memory had been tainted.

He brought the flowers into the house, arranging them several different ways before he was satisfied.

Rory tried reading a book to pass the time until Mari returned, but he felt like a child on Christmas Eve. He couldn't keep his mind focused on the words and read the same page for over an hour.

When he finally heard his truck pull into the lane-way he ran to the door and threw it open. Mari hopped out of the truck and pulled a paper bag full of groceries from the passenger seat.

She saw him waiting for her and gave him a big smile. Rory felt his heart quicken just a little.

"You look happy to see me," she said.

"I am."

Mari patted him on the cheek and walked past him into the house. It felt more comfortable just to have her back in the house. Not that he thought she might have lied about coming back, just that it felt better to be in the same room with her.

Mari busied herself in the kitchen for over an hour. Every time Rory tried to get into the kitchen and help, she'd wave him off and send him to sit back down. Again he tried to read. It was a little easier this time, but he stopped every few pages to peek at his wife or make another attempt to get into the kitchen.

They dined on steak and baked potatoes, corn, and sweet carrots. After nearly a lifetime of eating fish stew, with the occasional meal of mutton, the steak tasted like pure ambrosia.

Mari had also bought a bottle of sparkling water, flavored to taste like wine. Even without the alcohol, it tasted a little bitter on his tongue, but he drank every drop Mari poured for him.

When their meal was done, Rory read to her by the fire until the late hours of the night. They laughed as one yawn turned into an unending string. They crawled into bed and held each other.

Rory lay in bed and fantasized about a life filled with dinners for two, sitting together by the fire, and making love before falling asleep.

His last thought as he fell asleep was that he could have lived that fantasy every day for the past thirty years. That was his fault, but there was time to make up for it.

*   *   *

Mari was up before he was the next morning. When Rory woke up, he dashed out of the bedroom, again, afraid that she had left. She hadn't. She was in the kitchen cooking breakfast. Even though he hadn't voiced the fear, he felt embarrassed by his constant paranoia. It would stop eventually, he hoped.

"I'm leaving this afternoon," she said in the middle of their breakfast.

Rory choked on a mouthful of egg. He had been right to be paranoid! Once he got his coughing under control, he looked at her with wild eyes. "Oh, Lord, Mari! Why?"

"Don't be alarmed, love. I want you to come with me."

"Where?"

"Our house, in Glasgow."

"You still live in that house?"

She nodded.

Rory stood, his mouth hanging open in shock. He turned in a slow circle taking in his small home. It wasn't much of a house, but it was his. "I've been here for more of my life than anywhere else," Rory explained. "I'm not sure I can pick up and leave that easily."

"We'll take it slow. Come with me today, stay for a month, a week, a few days even. Anytime you want to come back here for a visit, we'll come together. It can be our little vacation spot."

"I've got a job here. And what about Gra . . . Nester?"

"Nester can come with us, and you won't need a job. I've got enough money saved up for us both. It'll be like we always talked about. A modest life, but our life."

The support from Mari helped, but the idea of leaving his house and the loch, still made him nervous.

He wandered around the house looking at the few things he had collected over three decades. There wasn't much: A framed picture of Graham, a golf ball that had been hit by Sandy Lyle, and a few interesting rocks he had found around the loch.

If these items were the culmination of the life he had been living, has he really been living at all?

"Ok, Mari. I'll go."

* * *

Rory walked into the pro shop, barely concealing his giddiness. Claire saw him coming and greeted him with a smile.

"Hello, there! You're certainly happy today."

"Am I?" he asked.

"To tell you the truth, I don't think I've ever seen you this happy."

"I'm about to go on a little vacation," he said with a sheepish grin.

"And you've never taken a vacation during all the time I've known you."

"Is that all right?"

"Of course, Rory! Of course! Where are you going?"

"Glasgow. With my wife." He nearly began giggling.

Claire's face went blank, her eyes widening slightly.

"You have a wife now?" she asked.

"I've always had a wife," he informed her. "We just haven't really been together." He considered going deeper into the story, but the details always made him feel ashamed.

"How long will you be gone?" she asked.

"That's the sticky part, Claire. I might not be back for a couple of days."

"Okay. A couple of days is no problem. We'll find someone to cut the grass while you're gone."

Rory forced himself to look Claire in the eye. "It's also possible that I might not come back at all."

"Let me just say one thing," Claire said. Her voice shook and she had trouble keeping eye contact. "If things don't work out between you and your wife, I'll be here for you."

"Thanks, Claire," Rory said with a smile. "You're a good friend."

"No," she said, "you don't understand. I'll be here, waiting. For you."

Despite always wanting her flirting to be real, he felt shocked at the admission. They had been working together for years. Why had she waited until his wife had returned to say something?

A part of him liked the idea of Claire waiting for him, but he pushed it away. His wife was back and they were going home.

* * *

They decided to take the train instead of driving. That was more relaxing for Rory who still wasn't completely comfortable with leaving. Graham stayed at home. If Rory decided to stay in Glasgow, he'd bring the dog then. In the meantime, Rory left him outside where he could get his own meals by chasing down fish and the occasional bird. If he decided to stay with Mari for more than a few days, he'd need to get someone to feed the sheep. By then he would be looking for someone to buy his property. *Maybe Chase would buy it to use as his tent*, Rory thought with a grin.

The train ride gave Mari time to tell Rory all about how Glasgow had changed over the years. The way the neighborhoods had grown, how some of their favorite stores and restaurants were different stores and restaurants while others were torn down to make way for car parks.

Again, he was content to listen. His stomach turned at the mention of some people he used to know. He never thought about having to face old friends and explain where he had been for three decades.

It was a short walk from the train station to the house. Rory barely recognized his old neighborhood.

Their house looked different yet somehow the same, as if he was looking at the physical house side-by-side with an old photograph. He walked up the front steps, caressing the handrail. The front door had been repainted, probably more than once.

Something else was new. Rory pushed a shiny, new button beside the door and listened to bells chime from inside the house.

Mari and Rory giggled with each other.

"Doesn't anyone use knockers anymore?"

While they still joked and laughed about doorbells and knockers, a young woman pulled the door open and looked at Rory warily.

"Oh, hello, dear!" Mari said, hugging the younger woman. "We were just having a bit of fun with the doorbell. Didn't mean to bother you."

"That's okay, Mom," the younger woman said. "Glad to see you made it back safe."

"Mom?" Rory whispered.

"Oh, Rory!" Mari proudly put her arm around the younger woman. "This is my daughter, Lindsey."

Rory felt an insatiable smile growing on his face as he looked at the younger woman. She had so much of her mother in her. Her hair, lips, nose, but her eyes.

"It's a pleasure," Rory said, taking her hand in his.

"Nice to meet you," she said, smiling. She had her mother's voice and smile too, but those eyes.

Mari busied herself in the kitchen while Rory and Lindsey sat in the living room. Rory couldn't take his eyes off of the beautiful daughter that sat in front of him.

"How was the ride?" Lindsey asked.

"Fine. It was fine," he replied with a smile.

"Good weather for travelling."

"Yes. Very good."

Lindsey continued attempts at small talk, but Rory kept answering her questions with no more than a word or two. She fell silent, smiling nervously when she looked up to see him staring at her.

"When's your birthday, love?" Rory asked.

"Um, March 23rd."

"Of what year?"

"1951."

Rory was filled with exhilaration as he counted backward from the date. Lindsey was born seven months after he left.

After the past two days, Rory thought there was no way he could feel any happier. He had been wrong. A beautiful daughter had just entered his life. There was a pang of sadness for all the years he missed, but he wasn't going to let past regrets ruin any more time.

He had a strong desire to dash over and hug the girl. The only thing that stopped him was the already uncomfortable look on Lindsey's face.

Mari quickly made another great dinner. Rory and Lindsey ate in near silence while Mari talked. She spoke to Lindsey about Rory and to Rory about Lindsey. Rory couldn't stop smiling. It didn't matter whether he was looking at Mari or Lindsey. He felt like the luckiest man in Scotland.

Rory and Mari washed the dishes after supper, playing flirtatious games with one another, and giggling.

"I'm going to go, Mom. I'll see you tomorrow."

"Okay, dear. I love you."

"Love you too. It was nice to meet you, Rory."

Rory quickly dried his hands and pulled Lindsey into a hug. She felt stiff in his arms, but he enjoyed the embrace, regardless.

"We'll see you soon," Rory said, stepping back and putting his arm around Mari.

"She's so lovely," Rory said after Lindsey had gone.

"I'm glad you like her," she replied, wrapping her arms around him.

"Like her? I can already tell that I'll come to love her. I can't wait to get to know her, spend time with her, become a family."

Mari's smile widened and she had tears in her eyes.

"That's all I've ever wanted!"

*   *   *

When Rory woke up it was late in the morning. He hadn't slept-in that late in years. The house was empty, which was disappointing. He had hoped that either Mari or Lindsey would be around to talk with. Their absence made him feel the paranoia of abandonment.

The phone rang. Rory went to answer it, but stopped himself. It didn't feel like it was his house anymore, which made him uncomfortable about answering the phone. After the sixth ring, a small box, which sat underneath the phone, clicked. Then he heard Mari's voice coming from the box.

"Hello! I'm not home right now, but if you leave your name and number—"

"Mari?" Rory asked as her voice continued. "Mari, it's Rory. How do I turn this thing—"

The small box emitted a loud beep and Mari was gone. A man began talking.

"Hi, Mari, it's George. Just needed to ask Lindsey something. Thought she might be there."

"Lindsey's not here, George," Rory said loudly toward the box.

"Call me when you get this, okay?" The message concluded.

"Call you when we get what?" Rory looked closer at the box to see if something would come out of it.

There was another beep and a click from the box. Rory waited to see who else was going to talk, but no other voice came. He took his hands off of the box, worried he might break it.

He wandered into the living room where he used to spend so much time sitting in his easy chair reading the paper or listening to the radio. His chair was gone, though another sat in its place.

It was comfortable, but he had no paper to read. The old radio was gone as well. Across the room from the chair was a television. Rory had seen them in stores, but never thought about owning one.

He took the remote control off the small table beside the easy chair and studied the buttons as if they were letters from an alien language. He stabbed at a few of the buttons with his finger until the television's screen came to life.

The glowing screen showed only static and made a horrible, unending noise that made Rory slap a hand over his good ear while the other hand desperately punched more buttons. The noise continued and grew louder.

Finally, Rory dashed over to the television and pulled its plug from the wall.

"Not so good with technology, are you?"

Rory turned and saw Lindsey walking into the room. She took the power cord from him and plugged the television back into the wall. Then she grabbed the remote, punched a couple buttons and a newsman appeared on the screen.

"Looks like you are," Rory replied.

"It's not that hard," she said. "You'll get it."

"How about we sit and have a coffee instead?" he asked. "You know, get to know each other."

She smiled politely, which told Rory that she really didn't want to, but was going to agree anyway.

"I was actually on my way back out. Just stopped to get my purse. We could head to a coffee shop."

"Love to!" he said, smiling at his new daughter again.

They walked side by side down the sidewalk into a small shopping area. Rory craned his neck continually, looking for the stores he used to know and finding strange new signs instead. There were only two places he had ever lived, and he felt like a stranger in one of them.

"It can't be!" a man's voice called out.

An older gentleman, using a cane to walk, was staring at Rory, a smile growing on his face.

"Rory Stewart?" he asked.

Rory looked at the man as he approached. He looked past the years that had reshaped the man's face and reached back into his memory.

"Hugh?" Rory asked. "Hugh Lambert?"

The old man laughed and grabbed Rory's hand in a handshake. "Yes!"

"This is my," Rory stopped himself from saying daughter. He didn't know how much Lindsey knew about him yet. "This is Lindsey. Hugh and I worked together some time back."

"Some time?" Hugh asked. "More like a lifetime!"

Lindsey excused herself to buy a few groceries.

"How long has it been, Rory?" Hugh asked.

"Long time," Rory replied. He knew just how long it had been, but was reluctant to say it.

"Where did you go? What happened?"

This was exactly what Rory didn't want to happen. How much should he tell people? Should he even tell them the truth?

"I left to deal with my son's death," Rory said, hoping the man wouldn't probe into an open wound. "Mari and I reconnected a few days ago, and I'm back."

"Yeah, but where did you go?"

Rory smiled to hide his annoyance. "I just kind of floated around."

Hugh continued to ask questions, and Rory continued to dodge them, until Lindsey came out of the store to rejoin them.

"Oh, gotta go, Hugh. Nice talking to you."

He walked on, pulling Lindsey's elbow as he went.

"What's wrong?" Lindsey asked. "That man seemed like a friend of yours. Why don't you invite him to join us for a coffee?"

Rory shook his head and continued on without looking back.

"We worked together. I wouldn't say we were friends. Besides, he talks too much."

Lindsey took Rory to an outdoor coffee shop that she called a café. Rory thought they only had cafés in France, but Lindsey explained they were popping up in most countries. The coffee was expensive and came in small cups, which didn't make much sense to Rory, but that didn't matter. He was only there to get to know his daughter.

As they drank their coffee, Lindsey began to open up,

dropping the polite tones reserved for strangers. He asked questions about her version of Glasgow and told her stories about his. She listened politely when he spoke and laughed at his jokes, even if they weren't very funny. He felt like he was talking to a younger version of Mari.

When they stood to go, Lindsey collided with a man walking by carrying a coffee. The drink spilled on both Lindsey and the man.

"Ah, shit. Look at this!" said the man.

"Oh, my God," Lindsey said. "I'm really sorry!"

"Damn right you are. This shirt is ruined."

Lindsey started to say something else when Rory cut in.

"You should have watched where you were going!"

"Stay out of this, old man, before I come over there and knock you out."

"Don't pick on him like that," Lindsey fired back.

"Shut-up, bitch. You're going to pay for this shirt."

Rory put himself between Lindsey and the man.

"That's not how you talk to a lady," he said in a low voice. "You should apologize and be on your way."

For the first time, the man didn't throw an insulting come back. He studied Rory and gave a nod. Instead of an apology, he balled up his fist and punched Rory in the left eye.

He didn't remember falling, but he was on the ground, a hand over his eye, with Lindsey crouched at his side.

"Get up, old man," the man taunted. "I'm not done with you."

Lindsey stood up and faced the man.

"What?" the man asked, spreading his arms out wide.

Lindsey's leg became a blur as she launched her foot into the man's face. He staggered backwards a few steps before falling onto his backside. He slapped a hand over his nose and blood ran through his fingers and down his face. He ran into the coffee shop without another word.

"We should probably go," Lindsey said, helping Rory to his feet.

"Where did you learn that?" Rory asked.

"I've taken quite a few self-defense classes."

They walked quickly until they were a few blocks away.

"When did people lose their basic decency?" Rory asked as they walked back to the house.

Lindsey wasn't able to answer. To her, people had been like that for as long as she could remember.

By the time they got back to the house, Rory's eye was purple and swollen. When Mari walked into the house she nearly screamed when she saw Rory stretched out on the couch with a bag of frozen peas on his face.

"What happened?" she demanded.

Rory started to explain, but Lindsey stepped in and saved him.

"We went out for a coffee and this guy came out of nowhere and started being a jerk. I thought he was going to hit me, but Rory stepped in and handled the situation."

"Handled the situation?" Mari said incredulously. "It looks like the situation handled him."

"Yeah, but you should see the other guy's face," Lindsey retorted.

Mari gave Rory a sly smile that he couldn't quite translate. It either meant she was proud of him and would reward him later, or that she knew Lindsey had left a part of the story out. Either way, she was willing to drop the conversation.

"What do you want for supper tonight, love?" Mari asked Rory.

"Doesn't matter to me. Anything you make is fine."

"Oh, so I'm the one who's going to be making supper?"

"I'll cook, if you like. I'm not very good at anything other than fish stew."

Mari laughed and gently probed at Rory's eye. He sucked in a breath at the pain that flared through his face.

"I'm going to go, Mom. I'll probably come see you again tomorrow."

"Staying with George tonight?" she asked.

"Yeah, I better go see him. He left me a message on the machine. See you later, Rory. Thanks for the afternoon."

"Don't mention it, love. I'll see you again tomorrow," Rory replied.

Rory sat up on the couch and hugged his wife as the front door closed behind Lindsey.

"Who's George?" he asked. "Boyfriend?"

"Boyfriend?" Mari asked. "No. George is her father."

The room spun as Rory slowly stood from the couch.

"Her father? But, I'm her father," he said, pointing a finger to his chest.

"I suppose in time she may become like a daughter to you," Mari reasoned.

"What do you mean 'become like a daughter'?"

Mari's mouth opened to speak, but only squeaks and grunts came out.

"Are you trying to say that she's not mine?"

She stared at him wide-eyed and fearful. Still unable to bring herself to words, she shook her head.

"No? What does that mean? No you're not trying to say that, or no she's not mine?" There were tears in his own eyes now, despite the rush of anger he felt.

"She's not yours." Mari's voice was barely audible.

He plopped down onto the living room floor.

"How can that be, Mari? Her birthday. She was conceived two months before I left." The obvious answer hit Rory like a punch in the stomach, and he closed his eyes.

Mari was sobbing, two small rivers ran down her face.

"I'm sorry," she cried. "I'm so sorry!"

"While we were still together, Mari?"

"Can you really blame me?" she screamed at him, standing from the couch. "Can you? One day my husband turns into an abusive drunk. I woke up each morning not knowing if I'd be ignored, yelled at, or hit. After months of that, a man comes around showing me respect and kindness. I just wanted to be loved again!"

Rory shook his head and stared at the floor.

"It was a mistake to come here," he said. "I'm sorry."

He didn't know what he was sorry for. Everything, he supposed. Being a terrible, abusive man in the first place, and for having to leave her a second time.

She stopped him at the front door.

"Are you really that incapable of understanding?" she asked.

"I could understand if you had taken another man after I left, but not while I was still here."

"If you leave now," she warned, her face scrunched up in anger, "I'm not coming to get you again. I'm not going anywhere near that God forsaken loch. And if you leave now, don't you even think about trying to come back here. You walk out that door and I consider you a dead man."

"I was just fine before you came and found me!" He was surprised to find he was yelling, but he couldn't stop. "You pulled me out of my life and showed me something so much better. You introduce me to this beautiful girl who I believe is my daughter." All his anger receded and sadness rushed forward like a dam had broken. Tears streamed down his face. "She's this incredible woman, and for the first time for as long as I can remember, Graham's memory isn't killing me from the inside. Then you pull it all away from me."

On his knees, by the front door, he sobbed. For what seemed like an hour, he sobbed. When he finally composed himself enough to stop crying and push himself to his feet, Mari was still standing there. She watched him, not trying to sway his decision in either direction. She just waited.

He reached out and opened the front door.

"You stupid, stupid man," Mari said before running into her bedroom.

Rory knew he should have closed the front door and followed Mari into the bedroom, but pride made him step out of the house and close the door behind him. He really was a stupid man.

He walked several blocks before he realized he was walking aimlessly without a way to get home. He had a little money, but not enough to buy a train ticket. He wished he had driven to Glasgow and that Graham had come with him so he had someone to talk to.

Rory found a late night diner and ordered a real coffee. He sat there for a long time trying to figure out a way to get home.

The waitress returned to top up his coffee and he forced a smile in thanks, though it hurt his face to do so.

"Looks like you've had a rough night," she said, nodding at his purple eye.

"Aye," he agreed. "Tried to make some lad show a lady respect. Didn't work out very well, did it?"

"A commendable effort."

"Do you have a phone I could use?"

She smiled and pulled a phone from underneath the counter and set it in front of him.

"Just no long distance, okay?" she asked.

"Of course," he lied.

"Okay." The waitress walked away to check on her other customers.

Rory began to dial, but then hung the phone back up.

"Uh, ma'am?" The waitress turned back to him. "I'm sorry. It's not a local number," he confessed, pushing the phone away from him.

She came back and pushed the phone toward him again.

"Just don't be long, huh?" she said with a wink.

Rory gave her a grateful smile and picked up the handset. He dialled the only number he knew and waited for the connection.

"Who is this?" demanded a voice on the other end.

"Rob. It's Rory."

"Rory?" he asked. "Do you know what time it is?"

"I'm sorry for the hour. I have a really big favor to ask."

"You think I'm going to do any favors for you?" Rob spat. "My kid lost his job after that little stunt you pulled, and you don't even have the courtesy to come and apologize?"

"I'm sorry about that," he said. He truly was sorry. Rory didn't mean for anyone else to suffer in the war he had waged against Chase. He supposed it wouldn't have helped to tell Rob they had ended the rivalry.

"It's too late to apologize, Rory. I'm not doing you a favor, and I think you should take your business somewhere else."

"I understand," Rory said. "I'm sorry to have bothered you."

After a quick consult with information, Rory dialled a hotel in Inverness.

"Evening. Could you connect me to Alex Stafford's room?"

236

-34-

The phone rang inches from Alex's face, making him sit straight up in bed before he was fully awake. He looked at the clock and wondered who would be calling at such a ludicrous time.

"Who is this?" he demanded.

"I've been hearing that a lot tonight."

"Who is this?" Alex asked again. The voice sounded familiar, but having been woken up so suddenly, he couldn't place it.

"It's Rory. I'm sorry about the hour."

"Rory," he said, somewhat relieved there wasn't an emergency. "How're things? How's Mari?"

"Things aren't good. I had to leave, and I'm not going back. Not ever."

"What the hell happened?"

"Not now. I need you to come and get me."

"Come get you? You've got to be kidding me," he said, laughing. "This is some kind of joke, isn't it? Couldn't you have waited until morning?"

"I'm in a bind."

Alex sat sputtering for a few seconds before he remembered how to form words again. "Even if I was willing to drive three hours to pick you up, which I'm not, I couldn't do it. I flew to Scotland. I only have a rental car and if I drove that far they'd charge me a fortune."

"Take my truck," Rory suggested. "It's sitting at the train station. The keys are in it."

"You leave the keys in your truck at all times?"

"Aye. Doesn't everybody?"

"No," Alex said, shocked. "No one does that. Except you."

"Alex, please. I've got no one else to call."

Alex grumbled as he dressed.

"Get into an old truck and drive for three hours! Probably because Rory did something stupid. Oh, wait! I forgot about the drive back. Six hours!"

*   *   *

The old man's truck could barely be described as running. It took Alex a half hour of coaxing before it started. Even then it constantly threatened to stall as he drove.

Coffee in hand and both windows down, Alex still found himself having to shake his head like a wet dog, or slap himself in the face to keep from falling asleep.

The drive should have taken three hours but ended up taking just over four due to the combination of engine trouble and fatigue.

Alex was grateful when he arrived at the address Rory had given him and found the old man waiting out front for him.

"You made it," Rory grumbled.

"Barely," Alex replied. "This thing's a pile of scrap."

"You just got to know how to stroke her the right way, that's all. Move over."

Alex slid over to the passenger side as Rory climbed behind the wheel.

"Are you going to tell me what happened?" Alex said.

"No matter how well you think you know a woman, you don't. And I'll tell you this . . . if you've got a good woman, treat her well and don't let her feel alone." Rory's voice broke a little.

Alex nodded, already thinking about sleeping all the way back to Inverness.

"You do have a girl, don't you? Back in London, right?" Rory asked.

"Yes," he replied with a smile.

"That smile means she's a special one, too."

"Yeah, I guess."

"You guess? Either she is or she isn't."

Alex thought about his night with the waitress and his shame returned. He did think Loren was special, but how could he do what he did to someone he thought was special?

Alex nodded. "She is. She's a little upset with me for working so much right now, but what can I do? It's my job."

"You know what we can do? Surprise visit. Women love that kind of thing. We're practically halfway to London. What do you say?"

"Halfway to London? More like a quarter of the way."

"Quarter, half. We're closer than Inverness. We could be there for lunch."

"No. Absolutely not," Alex refused. "I mean, I appreciate the thought, but no."

"Alex," Rory pleaded. "You've done me two huge kindnesses in a row now. Let me do one for you."

"I'll tell you what, I'll find something you can do for me back in Inverness. Don't worry about Loren and me. We'll be fine. Can we go back now?"

"Sure," Rory said, shrugging. "I could use my bed anyway."

"Speaking of which, wake me when we get there."

-35-

They made good time. Rory sped a little, no more than anyone else on the road, but it cut an hour off of their trip.

Alex was still asleep in the truck, fogging up the passenger side window with each rhythmic breath. Rory had one quick stop to make before taking Alex home.

He stopped at the first pawn shop he saw and slipped out of the truck. The store looked forgotten by time and consumers alike.

The inside was as outdated as the outside, which didn't matter to Rory. He was still the oldest thing in the store. A man behind the counter stopped sorting a box of records and studied Rory as he approached the counter. Rory looked at the items underneath the store's glass countertop with feigned interest.

"What are you looking for?" the man asked with an extremely unfriendly tone.

"I'm looking to get rid of something," Rory replied. He looked at the gold band on his finger for a few seconds before he plucked it off and placed it on the glass.

The man scrutinized the ring. Picking it up, he rubbed it with a small cloth and held it at eye level.

"Approximate worth?"

"To me?" Rory said. "None."

* * *

When Rory walked out of the pawn shop, Alex was standing outside of the truck looking at the surrounding buildings. He pointed at the old man and then at the buildings.

"We're in London!" he said.

"Sharp as a tack, even when you wake up."

"What the hell, man? You said we'd go back to Inverness."

"And we will," Rory said putting his hands up. "But while we're here, why don't we go surprise your girl?"

"Fine. We drop by on Loren, real quick, then we go back."

"Of course!"

Alex directed Rory through the streets of London until they arrived in front of his apartment building.

Alex sighed as they walked up the stairs and again as they stood outside of the apartment door.

They walked in and Alex called out, "Loren, honey, it's me!" He gave Rory a spiteful look. "I've come to surprise you."

Loren poked her head out of the bedroom and smiled when she saw Alex's face. "Alex! I'll be right there." She emerged from the bedroom a minute later. "Sorry, just had to throw on a sweater."

"It feels warm in here to me. Are you getting a bit of a chill?"

"I think so." She smiled and gave Alex a kiss. "I can't believe you're here. This is so nice."

Rory jabbed Alex lightly in the ribs and winked at the younger man.

"Loren, this is my friend, Rory."

Rory stepped forward with a smile, extending his hand. "Alex talks about you all the time. I just had to come with him and see one of the world's true angels."

Loren looked at Alex with a renewed smile on her face and bit her lower lip.

"Wow," she said. "I'm a little surprised to hear that."

"Nonsense, my lady. He can't say enough good things about you. And he says them so often I almost have them memorized myself."

Loren giggled and kissed Alex again.

"I'm glad you enjoyed our visit, but unfortunately, Rory and I need to get going. We've got to get back."

"Nonsense," Rory said with a wave. "I've been driving all night and morning. I was hoping you folks would do me the favor of allowing me to sleep under your roof. Then you two could spend some time together, maybe go out to dinner."

"You poor man," Loren said with a sound of sympathy. "Of course you can sleep. We have a couch in the study. You can close the door. It'll be nice and quiet."

"You're too kind," Rory said with a smile.

"I'll get you some blankets." Loren disappeared down the hall.

Alex turned and stared death at the old man.

"You said you'd go back," he said, his voice teeming with bottled anger.

"Soon," Rory said. "I really am tired. You wouldn't want to

get in an accident, and I know you don't want to drive that pile of scrap anymore."

Rory smiled at him, entertained by the situation he had put Alex in. *How mad can he really be?* Rory wondered. *He gets to spend time with his girl.*

Loren returned with some blankets and a pillow and showed Rory into the study. He thanked her again and kissed her hand.

She giggled at him. "You are so sweet!"

Once the door was closed he looked around the study and was glad to see a telephone sitting atop a desk. He didn't like to be deceiving, but he hadn't come to London just to bring Alex to see Loren.

During the four hours he had waited for Alex to pick him up, Rory had decided a few things. Things in the past were going to stay there. Whether he had handled things properly or not was a thought for another time, but nothing was going to change there. His focus automatically fell back to the one thing that had preoccupied his attention for thirty years. That meant his war with Harvey Chase would continue.

Somewhere in London, Chase had a factory making the substance that created the massive walls that were dividing up the loch. If he found that factory he might find some useful information.

Rory made a series of phone calls and through creative questioning he narrowed it down to two factories. When he called each one directly. The first claimed to be a soda bottling plant. The man who answered the phone at the second plant hesitated with his answers before claiming the plant was closed down.

"If the plant is closed, why are you there answering the phones?"

He heard a click before the line went dead.

* * *

"Are you almost ready to go, Loren?"

She poked her head out of the bedroom door. "Don't yell, you'll wake Rory up."

"Yeah, that'd be a real tragedy," Alex muttered.

Alex crept over to the study door and eased it open. The room was mostly dark, a small beam of light spilling in from the open door. On the couch was a motionless heap of a human being. He wondered if he should have checked for signs of life. Rory was an older fellow and a drive that far and that long takes an effect on the body. He decided against it, knowing if he woke Rory he'd get a verbally abusive rant for his concern.

Loren left the bedroom just as Alex pulled the study door closed.

"I'm ready," she said with a cheerful smile.

"You're wearing that?" Alex asked, trying to keep his tone polite.

"What's wrong with it? Are we going to a five-star restaurant?"

"Maybe not, but it is a nice restaurant, and you're wearing a baggy jumper."

"Well, Alex, this is how I'm dressed now. We can either pick another restaurant to go to, where this outfit will be appropriate, or I could go back into the bedroom and try to find something else to wear."

Alex considered the additional hour it would take for a new outfit to come together and compared that to the severity of his hunger pains.

"You know, I never liked that place anyway. Let's go somewhere else."

"What did you and Rory drive down in?" Loren asked as they walked outside.

"Oh, Rory's truck. It's a real rust bucket. Just terrible."

"I hope it's not that bad. Our car is in the shop for a few days."

Alex looked at the truck, and sighed. It was transportation, which meant its purpose was to get its driver and passengers from one place to another, and it did that—barely.

Fortunately, the truck started for him on the first attempt and only stalled once on the way to the restaurant. He considered that to be a good sign.

*　*　*

Rory waited for ten minutes after they left the apartment before opening the door to the den. He was grateful that they had left when they did. If he had to lay on the couch and pretend to sleep any longer he wouldn't be pretending.

His truck was gone, which gave him a moment of pause. He quickly walked to the nearest bus station and studied the routes. Within a few moments, he found which bus would take him closest to the factory.

His mind raced as he sat on the bus. His plan, if it could be called that, had no substance. Once he arrived at the factory, he had no idea what he would do. Everything else would have to be decided in the moment.

When he reached his stop, Rory quickly walked the three blocks to the factory, looking around for anyone who might see him. Fortunately, he was in an industrial part of the city near sundown; there wouldn't be any passersby.

A large metal gate surrounded the property. Rory walked the perimeter three times, never once seeing a security guard. Chase was likely pouring so much money into catching the Loch Ness Monster that he couldn't afford to pay for more than a minimal staff. The thought made Rory smile, but he knew that Chase would never run out of money.

Rory slid through a small gap in the gate, near the back of the property, and quickly ran to the building. Walking along the outside of the perimeter, he gave a gentle pull on the handle of each door he found. They were all locked.

He made one more sweep around the building, hoping there was an opportunity that he had missed. The smell of cigarette smoke made him stop. It was faint, minutes old, at least. Near the closest door he found dozens of stomped out cigarettes. He waited by the door, pressing himself against the building. He wasn't hidden very well, but as long as no one looked back as they walked out of the building he wouldn't be seen.

An hour passed before the door was pushed open and two men walked out, laughing and joking with each other. Rory slipped behind the men and inside the door before it slammed shut behind him.

He found himself in a packing area with several machines towering around him. Cases of Chase's miracle chemical, all boxed and ready to go, sat piled around him. The lights in the area were low, and the machines were unmanned. The packaging staff already finished their shift for the day.

Rory could still hear the two men outside. One of them let out a boisterous laugh, followed by a fit of smoker's cough. He didn't have much time. He had to get somewhere where he wouldn't be seen.

Cautiously, he moved through the packaging area toward a large doorway.

Each of the machines he passed had a large control panel with dozens of buttons, some of them lit with red or green. Sabotaging those would be near impossible. He wouldn't know what to press. Even if he had known, the machines were probably just as easily restarted. He moved on.

The next area was four times the size of the previous. It held several huge chemical vats. Above the vats were steel walkways circling the perimeter of the area with a single walkway leading out over the top of each vat.

An uprising of voices prompted Rory to dash behind one of the vats. It was a tight fit between the vat and the wall, but it was just wide enough for Rory to squeeze through. He waited for the voices to sound again, half expecting to be discovered before he could take another step.

When the voices arose again, Rory heard that they were sounds of laughter. No one was alarmed and, so far, no one knew he was there.

Rory continued to move toward the laughter, staying between the vats and the wall. A dozen men were standing around in a semi-circle; most of them had smiles half frozen on their faces as they watched one of their co-workers closely as he was handed a book of matches.

"Your turn, rookie," one of them said.

"Don't screw it up," another man called, causing a wave of laughter from the rest of the men.

Another man walked over to a faucet attached to the closest vat. He filled a paper cup and walked back over to the group.

"Ready?"

The 'rookie' tore a match out of the book and nodded. The cup was tossed, sending the clear liquid flying into the air.

In one smooth motion, the rookie dragged the match against the back of the matchbook and tossed it toward the airborne liquid. There was a bright flash of fire, intense flames hung in mid-air for a fraction of a second and then everything was gone.

Not even a drop of liquid hit the floor. Rory didn't even see any trace of the match that had been thrown.

"Nice throw," one of the men cheered, slapping the rookie on the back.

"How does it do that?" the rookie asked aloud.

"Who cares?" another man answered. "It's fun and it passes the time."

Fire! Fire could destroy Chase's walls.

Rory was about to leave with his information when he noticed a pile of matchbooks on the floor near the men.

He crept forward as far as he dared without a distraction. When the next man took his turn at throwing a match, he scurried forward and grabbed a handful of matchbooks and retreated while the men were still cheering at the newest flash of fire.

Stashing the books in his pocket, he moved away from the employees, still keeping close to the wall, until he found a ladder that led to the catwalk above.

When he was halfway up the ladder, the two smokers walked back into the building. With nowhere to go but up or down, and not enough time to do either, Rory thought he would be discovered, but there was a fresh flash of fire from the other end of the factory and the two men went running to watch.

Rory climbed the rest of the way up the ladder and stood over one of the vats farthest away from the men playing their game. He peered over the edge and was surprised to find Chase's miracle chemical looked like nothing more than water. He pulled a matchbook from his pocket and opened it. It was empty. So was the second and the third. He had grabbed a handful of empty matchbooks! He sat down and threw them over the edge of the catwalk one by one.

He was about to throw the last book when he saw the

slightest bit of red. Pulling it open, he saw there was a single match left in the book. Rory smiled and got back to his feet. He lit the match and absently wondered how safe he was standing directly over an entire vat of the stuff.

The men below threw a small cup full and it made an extremely bright flash of fire. An entire vat.

He walked back to the main catwalk, taking care not to let the match go out, and prepared to throw. Again, he reconsidered his position. Whatever the danger zone was, he probably wasn't out of it yet.

Before he could start moving again, the top half of his match broke away and fell toward the vat. Rory turned and ran as fast as his arthritis-ridden knees could handle.

The instant the match hit the liquid's surface, it turned the vat into a jet engine. Rory could feel the heat on his back as if his clothes were on fire. The roar of the fire completely muted everything around him. Even his footfalls on the catwalk seemed to be soundless.

When he was halfway down the ladder, a spark of the fire jumped from one vat to another. The impact and heat of a second jet engine threw Rory off balance and he fell from the ladder, landing hard on the floor. The impact sent blinding pain down his entire spine, as if each lumbar was a hot coal. Men were running out of the factory with their arms over their heads. He heard a third vat catch fire and thought he might not make it out of the factory alive.

* * *

Sitting through dinner was near torture. Alex did well to smile and nod at the appropriate times, but he wanted to get back to Inverness and continue the coverage on Chase's hunt.

Though, that wasn't the only reason he didn't want to be there. Loren was prattling on about work and her friends and all the television shows she had been watching recently and Alex couldn't stop thinking about his night with Betty. How could he sit here and face his girlfriend after that night?

He had given her grief about the way she was dressed, but even in his baggy clothes, Loren looked beautiful. Her smile wasn't one that could light up anyone's room, but it lit him up every time she showed it, especially when he was the reason for the smile. It was a shame that he could sit there remembering all the reasons he fell in love with her moments before potentially ending the relationship, but if it was going to continue Alex didn't want anything hidden.

"I have something to tell you," Alex said, cutting Loren off mid-sentence.

Loren looked around the restaurant with a smile on her face. It was more of a pub than a restaurant. The kind of place where patrons found their own seats, ordered from the bar, and every man looked over his date's shoulder for the week's footy highlights.

"Here?" Loren asked. "Now?" Despite the smile on her face, tears were welling up in her eyes. Did she know what he was going to say?

"It's not the best timing, but I'd really rather do it now."

Loren put a hand over her mouth, eyes growing wide. *She knows*, Alex thought. *Did she just giggle?*

"I've been unfaithful, and I'm sorry. I met a waitress in Scotland. We went out one night, it was all just friendly, but then we got really drunk and ended up at my hotel room. And . . . Loren, I'm sorry. I'm so sorry."

"You bastard." Her tone was calm and even, with a measured rage at the center. "I asked you not to go. You went. I asked you to come home. You stayed. You barely ever called and when you did you barely had anything to say to me. And now you tell me you've been fucking up with some waitress?"

"It was one time. I promise it'll never happen again. It was stupid. I was just so bloody drunk!"

The onslaught of insults continued. He deserved it all, but it was still torture to sit through.

"Loren, listen," He had to cut her off in her rant. She had grown louder and people were beginning to stare. Alex knew she wouldn't take it well, but she had never been this emotional about anything before. "I could have kept this from you. There's no way you ever would have found out, but I told you. I told you because I love you, and I didn't want to keep secrets from you. That should tell you something."

"Oh, I'll tell you exactly what it tells me—"

An explosion went off in the distance. The source couldn't be seen, but flames three stories high raged into the evening sky.

"My God," Loren whispered. "What do you think that is?"

Alex stood from the table and headed for the door.

"Alex! Where are you going?"

"This could be a major story. Make sure someone calls the fire department. I'll be right back."

Leaving was the worst thing he could have done, but he was desperate to escape Loren's scrutinizing. He'd have to deal with it soon enough, but he could use a momentary distraction.

Loren might even calm down a little, he thought. But as he pulled away from the restaurant, she stood outside screaming at him. *Maybe not!*

Rory's truck sounded like it was dying as it drove down the streets. Alex strategically made lefts and rights, each zig and zag bringing him closer to the source of the fire. A final right turn put him on a road leading directly to a building with a charred

Chase Industries logo on the side. Flames were still shooting out of the roof, though they weren't quite as tall now.

"You damn fool of an old man!" he yelled at the steering wheel. "You better not be here. You better not be here!"

He spotted a dozen men standing a distance away from the building, but there was no sign of Rory.

"Hey!" he heard someone say.

Alex looked at the men standing around, but none of them were close enough to say anything to him. A chorus of sirens sounded in the distance.

"Hey!" came the voice again. Alex turned toward the voice just in time to see Rory, covered in dirt and grime, coming out from behind a bush. His clothes hung off of him in burned shreds and he was hunched over more than normal.

"I knew it!" Alex yelled out.

"Keep your voice down and move over."

Rory got behind the wheel and took off down the street. The sirens grew louder and emergency vehicles passed the truck by. The sirens started to fade again as Rory pushed the truck faster.

"You stupid bastard," Alex said. "What the hell were you thinking?"

"Wasn't thinking too much, to be honest. I was kind of making it up as I went."

"And what the hell happened to you? You look like barbecue."

"I nearly was," Rory said with a laugh. "I honestly thought I was going to die. I had to crawl out of that place while it burned down around me."

"You crazy old fool. Take me back to the restaurant. I need to get Loren."

Alex directed Rory back to the restaurant but Loren was no longer there. One of the bartenders claimed to see her leave in a cab.

They drove back to Alex's apartment and got out of the truck.

"You stay here," Alex demanded, pointing a warning finger at Rory.

"I can help," Rory offered.

"I think you've helped enough."

Rory got back into the truck, muttering as he went.

Alex ran up the stairs and used his key to open the door. It stopped after a few inches, the chain keeping it from opening any further. Alex shoved his face into the narrow opening and called for Loren.

"Loren! Please let me in. Let's finish talking about this."

There was no answer in return.

"The silent treatment? Really? We're not in grammar school anymore, Loren."

He heard several stomping footsteps and then the door was crushing Alex's head. He cried out in pain and pulled his head from the opening just as the door slammed closed. He put one hand on his face and pounded a few times on the door with the other. His temples ached from a mixture of physical and mental pressure.

*   *   *

"Damn," Alex said getting back into the truck. "She's pissed off."

"Women get like that."

"What's this?" Alex shot back. "More advice from the expert?"

"Long night of driving," Rory said after a hesitation, and put the truck into gear.

The first hour, Alex wasn't talking. He spoke by the third

hour, but only with an occasional grunt when asked a question. In the middle of the fifth hour, Rory broke the silence.

"You ever been to a Scottish auction?" he asked. Alex said nothing. "I have. Right in the middle of the damn thing, they announce some rich man had lost his wallet with ten thousand pounds in it, and if anyone found it, the owner would give them a reward of a hundred pounds. Then some fella in the back of the room yells out, 'I'll give you one-fifty!'"

It was a terrible joke, but it was enough to elicit a laugh out of Alex.

"Hey," Alex replied. "How many Scots does it take to screw in a light bulb?"

"How many?" Rory asked with a grin.

Alex put on his best Scottish accent. "Och! It's not that dark in here."

They went on exchanging jokes until the end of the sixth hour. By the time they were able to see the loch, they were even laughing about the events from London.

Rory pulled into the parking lot of Alex's hotel.

"I don't know if I should thank you or apologize," Rory said.

Alex laughed. "Both, probably. I'd better go try to call Loren again."

They shook hands and Alex headed into the hotel lobby.

As he passed by the front desk, the man standing behind it put a hand in the air and called out, "A word, Mr. Stafford?"

"Sure."

"I regret to inform you that we can no longer allow you to stay in our establishment."

"What?"

The man brought a box up from behind the desk and placed it on top. "Your things have been collected for you. Please check them over and—"

"Does this have anything to do with my company credit card? It's maxed out on me before. You can just start using my personal card."

"Payment is not an issue. Please check over your items, and I would ask you to sign this form which acknowledges that nothing is missing."

"I'm not signing anything until you tell me why I'm being kicked out," Alex said.

"If you do not sign, then we're not responsible for any lost items."

"You have to tell me why I'm being evicted. It's the law," Alex threatened.

"No," the man said with an air of arrogance. "The law states that as a privately owned business, we may deny service to anyone at any time for any reason."

Alex grabbed his box of personal belongings and left the hotel, without signing their stupid form. The only thing he would be signing for that hotel was a complaint letter.

He went to the next closest hotel he could find. A woman behind the front desk smiled at him as he walked in.

"Hello, sir. What can I do for you today?"

"I'd like a room, please."

"How many nights?" she asked.

"Indefinitely. I'm here on assignment. I got a corporate card here." He passed the *UK Observer* credit card to the woman. She took it with another smile and began typing at her computer terminal.

"Your name, sir?"

"Alex Stafford."

The smile disappeared from her face and she handed the card back to Alex. "I'm sorry, Mr. Stafford, but I can't provide you with a room here."

"And why not?" Alex asked, annoyed.

"You've been flagged in our system. I'm very sorry."

"Flagged. What does that even mean?"

"I'm sorry, sir. I don't know, but I am going to have to ask you to leave the premises."

It was the same story at every hotel he tried. He was flagged. They couldn't let him have a room. And no one was able to give him a reason.

He was exhausted. All he wanted was to collapse into a bed and sleep for a day. He would need to call Loren first, but it wouldn't take long since she probably wouldn't answer the phone.

"Can I help you?"

"I'd like a room, please."

"Absolutely. Name?"

"Walter Flannagan."

That name wasn't flagged in their system, so the man had no choice but to process his request. Alex paid in cash to avoid any problems there. The man was just about to hand Alex a room key when a second hotel employee sidled up beside the first and showed him a piece of paper. The desk attendant pulled the key back.

"I'm sorry, sir. But we're unable to give you a room."

Alex snatched the paper away from the employees. Printed on the paper was a picture of Alex! In large font it had his name and warning not to provide any accommodations.

"Where'd you get this?"

"We're going to have to ask you to leave the premises."

"Of course you are."

Alex stormed out of the hotel with the paper still in hand.

-36-

Rory had been awake for a day and a half. Exhausted didn't begin to describe how he felt. His eyes felt like sandpaper and his head swam with every step. He collapsed into his bed and began to drift asleep. Graham barked outside. The single bark turned into several and then it was a constant stream of barking.

"Graham! Quiet down," he called. The barking continued.

With a groan, Rory forced himself to his feet. He ripped the door open and called out to the dog. "Graham!"

The dog continued to bark. Rory walked out of the house to find Graham barking at the sheep. He opened his mouth to yell at the dog again when he saw what was left of his sheep.

They couldn't even be called sheep anymore. They were just piles of bloody wool, meat, and the substance that Chase's dividers were made of. The dividers seemed to start in the stomachs of the sheep blowing the poor beasts to pieces from within.

He remembered seeing vats full of the stuff. It hadn't looked any different than water. Grabbing a box of matches from the house, he went back to the trough and dropped a lit match. What appeared to be water instantly became a flame. It was brighter and hotter than he expected, and he backed away with a hand up to shield his face.

He looked at the remains of the poor beasts. They had spent their entire lives knowing that when they wanted a drink of water, it was there for them. Even if they had been capable of the thought, none of them would have considered the next drink would tear them to pieces from the inside out. Even after the first few had dropped, the remaining sheep would not have learned to not trust the water trough. Poor, dumb animals.

Rory marched to his shed and grabbed his shears and a large knife. If he was lucky he'd still be able to salvage a little wool and meat. He was mad, but a part of him knew this was as much his fault as it was Chase's. This was retaliation.

*　　*　　*

As Alex walked through Chase's camp, everyone was looking at him. Annoyed glances, hateful glares, and menacing smirks.

When he finally found Chase, the billionaire was talking with three men. The trio all looked very interested in what Harvey Chase was saying as they scribbled in notepads.

If the notepads and mannerisms weren't enough evidence for Alex, one of the men, Grant Huxley, made it clear. Chase was talking to other reporters.

Chase shook hands with all three men before they walked away. Huxley gave Alex a cocky grin as he walked by.

"Right. So you're talking to other reporters now?" Alex demanded, marching over to Chase.

"That's right," Chase replied. "I'm talking to other reporters now."

"You told me, from the very beginning, that I had the exclusive," Alex said.

"I know I did." Chase put his arm around Alex's shoulders and led him toward the tents. "But with something this big, I couldn't keep it exclusive forever, could I? Eventually, I had to let others in to write their angle. It wouldn't really be fair otherwise."

"Well, I suppose," Alex said, though he didn't really believe it. "Could I ask a favor of you?"

"You may ask," Chase replied.

"A while ago you offered me a tent in your camp. I'd like to take you up on that, if the offer is still there."

"Well, now, that might be a bit of an issue."

They arrived at Chase's tent and walked inside.

"Are you full up?" Alex asked. "Because I'll share with some people. I don't mind."

"No, I'm not full up. There's plenty of room. The problem isn't with room, it's with content."

"I don't understand."

Chase grabbed a stack of newspapers from a box and handed them to Alex.

"I don't normally read the *UK Observer*, not even when I'm in London, but an associate of mine mailed me various copies that had been published over the last few weeks."

"And you have a problem with what I wrote?" Alex asked with an awkward smile.

"Just a few small things here and there." Chase began grabbing papers from the stack Alex was holding. "This one, for example, you describe my efforts as a pathetic attempt at a

PR stunt. In this one, you managed to call me an idiot, buffoon, and a tosser, all in one article. Very talented, you are. This one claims I'm blowing my family's fortune on something only a child believes. This one fooled me for a second when it said I was a mirror image of my father . . . in a house a wacky mirrors. But this one, this one, was my absolute favorite."

Chase held the very last newspaper in his hands, the rest scattered on the ground at his feet.

"In this edition you describe my plan as a retarded child about to place last in the Special Olympics. People aren't going to like you for that one, Alex. Extremely offensive. You can probably see why I'd be upset, why I decided to talk to other reporters, and why I have no place for you in my camp."

"Mr. Chase," Alex begged, "this is probably going to be hard to believe, but I didn't write any of those things. I would never write any of those things. I have a reputation for writing facts. All those terrible things, they're words of opinion. I don't publish my opinion."

Chase held the newspaper at arm's length so it nearly touched Alex's face.

"Isn't that your name there on the byline?

"That is my name, but I did not write those things."

"Then who did?" Chase said.

"My boss has had it out for me since the day he got there. It was probably him."

"Of course, the old, bitter co-worker excuse! It must have been him, right?"

"It's true. He's always trying to change my stories. Usually I'm at the office and I can keep it from happening, but being so far away—"

"Then maybe you should work for a different newspaper.

For now, you're going to leave, either on your own or with my security team."

Alex didn't have a choice. Chase had more power than anyone in the country, maybe the world. With power like that, Alex could quickly find himself kicked out of more than the camp. With that thought, his eyes widened and he turned to confront Chase.

"You're the reason no hotel in town will give me a room."

Chase smiled. "You'd be amazed how far of a reach I have. You should consider yourself lucky. I could have just as easily had you evicted from your place in London. I could have made sure no one would give you a job ever again. You'd have to move to America just to scrub toilets for a living. You should leave before I change my mind."

As Alex left the camp, he met every look he received with an angry stare of his own. He didn't know who made him angrier: Harvey Chase or Martin Edwards.

When he knocked on Rory's door, the face that opened it mirrored his own anger.

"That son of a bitch killed my sheep!" Rory said before Alex could even ask what he was upset about.

"He got me kicked out of every hotel in Inverness. Probably in all of Scotland."

Alex plopped down on Rory's couch and felt the cushions with his hands.

"This seems comfortable enough. Could I sleep here for a few nights?"

Rory stormed over and put a finger in Alex's face.

"No more of this middle of the road business. If you want to stay here, you're going to help me screw up that bastard's plans."

"I no longer have a problem with that."

If Alex didn't have the exclusive anymore, he'd have to get

his stories from somewhere else. Sticking with the man trying to stop Chase seemed like a good way to get interesting stories.

Rory and Alex shook hands on the pact and shared a sadistic smile.

"I've got to say, I'm surprised you don't just go home to be with your lady."

"That sounds perfect right now, but as mad as she was I think she needs some time. Plus, the reporter in me wants to see this story through."

"That's noble." Rory's words carried a bit of a mocking feel to them. "Can't do very well by you, though."

"A lot of people would say living by this loch for years is noble, too."

Rory looked away and rubbed at his chin.

"Maybe you'd find the bed of my truck more comfortable than the couch."

After a moment of silence, when Alex thought he really might have to sleep in a truck, both men broke into laughter. It was gratifying. Chase had attempted to squash the pair of them and all it did was bring them together and renew their want for a fight.

Alex leaned forward with a gleam in his eye. "What's next?"

- 37 -

"Poof!" Rory said, dramatically spreading the fingers on both hands.

"Just like that?" Alex asked.

"Just like that. As soon as the match hit, it was flames, then it was gone."

"That's kind of poetic, isn't it?" Alex mused.

"What are you blabbering about?"

"Water makes it bigger, and a fire destroys it."

"You could say the same of a tree," Rory shot back.

"Right. Think that I shall never see, a poem lovely as a tree." Rory only shook his head.

"Let's focus. How many sections have they drained so far?"

They had both stayed out of sight since returning from London, though they had been watching Chase's camp closely. Eighteen of the dividers were up and four sections had been completely drained. They consistently had two sections draining, one at the south end of the loch and one at the north, working from the ends toward the middle.

"Damn," Rory said. He had hoped Chase would have been forced to stop for a while. A burned down factory didn't slow the man's progress at all.

"We might be overthinking this. We know his weakness. We've got matches. Let's go put an end to this," Alex suggested.

They thought about destroying the walls at the north end of the loch, away from the camp, to give a sense of mystery. Chase would go insane trying to figure out how his dividers were disappearing. They decided against the stealthier approach. Rory wanted Chase to know who was doing it, and he wanted to see the look on the rich bastard's face when his plan dissolved into flames.

Since they knew security wouldn't let either one of them near the camp, they got into Rory's motor boat and headed toward the camp. Chase was near the shore talking with a few members of his team.

One of Chase's security staff walked over to him and pointed to the two men in the boat as they got closer, sidling up beside the nearest divider. Rory stood up in the boat and plucked a match out of the box.

"Hey, Chase!" Rory called.

"What?" Chase replied.

Just as he had seen the men at Chase's factory, in one motion, Rory lit the match and tossed it. His aim was true. The match hit the top of the divider. The match bounced off and fell into the water with a hiss.

Rory grunted his disapproval and grabbed another match from the box. Again he lit and tossed, hitting the divider, but nothing more happened.

He paddled at the water, bringing the boat closer to the divider. He lit a third match and laid it on the top of the divider, so it couldn't fall off. The match only sat there and burned from one end to the other.

On the shore, Chase and a few of his men were doubled over with laughter.

"Hey, Rory," Chase called. "How are those sheep of yours?"

That brought an even bigger eruption of laughter. Chase was laughing so hard he had to put his hands on his knees.

Alex took hold of the boat's engine and steered them back over to Rory's dock.

"That didn't go so well," Alex said.

Rory went into the house without saying a word. He walked straight into his bedroom, slamming the door.

Alex knocked a few times, to ask if the old man was all right, but received no answer. Alex even made an attempt at a dinner, which Rory didn't leave his room to sample. Even Graham only took a bite of the culinary disaster.

"It's that bad, is it?" Alex said to the dog.

Graham looked up at him and whined.

It wasn't until Alex was lying on the couch, fighting to keep his eyelids open, that Rory walked out of his room.

"There you are," Alex said, eyes popping open. "Is everything all right?"

"I've got a new plan, but I can only tell you your part of the plan. Beyond that, you just have to trust me."

Alex was silent for a moment, and then he nodded. "Okay. I trust you."

-38-

Rory strode into the Fort Augustus Golf Course pro shop with an extra bounce in his step. He was feeling good about his latest plan. Alex had a simple part to play, but it felt good to have an ally. In past plans, there was no one else to depend on. It certainly limited the kinds of things he could do.

Claire, who usually greeted him with a smile, looked like she was having a bad day. Her brow was furrowed as she read a newspaper and her eyes were glazed over with potential tears.

As Rory approached the counter, Claire looked up and shoved the newspaper away, underneath the counter.

"You're back," she said.

"Things didn't work out," he said with a sheepish smile. He remembered his last conversation with Claire. She had said she would be here waiting for him, and she was.

"I see." There was something odd in her voice. She wasn't

rude, but she spoke coldly to him. Perhaps she was embarrassed that she had told Rory about her feelings and then he left to another city with another woman. Rory still found it hard to believe she ever had feelings for him. He thought it was best if he didn't bring it up.

"I'll make my rounds. I saw the grass on seven was a bit long, but I'll check the rest."

"That's not going to be necessary," Claire stated.

"The rest are good then, are they?" Rory asked, moving to grab his keys from behind the counter.

"Listen, Rory." She sighed. "This isn't easy for me to say, but we've . . . I've found someone else. To cut the grass, that is."

"Okay. I suppose I'll just come back in a few days when the grass—"

"Rory," she burst in, "you've been replaced. Permanently."

"What do you mean replaced?" he asked. Betrayal formed as a tightness in his chest.

"I can't do everything, Rory! I needed someone to cut the grass, I got someone to cut the grass."

"I was only gone for two days!" he argued.

"How was I to know that? You told me you might never come back."

Rory searched his mind for something to say; something that would make Claire change her mind.

Instead, she opened the cash register and pulled out an envelope and placed it on the counter in front of Rory.

"That more than covers two weeks' severance pay. I suggest you take it and not push the issue any further. And please . . . spend it wisely."

Rory's pride begged him to walk away without taking the money. If he still had a herd of sheep, he might have. Even more than that, he wanted Claire to say it was all some kind of prank. That he still had his job and she was still waiting for him.

Shame stung him as he reached to grab the envelope. He left the pro shop with his eyes on the ground and refused to look back over his shoulder.

Rory drove straight home and continued discussing tactics with Alex. He wasn't happy about losing his job, but it freed him to devote all his energy into the night's plan.

-39-

Rory lay prone, twenty yards outside of Chase's camp, waiting for Alex to execute his part of the plan. It was minutes before midnight. He didn't like keeping his role in the plan secret, but he couldn't tell Alex the rest. The reporter might not have agreed to it.

Rory checked the knife sheathed at his right hip. Then he checked his son's service revolver, holstered on his left. It was better for Alex if he could plead ignorance afterward.

Just as Rory checked his watch again, Alex went running past him, yelling long strings of profanity, slurring his words in the appropriate places.

As they had anticipated, Mervyn and Melvyn reacted before Alex could bother anyone. They stood in his way, keeping him from entering the camp, and attempted to calm him down.

The distance separating Rory from their men turned

the voices into mutters, but by now Alex would be spewing a story about being betrayed by Chase. In mid rant, Alex threw his arms into the air and was running again, with the security men chasing after. It was like watching a comedy. The large men almost collided as they tried to follow the reporter as he zig zagged, and ran in circles.

Rory smiled and pushed himself up from the ground. He kept to the shadows as much as he could and ducked behind a tent whenever he heard voices approaching. Mervyn and Melvyn weren't the only ones in camp still awake.

He remembered finding Chase's tent before he went to Glasgow. Counting tents as he went by, he prepared to dart between two tents when he heard approaching footsteps. Whoever it was, he was dragging his feet.

There was a shout further off and the owner of the footsteps called back. "Yeah, yeah! I'll be right there."

There was a zipping sound, then the man let out a sigh as a stream of urine hit the ground a foot from Rory's foot. Rory was one tent corner away from being spotted. He took a step back, to lessen his chances of being caught and to distance himself from the growing pool of piss. Another sigh and a zip and the man dragged his feet away from the tents.

Rory let himself breathe, but held his breath again as he smelled the results of the man's bladder break. He stepped over the puddle and resumed his search for Chase's tent.

He arrived at the tent and stood around the corner from the entrance. No one was watching. Rory edged around the front and slipped inside. Chase was asleep on the bed. Rory placed a chair in front of the entrance. It wouldn't stop anyone from coming in, but it might trip them up long enough for Rory to make an escape.

He turned and looked at his sleeping target.

Drawing the service revolver, Rory stepped close and pointed the barrel at Chase's heart. Second thoughts hammered at his confidence. If Rory didn't hit the heart directly, Chase could survive. He changed his target to Chase's head.

Again, he reconsidered. Even if the shot provided an instant death, the gunshot would alert the entire camp. He holstered the gun and pulled out the knife. Much quieter.

It's no different than a sheep, he tried to tell himself. The knife shook as he extended his arm toward Chase. This would indeed be quieter, but it would be even more difficult to strike an instantaneous killing blow. A stab couldn't be heard, but a screaming man could be.

Frustrated, he sheathed the knife and looked around the tent. An extra pillow lay beside Chase's head. Rory carefully reached to grab it. His arm was so close to Chase he felt the man's hot breath on his wrist. He snatched it off the bed and held it in both hands. It seemed thick enough.

Again, a flaw presented itself. Chase was younger, and probably stronger. Even with surprise on his side, would Rory be able to hold him down long enough?

Rory started to think of a combination of attacks. He could stab Chase in the heart and use the pillow to suffocate whatever life was left in him. Or maybe he could use the pillow to muffle the explosion of the gun.

He stood there staring at the man that had been his focus for weeks. The same man that was trying to destroy one of the only things Rory was living for. Was he really willing to go to the length of murder to end their war? His hatred renewed every time he looked in Chase's direction, but still he felt weak in his resolve.

Rory sheathed his knife and let the pillow fall to the floor.

On several occasions, Chase had made Rory feel pathetic. This time Rory did it to himself.

"Are you going to kill me?" Chase asked. The sudden sound of his voice made Rory gasp and his heart rate doubled.

Chase was looking at him, eyes slightly wide in either fear or surprise.

"I was," Rory replied, surprised at how easily he had admitted his own guilty intentions.

"Was?" Chase asked. He pushed himself up into a sitting position, still watching Rory carefully.

"I'm not a killer."

"I am," Chase said. It wasn't a response born of pride. It was factual. "Not of people, of course."

"Your fair share of sheep, though?"

Chase smiled.

"Among other things. I've told you before that the monster from this loch isn't my first hunt."

Feeling an ache radiating in his knee and sensing a lengthy story, Rory pulled the chair closer from the tent's entrance and sat.

"A few months back, I was in America. You've heard of Bigfoot, yeah?"

"Of course," Rory replied.

"Well, I caught it."

"You did not."

"I did. I had a team up in these mountains. We laid traps and waited it out for days. The damn thing kept distracting us and taking the bait. If I hadn't been so frustrated I would have been impressed. Eventually, one of my men spotted it and we followed him into a cave.

"My men were hesitant to go after it, but I had faced CEOs more frightening than some kind of hirsute monkey-man. I thought I would find some kind a feral, unthinking beast but, whatever its intelligence, it built its own fire, so I guess it deserves some credit for that.

"This Bigfoot, this legend, was just sitting on a log in front of the fire. When I walked in, it barely gave me a glance. It was just sitting there with its head hung low. Then I looked across the fire and I saw another one, lying down. At first I thought it was sleeping, but as I got closer I saw it was dead. It was slightly smaller, a female, I assume.

"All the bait that had been stolen from our traps was sitting in a pile beside the female. It was as if the female had died and the male thought if he brought her enough food and things she liked, she'd come back to him. I examined the body very carefully. I didn't want the male to get upset with me for being too close to his mate, but he didn't move. He only watched and I found the cause of death. A bullet hole. One of the other men had fired at something unseen earlier in the hunt. We thought it had been nothing at the time, but it turned out he had hit something.

"When I turned back to the male, he was looking at me. We made eye contact. Neither one of us looked away for what felt like an eternity. A spectrum of emotions passed through those eyes. Confusion, fear, hatred. A lot of hatred. Then he cast his eyes back down to the ground, where his mate was. That's dominance in the animal kingdom. We took him alive, but he died in transit. The remains of their bodies decomposed so fast that by the time my plane had landed the evidence was nothing more than dust. No one was convinced by dust."

"What's the point of telling me all of this?" Rory asked.

"These creatures have been around a long time. Centuries. People have been hunting them as long as their legends have been told. When I looked into the eyes of that creature, something occurred to me: They don't want to be here anymore. They don't want to keep running and hiding. I tell you, the way he looked at me when I walked into that cave." Chase shook his head. "We may not be alone, but they are, and they're miserable. Death is a mercy."

"You actually believe what you're saying, don't you?"

"Think what you like, but I saw into that beast's eyes. Have you ever seen into her eyes, Rory?"

Rory dropped his eyes to the ground. He remembered the night he had seen her, or at least thought he had seen her.

"I know you feel a connection with her, Rory, but she doesn't feel the same. She doesn't love you. She's not your friend. From what I hear, you don't have any friends."

"Alex," Rory shot back. "Alex is my friend."

"Oh. Him," Chase said with contempt and stepped out of his bed. "I have something for you to see."

Chase turned on a lamp and sorted through a pile of newspapers.

"Like you, I thought Alex was a friend of mine. Then I took a few moments and looked at some of the things he was writing about me. They weren't friendly. He claims a man at his office did it, but really, could he have a worse excuse?"

Chase handed one of the newspapers to Rory.

It was turned to one of the inside pages where a small column featured a black and white picture of Rory standing near the loch. The title of the story was, *The Real Monster of Loch Ness*.

He read through half of the story, but couldn't bring himself to finish. His conversation with Claire suddenly made sense. The way she had tried to hide the newspaper when he walked in, and the way she had suddenly turned cold. Rory tried to hand the paper back, but Chase shook his head.

"Keep it," Chase said. "To remind you how precious trust is."

Chase poured himself scotch and swirled it around the base

of his glass, the amber liquid reflected and refracted the light as it moved. He stuck his nose into the glass and breathed deeply, his face melting into a smile.

"This scotch is a single malt, aged ten years; a fairly expensive bottle to the average man. But the day we bring in the monster, we'll be using this stuff to clean the boats."

Chase pulled a crate out from under his bed and removed the lid. Unlabeled bottles had been laid in a bed of wood shavings, pure gold shone from inside the glass.

"On that day, we'll drink this. It's the kind of scotch that's made for celebrating once in a lifetime achievements."

Chase pulled one of the bottles from the crate and put it in Rory's hands.

"This one's for you. So that when it happens, you'll be able to celebrate with us, even though you'll be all alone in your little house."

Rory didn't remember leaving, but he suddenly found himself standing outside of Chase's tent staring at the bottle of scotch still in his hands. He walked back to his house staring out at the loch, as if just to prove Chase wrong, Nessie would appear for him.

Alex was sitting on the couch, finished with his half of the plan long ago.

"How did it go?" Alex asked.

"Not well."

Alex's eyes touched on the gun and knife at Rory's hip.

"My God! You killed him, didn't you?"

"Of course not," Rory shot back.

"Then what was the plan?"

"It doesn't matter. Here." Rory tossed the newspaper in Alex's lap. "In case you're looking for some bedtime reading."

Alex looked at the paper, and put a hand over his eyes.

"Listen, Rory, I'm really sorry that you had to see that."

"Let me guess," Rory interrupted. "Someone at your office wrote that and put your name on it."

"That has been known to happen," Alex admitted. "But I'm going to be honest with you. This story was completely my doing."

"He admits it!" Rory said to the ceiling of his house.

"I wrote it the night you kicked me out of your house. After you almost took my head off with a plate."

Rory said nothing in return.

"I regretted it immediately, though," Alex continued. "That's why I went to find your wife for you. I wanted to set things right."

"That turned out well, didn't it? And now Chase wants nothing to do with you either. You might as well be a leper as far as anyone around here is concerned."

Rory opened his front door wide and motioned with his head for Alex to walk through it.

"Rory, can't we talk about this a little more? I've got no other place to go."

"You wrote that I contribute nothing to society, that I should be committed, and that I frequent whorehouses. Talking to you has caused me no end of trouble. You got no place to go? That's not my problem."

Once Rory had been standing at the front door long enough to prove that he wasn't going to give up, Alex stood and collected the few belongings he had brought into the house.

"Enjoy your scotch," Alex spat as he walked out of the house.

Rory looked at the bottle he was still holding in his hand. He had forgotten about it. Even a glass of it would be the most expensive, highest quality drink he had ever had. He thought about opening the cap, just to experience the smell of a scotch of that quality, but he knew he wouldn't be likely to stop at a smell.

A strong man would have poured it down the drain. Rory set it on the kitchen table and stared at it. With everything he had been through, the constant battling with Chase, Mari coming back into his life and leaving as quickly, his friend Rob not wanting anything to do with him, losing his job, his sheep being murdered, having a terrible story published about him by someone he thought was a friend, and just his depressing life in general, why shouldn't he have a drink? People got drunk for far less.

The bottle was left on the table and Rory got into his truck, spitting stones from the rear tires as he drove away.

*   *   *

Rory marched into the brothel and leaned on the receptionist's desk. She held up a finger for him to wait while she finished speaking on the phone. Rory drummed his fingers on the wood and looked around the reception area.

"What kind of brothel has a lobby? And a receptionist?" he spat.

The receptionist shot him a challenging look.

"You think you're fooling someone into thinking you're a real business?"

When the receptionist hung up the phone, she stood from her chair, standing an inch or two taller than Rory, and addressed him with an impassive expression and tone.

"What can I do for you?"

"Is she here?"

"Do you have an appointment?"

"No! I don't have a damn appointment. Would I ask if she was here if I had an appointment?"

"Well, without an appointment—"

"Don't give me that. I didn't have an appointment last time."

The receptionist picked up her phone and dialled, all while returning Rory's angry stare. She spoke into the phone, too quiet for Rory to overhear. She hung up and forced a smile.

"Go on up."

As Rory turned to climb the stairs the receptionist reached out and grabbed the sleeve of his coat.

"But if you ever come in here again behaving like you are now, you won't be welcome here anymore."

Rory yanked his arm free of the receptionist's grasp and went up the stairs.

Brandy's door was open a crack. Rory spied through it to see her lying on the bed, waiting. His lust rose as his eyes slid along her curves. Heart and breath sped up in unison and he staggered into the room.

She looked up as he entered, greeting him with a smile.

"Rory. Melanie was right. You look a little out of sorts." She patted the bed beside her. "Why don't you lie down and we can talk all about it?"

"No," Rory stated.

He walked to the bed and pushed her onto her back. Only bothering to lower his pants and underwear, before mounting Brandy.

An event normally treated with as much tenderness as could be given between professional and client became a primal act between a woman and an animal. Frustration fueled rough pumping. Brandy put a hand on Rory's chest and began to push him away, an expression of pain on her face. Rory imagined that look on the face of his ex-wife. Then the face became Claire's.

"Easy, Rory. Take it easy."

Rory flipped Brandy over and took her, leaving behind the rest of his human side. He pushed faster now, no longer interested in the progress as much as the result. When it came, he nearly howled, head thrown back and eyes squeezed shut.

He collapsed beside Brandy, who scrambled off the bed and over to her dresser. She kept her back to him, refusing to look back.

Rory felt his senses return to him within a wave of shame. He pushed himself to his feet and pulled his pants back up.

"Uh . . . I don't quite know. I'm sorry." He reached a hand out toward Brandy.

She whirled on him, nearly slicing into his stomach with the knife in her hand. She gripped it tightly enough to turn her knuckles white.

"Get the fuck out of here! And if I ever see you again, I swear I'll cut your tiny cock off!"

*   *   *

The bottle of scotch was waiting for Rory when he walked back into the house. It hadn't moved. Not only was it not willing to leave him, it wasn't angry with him, didn't expect anything from him and, in fact, it only invited him to do something selfish for himself.

Just as his fingers gripped the lid and prepared to twist, there was a knock at his door.

There had been more knocks at his door in the past month than there had been in the past three decades. With all of his friends at ends with him, and the time of night, there was only one person he could imagine standing on the other side of that door.

"If I open this door and you're on the other side, I'm not going to be able to control my temper!" Rory said, yanking the door open.

To his surprise, instead of a young reporter, it was a grizzled old man, much like himself, with a miserable look on his face, also much like himself.

"My name is Ryan Maxwell," the man said. "I understand you could use some help."

– 40 –

Martin Edwards panted as he climbed two flights of stairs, a feat that would normally have stolen a little less breath if his nerves weren't tingling. He had been called up to Gary Whitson's office, which was rarely a good thing.

When Gary had something good to share, he went out of his way to find the recipient of the good news. When the news was bad, someone was summoned.

He stood in the stairwell for an extra moment, catching his breath and mopping the sweat from his forehead. Just because he was nervous didn't mean he had to look nervous.

Once he had collected himself, he approached Gary's secretary who directed him to sit and wait. The waiting was worse than the stairs. He continually wiped his forehead, hoping Gary's secretary didn't notice.

"Is that Martin out there?" Gary called from his office.

"Yes, Mr. Whitson."

"Come on in, Martin."

Edwards hurried into the office and bent to sit in one of the chairs opposite to Gary's desk.

"Close the door before you sit down, will you?"

That wasn't a good sign, but Edwards did as he was asked, then sat down.

"Nice afternoon, isn't it?" Edwards asked with a smile.

"What's been going on with Alex lately?" Gary asked. "His articles have been getting some negative attention. I don't care too much about that. Readers are readers. The reason they pick up a *UK Observer* isn't that important, but it's just unlike him."

What Edwards thought would be a painful meeting turned into a massive opportunity.

"I've been asking myself that, Gary. The articles he's writing are getting more hateful with each submission."

"And the quality of the writing in general is pretty bad."

"Well, I didn't see a problem with that, but things are getting worse. Add to that, he hasn't checked into the office for days. I tried to call his hotel and they claim he's not there anymore."

"When was the last article we got from him?"

"Five days ago."

"Five days?" Gary asked, eyes widening.

Edwards nodded.

"Christ! What has he been doing?"

"I've been trying to figure that out. It's like he's abandoned his assignment."

"Abandoned?"

Edwards shrugged and looked mournfully into his outspread hands. "It happens with some reporters. The ones that lose their edge, at least. First, their work starts to suffer, then they turn their back on the job."

"Just because his last few articles haven't been his usual—"

"I'm afraid it's been longer than that, Gary. I've been fixing up his stories for some time, but I can't keep doing it. I don't have the time, and it's not fair to him or the paper."

Gary sat back in his chair like a man who was just told his dog had died. Edwards sensed that with another little push he could convince the man to destroy Alex Stafford's career path.

"What would you recommend?" Gary asked.

"I would recommend some staffing changes around here."

Gary sat forward in his chair, leaning on his desk as the words soaked in.

"All right," Gary agreed. "Let's make some changes."

* * *

Alex tried to find a comfortable position in an airport chair, but failed with every attempt. It didn't matter. He was going home. Even if a flight to London hadn't been available, he'd still be waiting for a flight. He would have gone anywhere that wasn't Scotland and he didn't care what the *UK Observer* or Martin Edwards thought about it. The waiting was torturous, but it was still a better option than another eight hour drive. With nothing to do, he found himself people watching and listening to the conversations around him.

Two men sitting behind him were discussing politics in the UK, which bored him, but he would have much preferred to hear more about politics rather than—

"You been out to see the setup that Chase fella has out there?"

Alex couldn't escape it. Even once he left the country, he had a feeling it would be waiting for him somehow in London.

"Nah. I've heard about it, but I'm not going out there. The whole thing is ridiculous."

"What's ridiculous about it?"

"Are you kidding me, Steve? The Loch Ness Monster?"

"You don't believe?"

"Oh, of course I believe. But there's no way anyone's going to catch her. Santa Claus will open the portal to outer space and they'll wait until it's safe to return."

"I'm just saying it's possible. She could exist."

"Yeah, yeah, yeah."

The men fell silent and Alex started to rethink his decision to leave. He was giving up writing on an event that was being discussed and debated in public. This was Scotland though, and he wanted to write for London. Besides, Chase was only the catalyst that led the men to debate the existence of a myth. Those discussions had been happening for decades, if not centuries, and his writing had nothing to do with it.

Even if he was willing to stay, no one at Chase's camp would talk to him anymore, and there wasn't a hotel, couch or cot where he could lay his head.

He thought about what the twenty-year-old reporter in him would say; the reporter that went wherever the story was even if it meant going someplace dangerous and sleeping in his car.

I was desperate then, he told himself. *I needed stories. Now I have a career and a following.*

"I used to know him, you know," said the man named Steve.

"Who?"

"Harvey Chase."

"You did not."

"Did so. I used to go out ghost hunting with him."

"Ghost hunting? I thought it was cryptozoo-whatever."

"Not always."

"Excuse me," Alex blurted out. "I couldn't help but overhear you say you knew Harvey Chase."

"That's right," the man said.

"Well, my name's Alex Stafford, and I—"

"You're the one that wrote all them articles in that London rag?" the man cut in.

"Yes," Alex replied with a sheepish grin.

"Look at that, Dave! We have a celebrity sitting with us." Steve elbowed his friend enthusiastically.

"Well, then, big shot! Go ahead and tell 'em, Steve," Dave said.

"Harvey Chase used to go ghost hunting?" Alex interrupted the argument before it escalated further.

"Oh, sure," Dave replied. "He went after any ghost he heard a story about, whether it was well known or not. We went after the woman in white a few times. Those barghest dogs at least a half dozen times. Those things used to scare the pants off me when I was a kid."

"Me too," Alex admitted. "I'm guessing you never captured a ghost."

"Of course not," the man said. "You can't capture something that never really existed. I never believed, but I'll tell you one thing. That Chase fellow, he believed more than any of us."

Chase may have taken the exclusive away from Alex, but that didn't mean he couldn't still get it his own way. This story had started out as Alex's, and it would end that way even if he had to write the discrediting, public relations disaster of a piece that Chase feared most.

"Sir, would you mind if I quoted you?"

-41-

Rory sat in his living room with the man who had introduced himself as Ryan Maxwell. They looked at each other, calmly, making silent judgments based strictly on appearances. In a sense, entire conversations were taking place between them, with their eyes doing all the talking.

When the newcomer had been standing on the porch, he had appeared to be of an age with Rory. In the light of the house, Ryan appeared to be younger by ten years, maybe even fifteen.

"What's this help you think I need?" Rory asked, breaking a twenty-minute silence.

"You know the help I'm talking about. You're a protector, like me."

"I'm afraid I don't know what you're talking about. What the hell is a protector?"

"So you've been living on the shore of Loch Ness, the famous spotting grounds of the Loch Ness Monster, to raise sheep and catch the occasional fish? That's all a coincidence, huh?"

Rory gave no reply.

"I also know that there's a fella by the name of Chase who's hunting your charge and it seems to me like he's closing in."

"You called yourself a protector?"

"Well, I was."

"What happened?"

"Chase happened. He caught wind of the Mothman Prophecies. You've probably heard of them by now, too. He was a tough one to protect, old Mothman. He was always getting away from my line of sight. Surprising people. There are a lot of rednecks in that area that like to get drunk and try to find Mothman, and they all have guns. I've had to chase away dozens of people after Mothman got grazed by a bullet or took some buckshot in an arm or a leg. I'd always bandage him up, but by the next time I saw him, there wasn't even a mark."

"Wait a second," Rory cut in. "You've actually seen this Mothman?"

"Of course. Hundreds of times. I don't know for sure if he knew I was protecting him, but he never attacked me, so I take that as something. Why? You must have seen Nessie just as many times."

Rory ignored the comment. "So what happened to your Mothman?"

"When Chase came around, he brought a dozen armed men. The locals in the area got all excited and joined the son of a bitch. More than a hundred people went looking for Mothman every night for a month.

"He was a curious thing, Mothman was. That many people

in the area, he couldn't resist taking a look. He was spotted one night and the mob let loose with their guns. Once they winged him, he couldn't disappear on his own. I found him and tried to help him find a place to hide. But Chase's men were closing in on us. Just when I thought they were going to cut us both down, Mothman pushed me away from him and flew directly at the mob. I was supposed to protect him and his last act was to protect me."

Ryan's voice cracked with emotion and his eyes became glassy. He put a hand to his face to shield his eyes from being seen.

"What happened then?" Rory asked, spellbound.

"Chase tried to take the body. But when the Mothman died, he turned into a husk. Chase's people tried to move him, but the husk crumpled in their hands and floated away like ash."

Rory sat silent for some time, thinking there would be more to Ryan's story.

"I'm sorry for your loss," Rory said, his voice no more than a whisper.

"I vowed I wouldn't rest until I found a way to stop that man from hunting anything else."

"What would you suggest?" Rory asked.

"What's happened so far?"

Rory gave a summarized version of all the plans he had tried and how each had failed. He also talked about his visit to Chase's factory in London and how he watched men eviscerate the chemical with nothing more than matches.

"That fire is interesting," Ryan commented.

"I thought so, too, but I threw half a dozen matches on those damn dividers. Something must have changed when it hardened."

"Or," Ryan said, unzipping a duffel bag he had brought with him. "Maybe you just didn't use enough fire."

Ryan pulled a rectangle of plastic explosives out of the bag and waved it at Rory with a menacing smile.

-42-

Alex walked into Chase's camp with his head held high and his chest puffed out. Someone watching him may have thought he was trying to be intimidating, but the truth was he was trying to hold onto his nerve. Every instinct he had told him to get back in his car and drive back to the airport. He was doing his best not to listen.

A security guard called out to him, but he ignored the call. The guard sped up his pace and Alex matched it, heading for Chase's tent. He had to run to keep ahead of the guard, and still when he reached the tent the guard was two steps behind.

Bursting through the tent flaps, Chase and Jerry both flinched, eyes widening. The security guard was there a second later.

"I'm sorry, sir. I'll get rid of him," the guard stated.

Alex would have argued, but he was still trying to catch his breath. Instead, he held a finger up to Chase and put his other hand on his knee, breathing heavily.

Chase grimaced and folded his arms over his chest.

"I'll hear what he has to say," Chase said. "But stay here. I'll probably have you throw him out immediately after."

Alex gave Chase a look of surprise, but the man only stood with his arms folded waiting for Alex to speak. No trademark smile. Not even a grin.

"I want my exclusive rights back," Alex said, still short of breath.

"I'll bet you do," Chase mocked. "But that's not going to happen."

"Oh, I think it is," Alex said with a smile. "You remember a gentleman by the name of Lawson? Probably not. He's not important enough for you to remember, but that doesn't matter. He assisted you with a number of," Alex paused, letting his eyes make contact with each man in the tent, "ghost hunts."

Chase's face barely moved, but there was a change in color. He calmly looked at the security guard. "Back to your duties."

Alex allowed the silence to continue. Whatever they were thinking was probably worse than any threat he could come up with. Alex sat in one of Chase's chairs and put his feet up on Chase's bed.

While Chase's face turned bright red, Jerry spoke.

"I'm not quite sure what that—"

"What that means?" Alex finished Jerry's question. "What that means is that I could go to print with all kinds of stories about you trying to be a ghost hunter. I know you don't want that out there since you've been working so hard at trying to make your hunts seem legitimate."

"You have no proof," Jerry continued. "All you have is one man's word."

"You're right. All I have is his word," Alex agreed. "But having his word means I can print it as a quote. Whether it's true or not, and despite any PR efforts you make to battle those quotes, they'll still be out there. They'll be on people's minds and on their tongues. This is the kind of thing people want to believe. They want to call their friends and say, 'Did you hear Harvey Chase believes in ghosts?'"

"You still can't have exclusive rights," Chase said through gritted teeth. "But if you swear not to print this ghost nonsense, I won't kick you out of the camp anymore."

"And you'll answer my questions?" Alex asked, nearly demanding.

"No. I won't say a bloody word to you!" Chase snapped.

Alex made a noise of disapproval and pretended to scribble something on a notepad. Chase stepped forward, as though he intended to hit Alex, but Jerry stopped him with a hand on the shoulder.

"I will answer your questions," Jerry blurted. "Me or someone else. But Harvey is off limits."

Alex knew the offer wasn't going to get any better than that. In truth, he didn't want to print anything about Chase being a ghost hunter. Constant stories about the Loch Ness Monster were odd enough. Stories about ghosts would effectively turn the *UK Observer* into a tabloid rag.

"Deal," he said, after making a show of considering the offer.

"Now get out of my tent," Chase growled.

– 43 –

Rory and Ryan slid across the loch in Rory's boat. They used paddles to propel the boat, instead of the noisy motor. They had planted a total of six bombs along the tops of two of Chase's walls, three for each. They had chosen dividers that were separating a full section from an empty one. They knew they weren't going to destroy entire walls, but they hoped to create large holes and let water drain back into the empty sections.

Ryan worked diligently to attach the final bomb to the wall.

Rory watched and wondered if they were using too many explosives. He had no experience with bombs. Ryan had assured him that it was better to make too big of a mess than to not have enough to get the job done.

When Ryan finished with the last bomb, they paddled back to shore and put the boat into the back of Rory's truck.

Ryan pulled the remote detonator out of his pocket and poised his thumb over the button.

"Wait," Rory said. "Will they be able to see the explosion in Chase's camp? Or at least hear it?"

"Hell!" Ryan said with a laugh. "They'll hear it, see it, and they might even smell it."

"Let's go over by their camp before you hit that button. I want to see their faces."

"Good idea, Rory," Ryan said.

They drove back to Rory's house and walked across the field. They stood on the outside of Chase's camp, looked at all the tents, and felt like Gods about to rain destruction upon the people of the earth.

"Now?" Ryan asked.

"Now."

A simple push of the button resulted in a mighty explosion. Rory was glad they had distanced themselves from the bombs. Had they stayed in their original positions, Rory would have lost his windshield and the ability to hear for the rest of his life.

The fire from the bombs was bright enough to bathe the camp in fire light. People emerged from the tents. Chase's security led the group of confused and curious.

Ryan saw them coming toward him and gave a savage cry as he ran at them. He pulled a knife, seemingly from nowhere, and spun with a grace unsuspected from a stocky man.

The knife bit the side of one of the guards, who dropped to his knees holding the wound. Ryan continued to spin, sinking the knife into the other man's shoulder. He kicked the first man in the back of the head sending him face first onto the ground, motionless.

A low spin kick put the second man on the ground. Ryan

crouched and pulled his knife from the man's shoulder only to plant it in the man's opposite shoulder blade.

"Ryan!" Rory cried. "What are you doing?"

When Ryan looked back at Rory he no longer seemed human. The eyes of a wild animal stared back, and his teeth were bared, thirsty for blood.

"They've got to pay, Rory. They all have to pay!"

Shouts rang out from the camp. Other members of Chase's crew were running to help the injured security guards.

Ryan gave another battle cry and ran to meet them. Rory sank to his knees horrified as Ryan jumped on a woman, letting his own bodyweight bring them both crashing to the ground. He punched the woman in the head three times, and then sprang up to meet a man who tried to throw a punch. Ryan took the man down with a quick judo flip.

Another man ran toward him with a canoe paddle raised above his head. Ryan deflected the blow and backhanded the man, sending him sprawling face first onto the ground. He straddled the man, grabbing handfuls of his hair, and began smashing the man's head into the ground over and over again.

Rory had tears leaking out of his eyes. He never meant for anything like this to happen. Pushing himself to his feet, he formulated a plan. He had agreed to work with Ryan, it was his job to put a stop to the man's rampage.

Rory crept up behind Ryan and wrapped an arm around his throat and the other around his forehead. If he could hold on long enough, he might be able to weaken the man or even make him pass out.

Ryan was lightning quick. He grabbed Rory's arms and threw himself forward into a front flip. When they landed, Rory was on the bottom. His lungs emptied from the impact and his arms went limp, allowing Ryan to easily roll away. As Rory lay there, gasping for breath, Ryan hovered over him just long enough to say, "Stay out of the way, Rory. This has to be done."

Ryan turned his attention back to one of his victims.

Rory gazed toward the camp, where people who could have been trying to help all stood back and watched in horror. Some were crying out for someone to do something.

Pain coursed through Rory's entire body, as though it travelled with the blood in his veins. He rolled onto his stomach and pushed with all his strength until he was standing once again.

Ryan was on top of another victim, crazed and throwing punch after punch into an unconscious face. Rory had to do something before someone died, if it wasn't already too late.

The canoe paddle that someone had tried to use as a weapon was nearby. Rory snatched it up and ran at Ryan. It wasn't a fast run. It was more of a lumber. His lungs hurt to breathe and his knees, which weren't much use for running in the first place, ached with each step.

Once Rory was close enough, he swung the paddle with all the strength he had left in his arms and connected with the back of Ryan's head. The man went sprawling forward.

Rory breathed a sigh of relief, until Ryan started to push himself to a standing position. Rory wasn't about to give the man a fair fight.

While Ryan was still on his knees, Rory hit him in the back of the head again, sending him flat on his face. To Rory's shock, Ryan placed his palms flat on the ground to push himself up once again.

Before Ryan could get to his knees, Rory brought the paddle down hard, and the crazed protector was still.

Rory threw the paddle down to the ground and then fell onto his rear. The people who had been standing around the camp suddenly grew brave and ran over to check on their injured co-workers. Two men roughly grabbed Rory's arms. He didn't fight back.

Chase was suddenly there, white-faced among all the carnage. He approached Rory and held his arms out, as if to encapsulate everything around him.

"Is this worth it, Rory? Is it worth it?" he screamed.

Rory shook his head.

When the police arrived, Ryan was loaded into the back of a car. When they tried to put Rory in the same car he turned and pleaded with him.

"That man's insane. I'm the one who gave him that bump on the head. Please, don't put me in there with him."

"You should have thought of that before you attacked these people," one of the policemen said.

Jerry heard the exchange and interjected himself into the conversation.

"Officer, some of my people claim that Mr. Stewart didn't attack anyone except that man," he said, motioning to Ryan. "If you put them in the same car, you'll be endangering Mr. Stewart's life."

The officer grimaced. If it weren't for the legal implications of endangering Rory's life, he probably would have put him in the same car as Ryan. Rory gave Jerry an appreciative nod.

At the police station, Rory also got his own cell. They were side by side, but having the bars in between them made Rory feel better about the situation, especially when Ryan sat in the middle of his cell, staring at him. There wasn't any confusion in that stare. If Ryan managed to get his hands on Rory, it would be the old man's last night.

It was a relief to get away from that stare when the police came to bring Rory to an interrogation room.

His interrogator introduced himself as Officer Jacobs.

"What do you know about this Ryan Maxwell?" Jacobs asked.

"Not much," Rory replied. "He showed up at my house and told me he could help me stop Chase." He hesitated for just a second when he realized he was about to say, 'from hunting her down.'

"Stop him from what?" Jacobs asked.

"From ruining the loch!"

"You knew nothing about this guy, yet you made and executed a plan with him?"

Rory had no answer. He felt foolish to have gone along with that lunatic's plan.

"Okay, here's the deal," Jacobs said. "We have enough eye witnesses that have said you didn't attack any of Chase's people, and that you were the one that stopped Maxwell, so that counts for something."

The door to the interrogation room was thrown open. Chase strode into the room, with Jerry close behind.

"Excuse me, officer, but I believe I have the right to talk to this man."

Jacobs grudgingly stood, but leaned against the wall beside Rory.

Chase stared hatred at him and flicked his head toward the door. Jacobs only shook his head in reply.

"Fine," Chase spat. "Jerry. Close the door."

Chase's eyes were wide with rage as he sat down opposite of Rory. They almost reminded him of Ryan's eyes when he had been attacking Chase's crew.

"Five people injured," Chase spat. "Three of them critically. A person might die because of this. Because of you. What do you have to say for yourself?"

"I never laid a hand on those people, and I'm very sorry they got hurt."

"You're sorry? What a load of shit! I'll bet you're not the least bit sorry."

Rory didn't really have a right to be mad at Chase, but the way the man was talking to him, it was hard not to be. He turned to Officer Jacobs and said, "What's the law say about killing another man's sheep."

Chase slammed his fist down on the table. "You shut up! What am I supposed to tell the families of the people that are in the hospital right now?"

"In case you haven't heard, I was the one who stopped it from getting worse. If it wasn't for me some of those people might have died."

"Bah!" Chase said with a wave of his hand. "Staged for appearances."

Chase stared at him for a long time, fatigue and stress obvious in his face. Large, purple bags hung under his red, droopy eyes. His hair was messy for the first time since Rory had first seen him.

"Despite what I think," Chase continued, "I'm told that no assault charges are being pressed on you."

Rory allowed himself a small smile, which seemed to enrage Chase further.

"But there's still charges of property damage. You're still going to jail! You're still going to be out of my way! You planted bombs, *bombs*, on my walls. My property. You'll be held here until the authorities investigate the situation. Even if you don't get any jail time, I'll be done and on my way back home with my prize."

Chase smiled sadistically as he stood from the chair. Before leaving, he stood in the doorway and flashed a huge grin at Rory. "Enjoy your time in jail."

"I won't be spending any time here, Chase."

Chase stopped mid-step and turned back to Rory, disbelief evident on his face.

"Not if you're a man of your word," Rory continued. Chase looked at Rory, confused. "I'm calling in that favor. The one that you owe me for saving your life. You said you'd give me anything in return. What I want, is for you to drop the charges."

Chase looked at Rory for a long time, struggling with his reply. Without another word, Chase stormed out of the interrogation room with Jerry following closely behind.

-44-

For the third time since he sat down in the police station, Alex jerked awake just before falling out of his chair. Three hours ago he was awoken from a fitful sleep in his car by a massive explosion.

He was parked, and technically living, a short distance away from Chase's camp. Starting up his car, he drove to the camp and found a scene of carnage. At first, he thought Rory and another man were attacking the camp. Injured people were scattered on the ground. Then he saw Rory attack his supposed ally.

Now Alex sat in the Inverness Police Station's lobby, hoping to see any of the involved parties. He told himself that he was only there for the story, but he also was concerned for the old man. Concerned might have been the wrong word. Perhaps it was more of a curiosity.

Alex stood quickly when Chase suddenly appeared with

Jerry a step behind. A miserable, black cloud floated above their heads. Chase stared straight ahead as though he saw his path clear across the country.

"Harvey," Alex said as they walked by. "What's going on?"

Neither man slowed his pace or even glanced in Alex's direction. He wasn't surprised, after their last conversation.

Alex watched them leave the station, then sat back down.

*   *   *

Officer Jacobs sat making polite small talk with Rory while they waited for a decision on whether Rory was a prisoner or free to go.

"I shouldn't really be telling you this," Jacobs whispered, "but in your situation, it could really go either way. There's enough to arrest you, but with the witnesses claiming you helped, the whole thing could be looked over easily enough."

"And, uh, what will be the deciding factor?" Rory asked.

Jacobs shrugged. "Some days it's nothing more than the Captain's mood."

"And his mood is usually—"

Jacobs's face sank, but before he could answer the question, another cop entered and gave a curt nod to Jacobs.

"Captain," Jacobs responded to his commanding officer.

The captain took a seat at the table, across from Rory. He casually flipped through Rory's file without a word.

"Did that son of a bitch drop the charges?" Rory asked.

"No, he did not," the commanding officer said in a matter-of-fact tone. "He walked out of this room and right out of the station."

"That bastard," Rory cursed. "He claims to be a man of his word. Well, I'll tell you something, his word ain't worth shit!"

"Well, I don't know much about all that," the captain responded without looking up from the file.

"I suppose I'll be spending the night here, then?" The thought gave him a chill. Especially if he had to sleep in a cell next to Ryan Maxwell. The man would surely try to find a way to kill Rory in his sleep.

"No," the captain responded. "You'll be going home."

"What about the charges?"

"I'm having them dropped. I've looked over your file, all the eye-witness accounts, everything. I don't think you're dangerous, but I want you to stay out of trouble from now on. I'm really sticking my neck out to make all of this go away."

"Why?" Rory asked. "Why are you sticking your neck out for me, Captain . . ."

"McGivern. Captain Derek McGivern. I'm sticking my neck out because when I was a rookie, and my co-workers put me through a stupid initiation, I almost drowned until an old man pulled my ass out of the loch." He nodded, his mouth curling into what was barely a smile. "Now we're even."

*   *   *

A young sergeant brought Alex a lukewarm cup of coffee. Despite its temperature and how watered down it tasted, Alex accepted the cup with far more gratitude than a tepid cup of coffee flavored water deserved. In his current state of sleep deprivation, and after a few days of sleeping in a rental car, the coffee seemed like a gift from a higher power.

The coffee kept him sated for a few moments, but impatience quickly set back in. He wandered up to the station's front desk where an officer sat filling out paperwork.

"Excuse me?" Alex said softly.

"Hm?" the officer said, without looking up from his work. Alex leaned over the counter and peeked at the man's important documents, which consisted of a crossword puzzle with a poorly drawn Popeye doodled in the margin.

"I was curious if you've heard anything about my friend," Alex explained.

"Your friend. Right. Who was that again?"

Alex looked around the station. They were alone. "Do you have anyone else back there?"

"I'm not at liberty to give that information, sir. If you could just tell me his name—"

"Rory Stewart." It dawned on Alex that he wasn't going to get anywhere without complying with a little bureaucracy. "If need be, I can post bail for him, or—"

"Bail hasn't been set. No charges have been processed as of yet."

"And none will be," said a new voice.

Two policemen led Rory into the station lobby.

Rory gave Alex a partial glance as he signed some papers with Officer Doodles.

"What are you doing here?" Rory asked.

Truthfully, Alex was hoping to get details about the night's event. That wasn't the kind of reason he could tell Rory. The only way the stubborn, old man would say a word is if he thought Alex didn't care if he heard it or not.

"I thought you might need a ride home," Alex said with a smile. It was a deceptive answer, but not completely false.

"Ha!" Rory replied bitterly. "Keep thinking on that."

One of the cops that had escorted Rory from the interrogation room spoke up. "You do have a ride home, don't you?"

"It's not that far of a walk. Nice night for one anyway," Rory said without looking up from the papers he was signing.

"Well," the cop said, "based on the night you've had already, I want you to let this man drive you home."

Rory looked at the detective defiantly.

"I could make you spend the night in one of our cells, you know. I don't want to, but I could."

Rory growled as he snatched his bag of personal effects, which appeared to be empty. "Come on, you," he snapped at Alex.

An awkward air surrounded them as they climbed into Alex's rental car. Alex looked at Rory expectantly.

"What?" Rory spat.

Alex pointed toward the passenger side seatbelt.

"What?" Rory repeated.

"Seatbelt," Alex said, pointing again.

"Yeah, I know what it is."

"Okay, then." Alex decided there was nothing he could say that would make Rory put on his seatbelt. Rory wasn't likely to do anything Alex wanted him to do, so he started the engine and pulled out of the police station.

The small clock on the car's radio told Alex just how slowly time was moving. After what seemed like a half hour, Alex glanced at the clock to find it had only been seven minutes. He needed to break the silence. Even if the old man wasn't willing to talk, trying to start a conversation might pass the time a little faster. It couldn't pass any slower.

"I've got to say, I'm surprised you're not in jail, after everything that happened."

As he expected, there was no response.

"I knew that other guy, the whack job, wouldn't be walking out of there tonight."

Again, there was no response. Rory didn't have any respect for the lunatic. If he had, he would have stood up for him.

"I don't know. I guess I just thought they'd see you to be just as guilty."

"I didn't do anything wrong!" Rory finally broke his silence.

"Sure. I know that. But the law . . ." He shrugged and glanced at Rory.

"I didn't even know the man," Rory said after another few moments. He laughed. "You'd think I'd be done with trusting people by now."

There were a hundred responses that Alex wanted to shoot back, but each one of them would have resulted in the old man's lips staying shut for the remainder of their drive.

"You didn't know him? From everything I heard, it sure seemed like you two were working together."

"I guess you could say we were." True regret resonated from Rory's words. "I didn't know he intended on hurting people. I never would have agreed to that."

They rode a little farther in silence. What had started as a subtle attempt to get story details had evolved into something else.

Everything that Rory was feeling was in his voice and on his face. His eyes seemed a little wider with pain, the corners of his mouth were pulled down more than usual, and disappointment was evident in his voice when he spoke. He wasn't hiding anything. It was rare to be able to know what Rory was feeling and Alex sympathized with the old man.

"Stop the car," Rory said, peering out the passenger side window.

"What for?"

"Stop the damn car!"

Before Alex had even brought the car to a complete stop, Rory was out of the car and hurrying toward the loch's shoreline. Alex found himself jogging to keep up with the old man.

When Alex reached the shoreline, Rory was standing on the very edge looking out at the water, his face a blank palette.

"It didn't do a thing," Rory whispered. "It didn't do a damned thing."

Looking out at the loch again, Alex saw it wasn't the water Rory was talking about. It was one of Chase's dividing walls. There were three pockmarks in the top of the wall, proportionally similar to those found on a golf ball.

"We put bombs all over this wall." Rory continued muttering to himself, too low for Alex to make out any of the words.

Might as well try to take down a bear with a BB gun, Alex thought as he looked at the wall.

"I guess none of it matters now, huh?" Alex said.

Rory gave Alex a haunting stare. There were tears in the old man's eyes.

"I just meant . . ." Alex scrambled for an explanation, "with Chase dropping the charges and all, I thought you two would just finally bury all this."

Rory continued to stare for some time. "He didn't drop the charges. Anyone who thinks this is over has his head up his ass."

Blood rushed into Alex's cheeks. "If that were true, I'd be smelling a lot of shit, right?" Alex burst out laughing at his own joke. Rory remained as still as a statue.

"I'll be walking from here," Rory said as he turned back to the water.

"But they told you—" Alex was cut off by complete silence.

He waited a while; assuming Rory would eventually change his mind and accept a ride the rest of the way home. After nearly an hour, Rory hadn't moved an inch. If the old man wasn't still standing, Alex would have thought he was asleep or maybe even dead.

*   *   *

Five hours later, Rory walked back into his house and plopped down on the couch. Graham gave a small whine, and rested his head on Rory's knee.

Rory wasn't quite a man defeated, but he felt as though he were flirting with the edge. It had been a long night. He didn't know his next step. In fact, he had no plan at all, but there was still something at his core driving him not to give up.

He wished he had been able to kill Chase when he had the chance. It wasn't the first time he had wished that since sneaking into the man's tent. He knew if he had another chance, he wouldn't take it. Even in anger, he wasn't a killer.

The entire walk home he had tried to come up with a plan, no matter how insane the idea might be. Most were pushed out of his head due to lack of resources or simple impossibility. There was no point to him sitting in his living room trying to force another idea. He scratched Graham's ears before shuffling toward the bedroom.

Being a man of meagre living, he knew where everything in his house was. He could close his eyes in any part of his house and navigate to any other room without putting a single foot out of place. That was what made it so surprising when Rory stumbled on something and fell to the floor with a painful thump.

Pain burned in his knees as he lay on the ground, cursing through gritted teeth. He looked behind him, to see what he had tripped on, and found Ryan Maxwell's duffel bag. And there were still a few tricks left inside.

-45-

Something woke Mona Chase from sleep. A sound, perhaps. One that echoed in her head, unsure if the sound came from the real world or that of dreams. At her age, she was usually only roused from sleep by a call of nature. She listened, waiting for the noise to repeat itself. If it didn't come again soon she would know it was nothing more than an echo from some dream, already forgotten.

Her eyes drooped, and she turned her head to a more comfortable position when the noise sounded again. Her eyes shot open and she looked around, but the darkness obscured nearly the entire room. A small sliver of moonlight spilled in through the bedroom curtains, but didn't reveal anything. Mona pulled the covers up under her chin and listened while she waited for her eyes to adjust to the darkness.

"Is . . . is someone there?" she let out in a whisper.

Another sound came from her bedside, and another and another. The sounds resembled crying. More specifically, a man crying.

She tried to contain her fear and spoke in a calm voice.

"Are you all right?"

The crying voice halted at the sound of her own, cut off with a breathless gasp.

"I'm sorry to have woken you, Ms. Chase."

"John!" she said, recognizing his voice. "What on earth is the meaning of this?"

He said something unintelligible among his sobs and sniffles.

Mona sat up in her bed and crossed her arms over her chest. Her eyes had adjusted enough to see John's silhouette, and she stared angrily at it. "Mr. Lasorda! You will take yourself out of my bedchamber this instant. In the morning, we'll have to discuss if you're going to continue working for—"

"They just wanted to be left alone!" he cried. The aggressiveness in his tone made Mona shrink into her blankets.

"What are you talking about, John? Who wanted to be left alone?"

"They just wanted to be left alone," he repeated, aggressiveness replaced with sadness. "They loved each other, and I loved them. They may not have loved me, but damn it I loved them."

John shifted and the moonlight fell onto something he was holding. Something long and metal.

"Oh, my God. Oh, my God, John. Is that a knife?"

She felt the sheets grow warm and wet under her bottom.

John's crying became louder and more intense as he stood. Between sobs he cried out, "I'm so sorry!"

- 46 -

Rory went over his plan again as he stood at the window staring at the loch. From the position of the empty sections, Chase was nearly done searching. Rory had lost too much time with distractions.

He laid out the elements of his plan on the kitchen table. Three more bombs had been created from the supplies in Ryan Maxwell's duffel bag. They hadn't worked the first time, but Rory realized that the bombs had been in the wrong spots.

He drove down the west side of the loch, until he saw a few of Chase's men setting up one of the large pumps on the shore of one section. Once the pump was set up, Rory watched the flashlights of the men move around for three hours. He sighed when he realized that they would be awake the entire night, watching the pump and looking out for saboteurs.

He dressed in his wetsuit and gathered his supplies, each

bomb sealed in a plastic bag. Rory fitted his oxygen tank and grabbed his waterproof flashlight and slipped into the loch.

Despite the suit, the water froze Rory to his core. He moved along the target divider strictly by feel. Chase's men might have noticed something if he turned his flashlight on too soon. A few meters deeper and the light wouldn't even be seen from someone directly overhead.

He kept a hand on the divider at all times. Bumps and crannies were constant, but he needed a more significant deviation.

After another few minutes, his hand sank into a small recess that hollowed inward and upward. It was tight, but Rory managed to squeeze one of the bombs into the open area. Once he was confident the bomb wouldn't slip out of place, he swam further down the wall.

Some distance down the wall Rory found a similar hole for the second bomb and another for the third, even farther down.

Rory turned his flashlight off and closed his eyes. He waited in the water with his arms spread wide and his eyes closed; not that he would have been able to see anything. He was reaching out with his mind, trying to feel a presence. Her presence. The only sounds were the occasional bubbles coming from his equipment and his own breathing. He realized, that though he had always wanted to see her again, he had a connection with the loch. Whether he ever met the beast again, he still had one love. The lady who was the loch.

Her embrace was cold, yet familiar. She would never let him see everything, but always allowed him to see enough. She was his provider and companion and unlike anyone else, mythical or otherwise, she was there every day.

Rory was so absorbed in the peace of his surroundings that he didn't notice he was slowly turning into an ice cube. Minutes had passed in the span of seconds and Rory was running low on his air supply.

A hiccup in his airline snapped him out of his trance. It wasn't an emergency, he wasn't going to die, but he didn't have time to swim back to his side of the loch before coming to the surface. He swam straight up, knowing he would be close to Chase's men, but not having an alternative.

Due to his loss of time, Rory half expected to see daylight when he got near the surface, but it was still dark. He broke the surface of the water smoothly, making less than a whisper of noise. Treading water, he watched and listened for any sound or movement. He was just about to make his way across the loch when he heard faint voices growing louder.

They couldn't have heard me, Rory thought. *Couldn't have seen me either.*

Rory pressed himself against the same wall he had sabotaged, leaving only his head above surface.

"I'm just saying it's possible," one of the approaching voices said.

The other laughed. "Do you even know what you sound like right now? Have you gone mad?"

"You don't think it's possible?"

"What's possible? You think that thing he's looking for is in this last little section of water?"

"It's not that little," the first man shot back. "I've seen lakes smaller than that with all kinds of things living in them."

The first man pointed his flashlight lazily at the surface of the loch, while the other laughed at the first's expense. Rory watched the beam as it floated toward him and prepared to slip under the water.

Something small hit the water a few feet away. Followed

immediately by another and another and another. Within seconds it was pouring rain.

"Ah, shit!" yelled out one of the men and Rory watched as their flashlights bounced away in search of some kind of shelter.

Finally, a stroke of luck, Rory thought. He swam across the surface of the loch to the west side and climbed into his truck. It took way more effort than it should have to undress, due to Rory's violent shivering. Once naked, he wrapped himself in a blanket and hugged his shoulders.

If the men he overheard could be believed, the section of loch he had been in was the very last to be checked, and it was already being drained. Chase would be done in a day, maybe two.

At least he would have been if not for Rory. Rory hit the button on Maxwell's remote and waited for a reaction.

There wasn't any blinding light or eardrum bursting explosions. There was a sound, though it was mostly muffled, and nothing could be seen. Rory thought he felt a rumble in the ground, though it could have been his imagination.

Chase's men noticed something, because the flashlights reappeared, bouncing around frantically. Rory smiled. The two sections that the damaged divider sat between would be half-full. If Chase's team didn't investigate, they wouldn't know anything had happened and they'd continue trying to drain. It would take quite some time before they realized why the final section wasn't draining.

By that time, Rory would have the materials for more bombs and repeat his plan as needed on other dividers. It would require a lot persistence, but with luck it would eventually frustrate Chase into going back to London.

He tried to imagine the holes he had created in the divider, hoping they were big enough to make Chase doubt that his prey was still trapped in any one section.

Once Rory arrived home, he fell into bed and drifted off to sleep instantly. It was late and he was exhausted, but also he felt satisfied. He finally had a way to fight back, one that yielded results, and that single thought washed away weeks of worry. His war with Chase wasn't over, but Rory felt like he had just won.

- 47 -

Rory was never fond of bragging, but he had to walk over to Chase's camp the following morning just to see the reaction. He was expecting confusion with some misplaced anger. What he wasn't expecting, was an empty camp.

No one met him at the edge of the camp to keep him from entering. No one was wandering from one tent to another. It was as though Chase and his employees had left without bothering to break camp. The thought exhilarated him, but he knew it was a dream. If they weren't here, they would be at the midpoint of the loch, investigating why the final section wasn't draining.

He chuckled as he got into his truck and drove around the loch. As he suspected, a large group of people were gathered at the shore of the loch, right around the divider that Rory had made into Swiss cheese.

As he approached the gathered crowd, he couldn't help

but notice that the people talking to one another didn't sound confused or distraught. They were fascinated and anxious. Rory slowly pushed through the crowd, working his way to the front.

Once at the front, he looked at the loch and felt his heart drop into his shoes. The final section of the loch was almost empty. One of the large security guards noticed Rory and put a hand on the old man's shoulder.

"Let him stay," said a wide-smiling Chase. "I'd like him to see my victory."

Rory looked to the wall where he had planted the explosives. There were three large craters in the side of the divider, but no holes. Once again, his plan had failed.

The old man fell to his knees and watched as the remaining water was pumped out of the last hiding spot she had. The fight had gone out of it. He wanted to physically attack Chase, for no other reason than to have the slightest bit of revenge, but couldn't force himself to stand and he couldn't take his eyes off of the loch.

A crowd of statues watched for two hours as the last of the water was pulled from the loch.

"There it is!" Chase called, with his arm extended toward the appearing bottom of the loch.

The crowd gasped, pointed and spoke in hushed tones of excitement or disbelief.

"There it is," Chase repeated. The smile on his face had never been so wide, or so genuine.

"Is it?" Rory said so quietly he was the only one who heard. "Oh, God, she's dead!"

A large, mound was slowly being revealed. It lied on the bottom of the loch, unmoving. The color was similar to that of the loch floor, but the shape and size told it to be more than mere mud.

"Get some men down there," Chase demanded. "Now!"

Another hour passed as a team went to work. Several divers waded into the muddy remains of the loch floor. They went without most of their gear, but kept their safety lines. Even though the water was gone, a man could drown in the soupy mud.

The men labored, slowly moving toward their target. A walkie-talkie on Chase's hip came to life.

"Almost there, sir. Still no sign of movement."

Back on shore, the large crowd of people didn't make a sound. The wind gave a gentle breeze and the birds sang their songs of the morning, but over one hundred people stood making less noise than a fly. All eyes were on the muddy shape on the floor of the loch.

"Take your time, son," Chase replied. "Don't dawdle, but don't get yourself into trouble."

"Yes, sir."

The crowd watched as the man reached the lump and cautiously touched it with his hand.

Jerry Triggs walked out of the crowd and tried to speak quietly with Chase, but was waved off like an intrusive gnat. Jerry tried again to speak discretely.

"Jerry, what?" Chase demanded.

"I need to speak to you."

"Speak, then." Chase didn't take his eyes from the loch floor.

"This is a matter better discussed in private."

"I'm not going anywhere right now. If it's so important just say it, Jerry. You don't have to be so damn secretive. As if you've ever had anything that damn important to say to me."

Chase's words slapped Jerry in the face, the sting visual on his face.

"All right, Harvey. Something has happened back in London. Your mother is dead."

"What?" Chase didn't look away from the loch.

"Your mother's been killed."

"Killed? Who would kill my mother? Who would dare?"

"The police have her new assistant in custody. Apparently he's some kind of sasquatch enthusiast who believes you killed two sasquatches."

This finally caused Chase to break his stare at the loch, only to shift the gaze to Rory. He seemed to be demanding an answer with that look. Then it seemed as though everyone was staring at Rory, so he spoke.

"Was it worth it, Chase? Was all this . . ." he motioned toward the drained section of the loch and at all the people he had employed to assist on his search. "Was all this worth your mother's life? Was it worth sacrificing everything else?"

Strangely, Rory felt he was talking to himself in a way. While battling with Chase he had sacrificed everything he knew. Was it worth it?

Chase stared back out at the loch.

"Was it?" Rory said again, louder and more assertive.

Chase continued to face the loch, his gaze darting from the water to the drained section and back to the water, as if the answer was there somewhere.

"Was it?" Rory demanded.

"Yes, God damn you, yes!" Chase exploded. "If it means catching the beast, it's worth anyone's life. It's worth your life. It's worth his life," Chase pointed to a random man in the crowd and began pointing to everyone else in turn. "And his, and his, and hers, and his, and hers, and his."

"We should go, Harvey," Jerry said, gently grabbing Chase's arm.

"We will," Chase replied, shaking Jerry off. "But not yet."

"No, Harvey. We're going now."

"Who the hell are you to tell me when and where I'm going? You are my assistant! You assist me!"

For the first time since Chase had come to the loch, Rory saw anger in Jerry Triggs' eyes. For a man who was usually offered good judgement, he seemed rattled. Some invisible line had been crossed.

"Harvey, I'm your father!"

The crowd turned mute at Jerry's outburst.

"No, you're not," Chase said. It wasn't denial. It was a stated fact.

"Yes, I am. Your mother and I—"

"I know all about you and my mother. Everyone did. Even my dad knew. We knew forever. It became a joke to us. You hear me? You were a joke. Are. You are a joke."

Jerry's mouth opened and his bottom lip quivered slightly, and his eyes turned glassy with tears.

"Don't you dare do that," Chase blurted. "Don't you dare cry. She was my mother, my father's wife, she was nothing to you except another man's wife that you took advantage of."

Jerry turned away from Chase just as a tear rolled down his cheek. He retreated from the crowd with shoulders slumped and shaking. No one watched him go as their attention was pulled back to the loch.

"What's going on down there?" Chase demanded. "Why haven't you reported anything?"

A hesitant reply followed. "There's nothing to report, sir." The man sounded scared. "There doesn't appear to be any tissue available for collection. Whatever this thing is, it's not . . . it."

Everyone's eyes turned to Chase. He was still breathing heavily from his emotional outbursts, but he was struck silent.

Staring at the large mound, he shook his head back and forth. Slowly at first, but building in intensity, indicating the next outburst was seconds away.

"Impossible." He continued shaking his head. "Impossible!"

"She doesn't exist?" Rory stared at the muddy bottom without seeing anything at all. Being defeated by Chase was difficult. Finding out he had been fighting for nothing, living for nothing, that was impossible to take.

Chase sank down to his own knees, directly beside Rory. "Impossible," he whispered.

People began to slowly drift away, driven off by the uncomfortable weight of silence as two grown men sat on their knees staring at the mud of Loch Ness.

"You work so hard to excel at everything you do and people only look at you and say, 'What's next?'"

Though Rory was the only person left to hear Chase's words, he didn't know if Chase was talking to him or just out loud. He didn't care. He had never experienced true heart break before, and it hurt.

"People want more, so you work harder and give them more. Soon people don't even know what to expect but they expect more, regardless. Then when you start doing things," he hesitated and motioned toward the loch with his arms, "things that are truly great, those same people call you insane.

"Mythological creatures, they say, fancies of the imagination. Maybe that's what I started after, but it became more than that. It became about finding something that would prove everyone wrong. Something that would show everyone that I'm not the one who's lost my mind. Validation. That's what it's all about."

Rory stood without a word, held his gaze on the drained portion of loch a second longer, then walked away leaving Chase to suffer by himself.

- 48 -

Dr. Darin Schnabel slid the dividers back into place in the small, tabletop version of the Loch Ness. He counted out the sections, pointing to each one with the end of his pen, and scribbling equations in his notepad. After making a few more calculations in his head, he scribbled another set of numbers before filling the miniature loch for a test.

Chase walked into the tent staring at the ground with his hands in his pockets and his shoulders slumped. He wandered around the tent without acknowledging Dr. Schnabel. It seemed likely he didn't even realize the doctor was there.

When he reached the table with the Loch Ness model, he crouched and placed his arms on the tabletop so he could look at the loch from the side.

Reaching forward, he stuck his hand in one of the sections, then another, and another, and another. His hand darted into each section with building aggression. He stood and jammed his hand into each section in order, water splashing all over the table. When he reached the end, he took the whole model and threw it. The black water hit the side of the tent before splashing to the ground. A small portion remained on the canvas then slowly dripped down to join the rest.

"Mr. Chase, I . . ."

Chase's head snapped in Dr. Schnabel's direction. He really hadn't known the other man was there.

"She's really not in there, is she?" Chase said.

Dr. Schnabel looked at Chase, puzzled. "She?" He reached into his shirt pocket and pulled out the small toy Nessie. "Are you talking about this?"

Chase smiled and gently took the toy. He walked around the tent staring at the toy and laughing to himself. "I think this'll make a good souvenir for this venture."

"I think I've figured out a way to sweep the loch again with less dividers in half of the time."

"That's great, Doctor, but I'm heading home. I have things to do."

"I'll stay here, then. Head up the team until you can return."

"Suddenly you believe in what we've been doing here? You believe in what we've been looking for?"

The doctor couldn't blame Chase for his disbelief. Dr. Schnabel had been the first one to voice negative opinions and skepticism. It had been some of the things he had seen, unexplained readings, that grew his curiosity. Chase's passion had been inspiring. He still couldn't admit to believing the Loch Ness Monster existed, but he was invested enough that he needed to find out.

"We're packing it up. All of us," Chase said.

"After all of this? All the work, the research, the time? It doesn't matter what I believe. We're making history here."

"You were paid. What do you care?"

"Don't you want to find her?"

"Listen to yourself. Finding her? As if she ever existed." Chase marched to the door and looked back at Dr. Schnabel. "You sound like a fool." Chase tossed the toy monster to the doctor. "A damned, stupid fool."

-49-

Rory sat in his old lawn chair, staring out at the loch. Over a day had passed since he first sat down. He hadn't eaten nor had he anything to drink. The expensive bottle of scotch that Chase had given him sat at his feet, unopened so far. Chase's men worked without rest taking deconstructing the dividers and shipping them away in dump trucks. It appeared uncomplicated. Easy. They pulled chunk after chunk out of the water, like a disassembly line. There was likely more effort into the work, but Rory hadn't been paying attention. It no longer mattered how the walls came down.

He sat there, in his usual spot, until he greeted the moon. A little while later the moon abandoned him and he sat with the sun. And still he sat there until the moon had returned to him once again.

Chase's crew had worked far enough down the loch to be out

of sight. Still, he continued to stare. He stared at nothing, and at the entire loch. From where he sat he could have seen its entirety if not for its length.

"And just what the hell am I supposed to do now, huh?" he asked the loch. "I changed my entire life, spent my entire life here." A tear rolled down Rory's cheek. More weren't far behind.

He thought of his wife and her daughter. The daughter that could have been his if he had stayed. He thought about his house and the comfort he could have been living in for decades instead of sleeping on a cot in an old shack.

He thought about the night he had been at his lowest. The night he had crashed his car less than a kilometer from where he sat. He hadn't reached a point of considering suicide, but he had lost everything that made life worth waking up for. Then he found something when he saw her for the first time. It had also been the last time.

He stood and staggered to the edge of the loch on legs that had fallen asleep a day and a half ago. The water's edge lapped at the toes of his shoes.

"My entire life, for you. And what have you done for me? Nothing. Not one thing. You didn't even care enough to let me know you exist," Rory demanded, taking a swing at the air. "Well, do you? Did you ever exist?"

A cold sensation crept up his legs, and when Rory looked down he saw that he was up to his knees in the loch. It only captured his thoughts for a split second.

"I've never hated like I hate tonight. I hate everything. I hate myself for being so stupid. I hate this loch for what it is and what I thought it held. I hate this country. I hate this life. And I hate you!" He swung his fist again, hitting the surface of the loch. It reached his chest.

His voice began to crack as he held back a sob. "And even

though I hate you, I find myself still loving you. And that makes me hate everything so much more!"

Fatigue suddenly struck him. The yelling, the cold water, and the raw emotion all added to his being awake for nearly two days. Rory Stewart was an old man who was talking to an imaginary being, or a body of water.

It wasn't until he turned to get out of the water that he heard it. Something had gently broken the surface of the water.

Rory turned slowly and saw a silhouette, a short distance from shore, sitting on top of the water. His heart began to pound and he felt thirty years younger. The moon was large in the sky, but it didn't do much to illuminate whatever was sitting there.

"It's you, isn't it?" Rory whispered. "I've waited so long. Please stay." Slowly Rory moved closer with one hand outstretched, continually begging "please stay," in hushed tones. His heartbeat echoed in his ears until he could hear little else.

The water grew deeper and Rory needed both hands to tread, but he still reached his hand out every few seconds. It was difficult to tell how close he was. Each time he thought he should have reached her, there was still some distance to cover. A spark of pain ignited in his chest.

Tears continued to flow as he kept moving repeating his plea. "Please wait."

Finally, she was right in front of him. He was so close, but he couldn't will his body to move. The spark in his chest was spreading fire into his lungs.

It was dark. Too dark to see any detail, but it had to be her. What else could it be? Treading water made it difficult to reach out with his hand, but if he could just touch her, just once, everything would have been worthwhile.

Inch by inch, his fingers grew closer as he struggled to keep his head above water. Despite the effort, his mouth continually dipped below the surface only to re-emerge sputtering.

Then all the difficulty seemed to melt away. Treading was easy and he stretched out a hand without any effort. His hand made caressing contact—his heart exploded with emotion—a smile grew on his face, and the world turned white.

– 50 –

Alex stared into his coffee, which wasn't as good as what they served at Betty's diner, but he preferred not to put himself through the torture of seeing her again.

The coffee was fine, but he couldn't seem to drink it fast enough. He wished he could absorb the coffee through his pores, or take it intravenously. Sleeping in the back seat of his rental car didn't do well for his energy level and gave him several aches throughout his body. His only solace was knowing that it was the last time he would sleep in a car for some time. Today was the day he was going home.

He decided to call the office and inform them of his travel plans. With no contact for nearly a week Martin Edwards was probably drafting a story headlined, *Loch Ness Monster real, eats beloved reporter.*

Alex ordered another coffee and shuffled to the pay phone at the back of the diner. Each coin dropped in with a metallic clink and after inserting enough coins to buy everyone in the diner their breakfast, he dialled the office.

"*UK Observer*," Doris answered.

"Hi, Doris. It's Alex. Martin busy?"

Doris hesitated, the line falling so quiet that Alex worried the call had been disconnected. He didn't have enough change to make another.

"Please hold," she said, a click coming through the phone before he could reply.

Within the time it took him to roll his eyes and let out a sound of frustration the line was ringing again and then a man's voice picked up.

"Hello?"

"Martin?" Alex asked.

"Alex! It's Gary."

"Gary? Where's Martin?"

"Martin's tied up."

Edwards was busy and had Gary Whitson handling his calls? Odd wasn't a strong enough word, but Alex was too tired to ask questions.

"Just wanted to check in, let you all know I'm heading back tonight."

"It's done?" Gary asked, his voice excited. "What did they find?"

"Mud," Alex stated. "My flight is pretty late, so I won't be in the office until sometime tomorrow."

"Yeah, I wanted to talk to you about that, Alex."

"Oh?"

"This is never easy, but we've decided to make some staffing changes around the office."

*   *   *

Alex returned to Chase's camp one final time. Not as a reporter. There was no longer a story there, and it seemed his life as a reporter was over.

It was a feeling of incompleteness that drew Alex back to the loch. The events leading up to the big reveal should have had a bigger climax. Alex had never believed the Loch Ness Monster existed, but he had been caught up in the final moments of Chase's plan, excited to see what would be uncovered. Then nothing.

There was little sign that Chase had ever been there, near the south end of the loch. He drove past some men still working toward the middle, hauling large white chunks from the water.

He sat, watching the water and writing a few ideas for his novel in a spiral bound notebook. Once the sky had grown too dark to see his scribbles, he turned on the headlights of his rental car and worked a little longer.

He was going to miss this place. He wouldn't miss the war between Chase and Rory. Their attempts to get at one another were amusing in the beginning, but had quickly grown tiresome.

What he was going to miss was the loch itself, mainly when it was quiet and he felt like the only human being in the country, treated to a gorgeous show of moonlight dancing on the water backed by a choir of nature.

It was too dark to see anything over by Rory's house. Even the house lights were dark. He had seen the old man sitting outside for quite some time after the final section had been drained. Either he was still there, or he had gone to bed.

The old man had been the original reason for Alex to be in Scotland. He was the reason Alex got the jump on the Chase story before any other reporter. The relationship between them had been strange. Alex could remember feeling like the old man's best friend at times, and his worst enemy at others. It didn't feel right to Alex that their last contact hadn't been a good one. He didn't think the old man would be receptive to an honest conversation and moving past the events of the past month, but he was going to try.

The walk was peaceful, the gentle lapping of the water on the shore was the only sound. The insects were quiet, the birds were asleep, even the wind seemed to have retired for the night.

Rory's lawn chair sat in the same place it had been when Alex saw him earlier. It was unlike the old man to have left the chair sitting out, but Alex continued on to the house.

He knocked gently and pushed the door to the old shack open. "Rory?"

After checking each of the rooms in the shack, Alex left, closing the door behind him. He walked back out to the loch and stood beside Rory's lawn chair. A bottle of scotch lied on its side beside the chair. That worried Alex until he saw it hadn't been opened.

"Rory?" he called out.

Something gently broke the surface of the water, making Alex turn around. His mouth dropped open and he fell to his knees.

"Oh my God," Alex whispered.

A short distance from the shoreline was Rory's body, floating and motionless.

Face down, only a portion of his back could be seen, but it had to be Rory. Who else would it have been?

"Rory!" Alex shouted as he rushed into the water. The freezing water stole the breath from Alex's chest as it hit his skin, and every nerve in his body begged him to turn around, but he continued thrashing until he had a handful of Rory's shirt.

He twisted Rory onto his back as he pulled the motionless old man to shore.

"Rory!" he continued to call. "Can you hear me? Wake up!"

Alex had always heard of the buoyancy of the human body and how light a person could seem in the water, but in that moment it all seemed false. He felt like he was pulling a small car.

When he finally got back to the shoreline, he laid Rory on his back and leaned over him. He listened for breathing, but heard nothing. When he thrust his fingers into Rory's neck to check for a pulse, Alex knew he was far too late.

Alex didn't know if he could truly call the old man a friend, but he felt overcome with sadness over Rory's death. Perhaps it was being the one to discover the body, or maybe it was because Alex could have been able to save the old man if he had come sooner.

He sat shivering beside Rory's body wondering who to call. Rory had mentioned only a few friends and those he had no idea how to contact. If he left it up to the government would they treat the death with respect or would he end up in some pauper's grave?

The water lapped at the shoreline, at Rory's legs, trying to pull him back into the water. Alex's eyes welled up and he nodded to himself. Rory's grave would be unmarked, but it wouldn't be some cold, random hole beside other people no one cared about. Rory didn't have a lot of friends, but at that moment he had Alex.

Alex solemnly walked to Rory's small shed, took three sandbags from the monster decoy and put them into the old man's boat. Next he dragged Rory's body to the boat and placed him in as gently as he could, hitting Rory's head on the side in the process.

"Sorry!" he said, realizing he was apologizing to a corpse.

Once he had Rory in the boat, Alex heard a bark and Graham ran over and jumped into the boat.

"Off with you boy, you don't want to be here for this," Alex waved the dog away.

The dog whined and lay down beside Rory.

"Okay. I don't know if you understand any of this, but maybe you should be here."

Rory had never mentioned a favorite part of the loch, but Alex imagined he wouldn't want to be too far from his home. Alex paddled a short distance out, still in sight of the old shack. He carefully tied the sandbags around Rory's waist. It was an odd chore. Alex found himself being careful not to tie the bags too tight as if it could still somehow injure the old man. After a half dozen reties he was confident the knots were strong enough.

Alex looked at Rory for the last time.

"We had our differences, old man. By the end you may not have considered me a friend, but I will forever count you as one of mine."

For the second time that night Alex heard a gentle break of the water's surface from behind him. Graham noticed it as well and let out a single bark. Alex turned slowly and saw something on the surface of the water. His heart began beating faster.

"Impossible," Alex whispered. "I've gone mad. Clearly, I've gone mad."

He squinted, trying to make out more detail, but it was too far away and the sky too dark.

"I don't know if that's you," he called out. It already felt awkward trying to have a conversation with a dog and a dead man. Now he was having a conversation with something that didn't exist. *It didn't exist a moment ago*, Alex thought. *It might still not.*

"If that's you," he paused. What was next? If he was looking at the Loch Ness Monster, what then? "Where did you go?" he wondered aloud. "They drained the whole loch. Where did you hide?"

Whatever was sitting on the surface made no reply. No sound, no movement.

Alex suddenly understood what made Rory live his life in a little shack on the shore of Loch Ness. The feeling Alex was experiencing just then was unlike anything he had ever felt. He was in the presence of something truly phenomenal. It was a feeling that couldn't be bought or reproduced no matter a person's resources. It was a feeling that couldn't be understood except for the few that have felt it. It was a feeling that was entirely real, even if Alex wasn't sharing a moment with any kind of monster, the feeling he was having was, and would always be, real.

Rory felt this once and spent the rest of his life trying to feel it again.

Alex had to force his eyes away from the unknown to deal with Rory. First he placed Rory in the water. The old man floated on his back beside the boat. Graham stood up in the boat, as close as he could to his master, and licked Rory's face, just once. Alex felt himself overcome with emotion again at the dog's good-bye and considered that Graham really did understand.

The first sand bag went in with a splash, followed by the second. Rory was just under surface now, only held back by the third sandbag in the boat. In the water, he no longer looked dead. He seemed to be enjoying the most peaceful sleep a man could ever have.

"Wherever you went," Alex said aloud, "he belongs with you."

The third sandbag went into the water and Rory sank, the dark water combined with the cover of night, quickly taking him out of sight.

"Please take care of him," Alex said as he turned back around, but whatever had been sitting on the surface had returned to the depths of the loch.

-51-

Harvey Chase was speechless.

He had bribed various officials, offered favors, dropped every name he knew, all to find himself sitting across from the man who murdered his mother. From the moment he found out his mother was dead, he fantasized about what he would do and what he would say to the man that took a member of his family away from him. Now that they were face to face, he couldn't bring himself to say a word.

Chase had imagined the murderer would stare across the table with all the malice and heartlessness it required to take a life. Instead, the man in handcuffs barely lifted his head to show his red, teary eyes. The only sound in the room was the occasional sob from the prisoner.

Why am I not the one crying? Chase wondered. *Why is he crying?*

Chase stood and turned away from the crying man, trying to work up his anger. He focused on the fact that this man was a murderer. A killer. This man had worked his way into Mona Chase's life, into a position of trust, and then used that trust to kill her.

He turned back, with fire in his eyes, but the pathetic state of the man in the chair snuffed out the flames.

"Don't you do that," Chase said. His voice was shaky. He tried to make it sound angry, but bitter was the best he could summon. "Don't you sit there and act like the victim. My mother was the victim. You killed her!"

"I know," was all the man said, his voice just above a whisper.

"I'm the victim. You took my only living parent, my only living family member, away from me." Truthfully, he had a few other relatives. The majority of them had stopped talking to him years ago when he stopped giving them handouts.

"I know," the man said again.

The man, this killer, didn't even look intimidating. He looked tiny. Frail. *I'll bet I could thrash him within an inch of his life,* Chase thought. Did he have enough money to make that go away?

"I'm sorry," the man whispered.

Finally, Chase got angry. "You're sorry? You're sorry?! Shut your mouth, you son of a bitch! You'll be sorry, but you're not sorry yet."

"No," the man responded, finally lifting his head. "I'm already sorry for what I did. Your mother didn't deserve to die. I was confused. It shouldn't have been her. It should have been you."

"Me?! You want to kill me?" Chase put his hands on his hips and felt a small pocketknife clipped on his belt. He didn't remember clipping the blade on before heading into the prison.

He pulled the knife off of his belt and slammed it down on the table in front of the man. "There you go. Kill me!" Chase was yelling at this point. Officials were watching through the two-way mirror, he knew. He wondered if the presence of the knife would bring them to burst through the door.

The man in handcuffs stared at the knife and shook his head.

"Who the hell are you?" Chase demanded. "I thought you were a killer. Where did the cold-blooded murderer go?"

"I'm done with killing."

"A changed man!" Chase mocked. "At the very least, do me a favor and tell me why I should have been the one on the end of your knife."

The man muttered something unintelligible, muddled by his sobs.

"For God's sake, man. Stop your damn mumbling."

His head snapped up, anger plain on his face. "You killed my family!"

"I've never killed anyone," Chase said.

"They were family to me," the man said, his head drooping once again.

"Who? Who was family to you?"

The man's tears renewed. "The world named them Bigfoot or Sasquatch, but I called them Harry and Mary. It was a joke at first, but then I grew an appreciation for them. I gave up my life, moved to be closer to them, protected them. After years I even began to love them. They never fully accepted me into their lives, but I think, in a way, they loved me too."

Chase actually laughed. "You think a couple of giant apes were family?"

"I've been dealing with people like you for years. You'll never be able to understand. No one will."

Chase nodded, the condescending smile still on his face, thinking of Rory.

"I know one man that might." The image of Rory on his knees, peering into an empty loch came to his mind. "Things ended in disappointment for him, too."

"Why? Did you kill someone he loved too?"

"Did I kill something he loved? No. He loved something that didn't even exist. He set himself up for failure. That must sound familiar."

"What do you want from me?" the prisoner demanded.

"I want to make you pay," Chase returned, his words took on a sadistic edge.

"I'll be in jail for the rest of my life. I have no family. I own nothing. There's nothing more to take away from me. If there was, I'd give it up freely."

"You're right. There's nothing I can take from you. Your freedom is gone, and you have no assets. You have no wife, no children." He paced the length of the room, carefully planning his next words. "But you do have a sister."

The man's head snapped up with some fire returning to his eyes.

Chase opened a file folder he had brought into the room and read from it.

"Oh, yes, I know about her. Back in North America, am I right? Shelly Williams, maiden name Lasorda, married to Frank Williams. Seems they had a son recently, too. I hope you got a chance to see him before you came to London to plan a murder. So, yes, I can't take anything from you, but I can take everything away from them!"

The door flew open and three officers rushed in, guns drawn. Chase hadn't noticed that the man had picked the knife up off the table, but it was in his hand.

With guns pointed, the officers repeatedly ordered John to drop the knife.

Chase put his hands out toward the officers, silently begging them to stay back. They kept their guns trained on the man, but stopped shouting.

"They've got nothing to do with this! These were my sins. My punishment. You leave them alone!"

"The same way you left my mother out of my sins?"

"Your mother was a nice woman and I regret misplacing my anger on her. I wish I had killed you."

Chase made a show of looking at the armed officers standing at his shoulders.

"Somehow I don't believe that's going to happen."

"It's not. I'm not made for killing the way you are. I'm done killing. I'm done everything. Done."

Lasorda thrust the knife out in front of him and pulled it back hard, burying it deep into his stomach. He collapsed onto the table in front of him, groaning in pain. Chase and the officers stood frozen in shock.

After what seemed like minutes had passed, Chase looked around at the officers. "Shouldn't someone be calling for help?"

One of the officers, who must have been the ranking official, nodded to the other two, who holstered their guns and left the room.

"We don't have to call anyone," the officer said.

"He's dying," Chase said. He wasn't concerned for the man. Only stating a fact.

"This is the man who killed your mother. Does it matter if he dies? He obviously wants to die."

"What are you saying, exactly?"

"Maybe we weren't in here when he stabbed himself. Maybe he was waiting to be taken back to his cell when he took the knife, that he had concealed, and stabbed himself. And maybe he bled out by the time we came back to bring him to his cell."

Chase nodded, taking the idea in. He paced around the room while Lasorda lay on the table, groaning. He leaned over, bringing himself face to face with his mother's killer.

"Is that what you think we should do?" Chase asked, assuming the killer had heard the rest of the conversation.

Lasorda opened his pain-filled eyes. His mouth opened with another moan. It took a few more efforts before he was finally able to whisper, "yes."

The man wished for a quick death, for an end to the guilt and the suffering. He wanted it all to be over.

At least there was one last thing he could take away from the man.

"Get a medic in here."

– 52 –

Alex drove through the night stopping only for gas, where he would get a new cup of coffee, and take a bathroom break to get rid of the last cup of coffee.

After he had dealt with Rory, Alex spent some time loitering in Rory's old shack, going through his belongings. It wasn't meant to be an invasion of privacy; he wasn't looking to steal anything. Alex was just trying to pay his last respects to the old man. The person that knew Rory best normally would have eulogized Rory and spoke about the old man's life, but Alex only knew a little about Rory's life. Everything he found in the house was like a new piece to the puzzle.

Tucked away in a drawer was a small picture frame with an old image of Rory's wedding day. Alex might have thought it had been there for years except that a thick layer of dust had recently been wiped away with a finger.

Rory's wedding ring was in the drawer as well. The ring had been absent from Rory's finger since the old man walked out of the pawnshop in London. Alex had assumed Rory had sold it, but its existence revealed the old man hadn't been able to rid himself of it.

Alex wondered what had really kept Rory by the loch for so many years. The feeling he had just experienced was exhilarating, but that could have been sought without Rory throwing away the rest of his life. He thought about the times when Rory had spoken about protecting the loch and the monster. There had been pride in his eyes and words. To him it was a job, and one that he was very proud of even though putting the job first had lost him everything else.

That was the moment Alex was pierced with a bolt of his own hypocrisy and he ran out of Rory's house to get to his car. He couldn't wait until tomorrow to get home, he had to go now. Only he had left the lights on and had a dead battery. Rory's truck sat in the lane-way with the keys in the ignition. He didn't have to drive alone, either. When Alex started to pull away, Graham jumped from the ground and into the truck through the passenger window. Alex smiled and rubbed the dog's head, not even considering telling the dog to get out.

The sun was rising as he neared the city limits of London. Alex fought to stay awake, resorting to slapping himself in the face. Lightly at first, but harder as his fatigue proved more resilient. Occasionally he got help from his passenger in the form of a big, wet tongue.

His mind wandered momentarily and he thought about his experience on the loch mere hours before. Something had been there on the surface of the water. There was no way for him to know what it was, and it really could have been anything. The reporter in him leaned toward some kind of fish, or some driftwood that bobbed to the surface and sank back under. His cynical side wanted to believe it was nothing more than his imagination. Another part of him wanted to believe he had seen her.

When Alex arrived at his apartment building, a moving van was sitting directly out front. Alex told Graham to stay in the truck, not knowing if he would listen at all. He dashed toward the door but quickly stopped when he passed the moving van. Sitting in the driver's seat looking back at him, and dabbing at her eyes with a tissue, was Loren.

"Loren? What's going on?"

"Hello, Alex. I'm somewhat surprised to see you remember my name."

This was something Alex could never have been fully prepared for, but he couldn't pretend to be completely clueless to her reasons. Things hadn't been going well recently. Not only had Alex been putting his job first, but he had barely made time to write her a letter, or call her to talk for more than a few moments. He didn't even want to think about the night he had spent with Betty.

"Please don't go," he said, letting all his desperation come through in his words. It was embarrassing to show that desperation, but he didn't care about feeling embarrassed. It was the least he deserved.

"I have to."

"Why?"

"You have excellent priorities in your life, most of them career driven, and then there's me, at the very bottom. I can't live like that anymore."

"You won't be at the bottom ever again. I promise."

"You'll try. And for a few weeks I'll be your main priority, but then you'll slip back into your old routine and I'll come last once again."

"I'm not a reporter anymore!"

"What?"

"I talked to Gary Whitson yesterday. They fired Martin for tampering with stories and he asked me to be editor. No more travelling."

Loren turned away from him, looking straight out at the road and started the moving van's engine.

"I'm very happy for you." Her tone implied that she wasn't. "Still, it's become painfully obvious to me that we can't be together."

Alex felt sick to his stomach. He had been lucky to catch Loren the minute before she left, only she was still going to drive out of his life. Except she wasn't driving out of his life. She hadn't started moving. Still looking straight ahead, she made no motion to put the truck in gear. She was trying to decide something. Was she waiting for him to keep talking or convince her?

A nervous tick caused Alex to slide his hands into his pants pockets. There in his right pocket he felt the small wedding ring he had found in Rory's house. He didn't even remember taking the ring. It must have been in his hands when he ran out of Rory's house.

Alex slowly pulled the ring out of his pocket and dropped to one knee. He extended both arms toward the driver's side of the moving van, offering the ring.

"I won't let you walk away from me. Don't go. Marry me."

Loren put her hands over her mouth and Alex thought he saw tears forming in the corners of her eyes. Alex wondered if she was crying out of happiness or because she had already made up her mind and he was just too late.

As he sat waiting, down on his knee, the absurdity of the

situation washed over him. His girlfriend was trying to leave him, due to his continual neglect and dishonesty, and he was trying to get her to stay by suddenly proposing with an old man's wedding band, which he unwittingly stole.

His hands started to fall, along with his spirits.

"Yes," Loren squeaked, barely audible.

"What?" Alex said, quickly standing. "Was that a yes? Did you say yes?"

"Yes!" she repeated with a smile on her face and the tears still in her eyes.

The door to the moving van swung open and Loren hopped down. A much bigger Loren than the one he remembered. Her stomach was swollen, which made him a little nervous, and her breasts looked bigger, which made him a little excited.

"You're . . ." was all he could say.

"Yes. Pregnant."

He took a quick step to her and warmly placed his hands on her arms. Looking from her face to her bulging belly, he smiled.

"Is it . . ." He couldn't bear to say the third word. He didn't believe she would have cheated, even though he had. She was better than he was. But the initial shock of her revelation had his brain working at half speed.

"Of course it is!" she said with a smile, hitting him playfully. "Speaking of, don't think that because I said yes I'm going to let you off the hook for cheating on me. You're in shit for a long, long time."

He didn't care. A smile was cemented on his face as he looked down at her stomach. Slowly he placed a hand on her bulge.

"Wow," he said in hushed wonder. "How far along?"

"About four months. I was just starting to show when you left for Scotland, but I was hiding it with baggy clothes. I wanted to tell you so many times."

Alex rested his forehead against hers. They both closed their eyes and Alex felt a level of contentment he had only felt once before, mere hours ago, on the Loch Ness.

"How do you feel about vacationing in Scotland?" he asked.

She laughed and gave him a quizzical look.

-53-

Chase sat in his favorite café at his favorite table. Over the years he had come so often and tipped so well that they left his table open for him every morning whether he was coming or not.

That morning was the first morning in months he had stopped in, yet it was still open for him.

His waiter brought him his usual espresso macchiato, a croissant freshly drizzled with chocolate, and the morning's edition of the *UK Observer*.

Normally, he would only pay attention to the financial section, but he was putting off his visit into the office. He was expected to interview and hire a new assistant in the next few days.

He enjoyed taking his time with the paper, flipping through casually, reading stories that captured his interest. He looked twice when he saw the words *Loch Ness* and took a closer look at the story. The full headline read, *Legend Finally Revealed at Loch Ness.* Chase couldn't help but smile when he saw Alex Stafford's name on the byline.

One would have to go a long way to find someone who's never heard of the legend that lives at Loch Ness. Certainly, you'd have to leave Europe, if not this entire planet. During a recent trip to Scotland, not only did I find out that the legend exists, but I had the opportunity to spend a little time in its presence.

His name was Rory Stewart and he was a protector of sorts. He lived the majority of his life on the edge of the Loch Ness and possessed a tenacity that would make most other men hang their heads in shame. Life was hard for Rory, but Rory was a hard man.

He stood up for the things he believed in, even if that meant knowing he was going to be knocked down. Rory would simply stand back up again. He was a man that knew that the right way was seldom the easy way.

Though he wasn't perfect, Rory was loved by a few that were close to him. The closest of whom were blessed with Rory's unwavering dedication which was only broken by the finality of death. As one who knew Rory a little, I can say that he died happy, surrounded by that which he loved.

Rory was a great man. He wasn't rich, or powerful, but great nonetheless. He lived a simple life that made an impact in his part of the world. Many people end up becoming a product of their surroundings, but Rory's surroundings will forever be a product of him.

Years from now people will come back from the loch and say that they saw him. Perhaps tinkering around his old shack, or scaring off a tourist, or swimming in the loch. As is the way with stories like these they're more likely to be tales of fancy or some kind of misunderstanding, but that's to be expected. That's what happens when a man becomes a legend.

Chase folded the newspaper and dropped it on the small café table. He stared off toward the park across the street and let the story wash over him.

A chuckle burst from Chase's lips, followed by another. More and more came unbidden and he found he could not stop as they turned into roaring laughter. With another shift the laughter converted to tears. Not tears due to the intense laughter; tears of sadness.

Chase realized that Rory had impacted his life as well.

With all of his money and all of his resources, he was battled to a standstill by an old man who had nothing but his wits. Chase had never found anyone who could match his heart, resolve, and tenacity. Rory topped him from all angles.

Chase was pretending to be a legend. Rory became one without even trying.

As much as they seemed to hate each other, Chase felt a connection with the old man and knew he was a better man for having known Rory. Chase felt a genuine sadness knowing Rory had died and he would never be able to pay him back for saving his life.

When Chase was finally able to take control of himself again, he wiped the last of the tears from his eyes and stood from his table. Resting a hand on top of Alex's column, he smiled.

"Well done, lad. Well done."

Dear Reader

Thank you for reading Living Legend. I hope you liked it. If you did, or even if you didn't, I want to hear from you.

- Leave me a review at amazon.com, iTunes, or wherever you bought this book from.

- Get on social media
  Facebook: facebook.com/jwmartinonline
  Twitter: @JDubMartin

- or e-mail me: joe@jwmartin.com

I don't have a staff or an assistant. I personally read every review, tweet, facebook comment, and email that comes my way. Writers love nothing more than hearing feedback from readers, so let me hear you. You'll most likely hear something back.

J.W. Martin spends his nights and weekends writing in Ontario, Canada. He has a very understanding wife and two hilarious sons, without whom he would get much more writing done. . . and would be completely miserable.